All We Once Had

ALSO BY
KATY UPPERMAN

Everything I Promised You
How the Light Gets In
The Impossibility of Us
Kissing Max Holden

PRAISE FOR
EVERYTHING I PROMISED YOU

★ "Emotionally raw and tender... Give to teens who love a good emotional tearjerker."

—*Booklist*, Starred Review

"Upperman's writing is engaging, and although the emotions are heavy, an undercurrent of hope snakes through the narrative... A poignant and romantic coming-of-age tale."

—*Kirkus Reviews*

"A story that will pull at the heartstrings of those longing for an epic romance."

—*School Library Journal*

All We Once Had

KATY UPPERMAN

sourcebooks
fire

Copyright © 2026 by Katy Upperman
Cover and internal design © 2026 by Sourcebooks
Cover design by Sarah Brody/Sourcebooks
Cover image © Ali Majdfar/Getty Images
Internal design by Tara Jaggers/Sourcebooks

Published by Sourcebooks Fire, an imprint of Sourcebooks
1935 Brookdale RD, Naperville, IL 60563-2773
(630) 961-3900
sourcebooks.com

Cataloging-in-Publication Data is on file with the Library of Congress.

Printed and bound in Canada.
MBP 10 9 8 7 6 5 4 3 2 1

For Bev and Phil,
whose warmth, support, and love are invaluable.

Piper

BRIGHT AND EARLY, I STAGGER into the kitchen in desperate need of a Red Bull and a few more hours of sleep, to find a strange man standing at the coffee maker. He's not a bad-looking man—attractive in a *The Hangover*–era Bradley Cooper way—but still.

A strange man.

He gives me a lazy shrug and a sheepish grin, then musses his already-mussed hair. I watch, stone-faced, as he pours coffee into my sister's favorite mug—not that this interloper would know the distinction. It's black with little white planets sketched over its surface, and it says I NEED MY SPACE! Which, yes, Tati almost always does.

The shower in her bathroom cranks on. I linger near the stove, wondering if she knows that the dude she apparently spent the night with is moving around our kitchen with the ease of someone who's been here a dozen times, filching a splash of creamer from the fridge, snagging a spoon from the flatware drawer, swirling it languidly through his coffee.

Well.

I go about my business because I'll be late for work if I idle any longer. Hopefully Tati's enjoying her shower while I awkwardly maneuver around this person who I have to assume is a one-night stand.

He leans against the counter, sipping from her mug while I pour Cheerios into a plastic baggie. He says, "You must be her sister."

I take a pear from the fruit bowl, trying to determine whether he's somehow so familiar with Tati that a mere pronoun will do, or he's forgotten her name.

"I am. And you're…?"

He gives my question a few seconds of thought before landing on, "A friend."

He doesn't offer his name, and I don't inquire. He won't be back. Tati likes sharp, well-groomed suitors who stand up straight, enunciate, and have jobs that serve the community: child welfare lawyers and ER doctors and firefighters. The last man she dated was a police officer, well respected in our little town. That relationship ended a week ago, and it ended badly.

This dude looks like a weathered fraternity brother with his disheveled hair, yesterday's wrinkled button-down (popped collar and rolled sleeves, naturally), and mirrored aviators hooked to his breast pocket. His face is tan, his teeth are bright

2

white, his smile so carefree that I wonder again where Tati met him, what she saw in him, and why she let him stay all night—definitely *not* her usual protocol.

"I'm Piper," I say to fill the quiet, pulling my sun-bleached curls into a topknot.

Blithely, like a stoned surfer, he says, "Cool."

Down the hall, the water shuts off. That's my cue to go. Hard pass on sticking around to watch my sister interact with her random bedmate.

I nod once. "I need to get to work. So…"

"So, I'll see you around."

Highly unlikely.

I grab a Red Bull from the fridge, then take my breakfast to go, making sure to let the door to our apartment slam on my way out.

———

My sister doesn't approve of my summer job. But she doesn't approve of the majority of my choices, so at least there's consistency.

Since school let out last week, I've been working at the Sugar Bay Marine Conservation Park, which—no offense to Disney World—is absolutely the most magical place on Earth. We have dolphins and seals and sea turtles and rays, and these are not animals who were kidnapped from their natural habitats. They're animals who've been injured, usually due to shitty human behavior, and are being rehabilitated for release back into the wild or cared for permanently because release isn't safe for them.

I work in Guest Experience, which means I do a bunch of grunt work deemed undesirable by the employees with college degrees. I earn pennies, practically, but it doesn't matter. I love being at the park, even when it's ninety-seven degrees and sticky-sweaty-humid, even when I'm emptying trash bins and hosing out stinky fish buckets, even when I'm stuck in the admin building stuffing envelopes for some huge PR mailing.

My parents helped open the Sugar Bay Marine Conservation Park almost thirty-five years ago, shortly before Tati was born. They were marine biologists and ardent ocean conservationists. The director of the park, a meek, altruistic man nicknamed Turtle (because he's passionate about them and kind of looks like one), mentored them both and still speaks warmly of them. When I applied for a summer job, he disregarded the *must be enrolled in a college program* requirement and brought me on as an intern to the interns.

I've been coming to the park all my life, first with my parents, then on my own, and now as a staff member. It's a safe haven. The place where I feel most like myself.

I spend the better part of the morning scrubbing and sweating and directing guests to restrooms and water fountains, encouraging them to *Have a sunny day!*, the catchphrase Turtle urges employees to use on the regular. My smiles come more easily here than anywhere else, and before long, I've forgotten about

4

my encounter with the kitchen intruder. I've forgotten about Tati, who more often than not feels like a tyrannical roommate instead of my sister and guardian. And I've *almost* forgotten about Gabi, my estranged best friend.

It guts me, thinking of her that way.

I shake off the bitterness I've felt every time Gabi has wandered into my mind since our friendship fell apart nine days ago, and take the Cobb salad I bought at one of the park's snack huts to the dolphin enclosure for lunch, since now there's a break between shows.

I haven't met any new friend prospects since I started my job—not that Gabi's friendship is replaceable. It's been her and me since fourth grade, an inseparable, impenetrable pair. I've never needed anyone else—never even wanted anyone else. But now I'm truly on my own. My sister is more my keeper than my confidant, and my fellow park employees are all in college or older. Forging bonds is hard for me, especially now that I've seen how swiftly a friendship can crumble.

And so I'll dine with the dolphins.

I clamber up the grandstand to one of its highest benches, then sit and pull out my phone. Maybe Gabi has seen the light and sent a text groveling for forgiveness. She hasn't, but my sister's sent three messages in the last hour: Your bathroom's a mess! and Chicken lettuce wraps for dinner? and Don't forget to drop the mail in the outgoing box.

Whoops—I definitely forgot.

I pocket my phone without responding, then devour my

5

salad while watching our trio—Luke, Leia, and Han—swim and jump and play. They seem so happy and carefree; lately, I've been envious of their companionship.

As I collect my trash, I spot Turtle climbing the steps. He's jutting out his chin, his expression curious but cautious. When he reaches me, he sits. "How's your first week been?"

"Awesome," I say, hoping he hasn't tracked me down because I screwed something up.

"You're a hard worker," he says, to my relief. "A lot of the staff has said so."

"Really?"

He nods. His face is lined and sun-spotted. He's as old as my mom's parents—Dad's died before I was born—lifelong New Yorkers who, in the wake of losing their daughter, became rather aloof. It's been years since they've visited Tati and me in Florida.

"I'm not surprised," Turtle says. "Your mama and daddy were hard workers too. So's your sister. Determined as all get-out."

"Determined," I say, wrinkling my nose. "That's one way to describe Tati."

He laughs, his green eyes glinting. He's been a surrogate uncle to my sister and me since our parents passed, checking in on us from time to time, sharing wisdom and stories about my mom and dad. He and his wife, Brenda, invite us for a Thanksgiving feast every year. Tati has a lot of respect for Turtle, which is why she agreed to let me work at the park despite the *meager compensation*. Her words, not mine.

6

"You're off at two?" he asks.

"Yep."

"Swing by my office before you go. I've got your first week's pay."

The Sugar Bay Marine Conservation Park is a utopia. Thriving animals, joyful guests, and fresh air, a slice of Florida that reminds me more of my parents than any other place on Earth. In a quiet area of the property, near the manta ray exhibit, is a medallion embedded in the concrete path: IN MEMORY OF TWO BELOVED COFOUNDERS AND CONSERVATIONISTS, STEPHEN AND CONSTANCE NIXON. The letters are worn a shiny copper color by the countless shoes that've passed over it during the last seven years. Turtle had the memorial installed after my parents' deaths, a tribute I get to witness every time I walk by. It still makes me teary when I let it. Not only is the park a link to my past, but spending my days here gives me glimpses of what my dream—a degree, a *future*, in marine biology—might be like. The pay, scant only by my sister's snooty standards, is the cherry on top.

I grin at Turtle. "I'll see you at two."

He squeezes my shoulder. "We're happy to have you, Piper. Keep up the good work."

———

After my shift at the park, I check in with Tati because she'll have a meltdown if I don't. Our phone call involves way more hassling

7

than I've got the energy for, and I bite my tongue, literally, to keep from retorting. The last thing I need is to have an argument on a public sidewalk. "Clean your bathroom before I get home," are her parting words, and then the line goes dead.

She's so lovely.

I stop by the bank, where, instead of depositing my paycheck, as my sister demanded during our call, I cash it. Turtle's giving me six hours a day, five days a week, which has amounted to close to three hundred dollars after taxes.

A windfall.

It's *hot*, so I stop at Clementine's, a shop with amazing donuts and smoothies only a few doors down from the bank. I treat myself to a Sunrise Acai Bowl, and I'm reveling in my first sweet spoonful as I push through the swinging door, heading toward the picnic tables outside, and nearly collide with Gabi.

She's trying to get inside, so I step—stumble—out of the way.

She's alone, thank god.

She gives me a long, cold look. Heart hammering, I think of this movie she and I watched about Jack Frost when we were kids. When he touched things—a window, a pond, a meadow— crystalline ice flowed from his fingertips, trickling over surfaces, overlaying them with frost. Her stare has the same effect. My insides have frozen over.

She steps around me, then away, like I'm infectious.

I should've avoided Clementine's. Gabi loves it as much as I do. My parents brought us in the earliest days of our friendship, after Gabi moved to Sugar Bay, way back when we were nine.

8

Not even a year later, her parents took over the tradition, treating us on Sunday mornings after sleepless sleepovers, maintaining a sliver of stability in my suddenly upside-down world.

I haven't seen Gabi in more than a week, since the Saturday following the final day of our junior year at Sugar Bay High. Her parents took her younger brother camping for the weekend, so Gabi invited a bunch of people over. It was fun until it wasn't. I drank too much, went swimming in my bra and underwear, and ended up pressed against Gabi's boyfriend, Damon. In Gabi's bedroom. Wearing only my damp underclothes. Gabi walked in at that moment—the *pressed against* moment.

She didn't take it well.

Still in the entryway, dizzy on my feet, I watch her glide to the counter and ask for a smoothie. Her minidress is white cotton, pretty against her brown skin. Her legs go on forever. On her feet are my shoes—espadrilles she borrowed for last weekend's party.

I think an uncharitable word—*bitch*—because how dare she?

I duck out of Clementine's holding my bowl of blended tropical fruit in shaking hands, blinking back tears.

I don't need Gabi.

I don't need anyone.

I walk until I've regained a fragile hold on my emotions. That's when I catch my distorted reflection in a hair salon's front window. Blue Sugar Bay Marine Conservation Park T-shirt, denim cutoffs, and white Vans purchased specifically for my new job. My hair's slipping out of its knot. Wispy blond coils frame my face like a halo.

9

I'm no angel.

Gabi will attest to that.

Inside the salon, a stylist wearing head-to-toe black is sweeping shorn hair into a pile. She looks bored. I push through the door, and the bell above it jingles. She looks up.

"Do you have availability?" I ask. "Like, right now?"

She smiles and points to her chair. "Have a seat."

Henry

MY DAD DRIVES A JACKED-UP cherry red Ram 1500 Big Horn with an upgraded exhaust system that roars like a pissed-off lion every time he accelerates.

I'm embarrassed on his behalf.

Even more so when the engine growls out of the parking lot of the tiny airport that serves the Florida panhandle. The land is flat and unchallenging, safely traversed by Subarus and Wranglers with soft tops. Dad's truck looks like it belongs on a rocky mountain, like an actual ram.

He's got the windows down as we rumble toward Sugar Bay, a resort town on the Gulf of Mexico. Its population is less than fourteen thousand, though that number balloons during the tourist season. Sugar Bay boasts a putt-putt course, a few nationally renowned golf courses, a go-kart track, a marine conservation park, a couple of arcades, and various pontoon rental shacks. There are a shit ton of beach-themed seafood restaurants, a bunch of hotels, and countless Airbnbs along the shore.

I know this because I've been to Sugar Bay once before, three years ago, for a weeklong visit a few months before my dad opened his sports bar.

"How was your trip?" he asks, his attention split between the highway and me. The sun's working its way toward the horizon, and the sky's blazing with light. Ahead, there's a line of scrubby long-leafed pines and somewhere beyond them, the beach.

I shrug. "Long. Boring."

I'd forgotten how long and how boring. The last time I was on a plane was two years ago, when my mom and I flew to Phoenix to visit my grandma. That was a single three-hour flight—easy. It's taken me a whole day to get to Sugar Bay: Washington to Utah to Georgia and then finally to Florida. My neck hurts from the kink I earned trying to sleep somewhere over Missouri.

Dad pulls his focus from the road. He's sporting the sort of mirrored sunglasses a motorcycle cop would choose. Even though his eyes are hidden, I can tell my lackluster tone has set off alarm bells.

"It was good," I amend. "Uneventful."

It was my idea to come to Florida this summer. I should play nice.

Dad moved here from Spokane, where he and my mom were born and raised, same as me. Four years ago, when I was thirteen, he decided it was his calling to open a sports bar—but not in Eastern Washington. He wanted to live near the beach. Other

12

than my single trip to Sugar Bay, I've seen him a couple of times a year: in September, when he treks back to Spokane to hang out with me for my birthday, and then at Christmastime, when we spend a few days shredding the slopes together.

I figured it was my turn to make an effort.

"You hungry?" he asks.

"Not really. I grabbed barbecue during my layover in Atlanta."

"Tired, I bet."

"I'm good. It's only, like, three back home."

His flinch is almost imperceptible, but I know it bugs him that I think of my mom's house as home. Not because there's drama between them—my parents get along fine—but because he's been suggesting I live with him for ages. Give Florida a shot. Visit again, at least.

I haven't, but not because I don't like my dad. He pays above and beyond what he owes in child support, calls once a week minimum, and gives me presents and cash on birthdays and holidays. He asks about my grades, my teachers, cross-country. He offers to help my mom in every way he can. The reasons I haven't visited are my own: I'm a creature of habit, and I feel bad about leaving Mom on her own.

"You really don't want to swing by the bar to grab a burger?"

"Maybe later?"

"For sure. I can't wait for you to see it. Football season was a round-the-clock party. And now that baseball's in full swing, we've got butts in chairs every night and all weekend. People visit Sugar Bay just to hang out at Blitz Brews. More and more often, I talk to customers who've come from Pensacola and Tallahassee. Last weekend, we had a crew in from Jacksonville."

This might impress me if I knew how far away those places are from Sugar Bay. Before my dad moved to Florida, all I knew of the state was Disney World, the Seminole War, and Ernest Hemingway. My knowledge base is still pretty limited. "That's cool, Dad."

Up ahead, a SUGAR BAY WELCOMES YOU! sign points toward an approaching exit. The Ram trundles off the highway and onto a quiet street lined with tall palms. We travel a few blocks, and then the Gulf of Mexico announces itself. The sand's sparkling white—it almost looks like snow—and the water's deep turquoise. The sky is cobalt and cloudless.

Dad makes a left toward a stretch of high-rise hotels and apartment buildings, then reaches over to jostle my shoulder. "Hey, buddy, about the whole *Dad* thing…"

I glance his way "Yeah?"

"You're practically a man now."

My eighteenth birthday's in three months. "Okay. And?"

"I was thinking…what if you call me by my name? You know, instead of *Dad*?"

I laugh—I can't help it. "Why?"

"'Cause in Sugar Bay, I'm Davis Walker, owner of Blitz Brews. You've spent a lifetime with me as your old man, so this is probably hard to imagine, but around here, I've got to maintain a certain reputation."

"Uh-huh," I say, trying and failing to sand the mockery from

.14

my tone. "And a teenager calling you *Dad* will screw that up?"

He turns a grin on me. "I knew you'd get it."

I swallow a snort. "Sure, *Davis*. Course I do."

Stupid as I find his request, arguing during our first hour together is a bad idea, seeing as I'll be living with him for the next two months. My mom has finally saved up enough to chase a Master of Science in Nursing, her dream for as long as I can remember. She needs space to focus on her coursework, and thanks to Dad, I can give it to her. That's not the only reason Sugar Bay has become appealing, though. Eight weeks ago, I dug myself out of the rubble of a train-wreck breakup with the only girlfriend I've ever had, Whitney. Since then, engaging with her has been a fucking nightmare so, cowardly or not, I fled.

My dad—*Davis*—turns into the parking lot of a beachfront apartment complex. There are two buildings, ten floors each, with a courtyard in between. Sugar Bay Luxury Towers is way fancier than the little bungalow Mom and I share in Spokane.

"Home sweet home," Dad says, pulling into a numbered space.

"It's as nice as I remember," I reply, because he feeds off accolades. He can afford to live in a luxury tower: He's made it.

Since the last time I was here, he's moved units. The one-bedroom he had originally was too small, so as soon as it became available, he snagged a two-bedroom with a balcony overlooking the gulf. The views are unreal. He's been telling me that for literal years, and I'm sure it's true, but what I'm really excited about is having my own room. When I last visited, I slept on the pull-out sofa.

We unload my bags, then head for the east tower. I'm trailing behind him when I spot a girl crossing the parking lot. She looks close to my age, and she's making her way toward the west tower. Her dark hair is a mass of shiny curls. She walks with confidence: spine straight, shoulders back, head high. She's wearing a blue T-shirt with an indecipherable logo and denim cutoffs.

She disappears into the west tower, but not before dredging up the memory of another girl. Not Whitney, but someone I met the last night I spent in Sugar Bay three years ago, a blond so pretty, fourteen-year-old me thought he'd died and stumbled across an angel. She was crying at the pool under a full moon. I had no idea what was wrong, and I was young and imbecilic. I saw tears and wanted to run. But she looked so heartbroken sitting there by herself. This protective instinct kicked in; I needed to make sure she was okay.

We ended up hanging out until dawn.

She was my first kiss, and she set a high bar.

We never spoke again.

God, I haven't thought about her in ages.

Dad and I reach the building's entrance. I follow him in, lugging my backpack and suitcase, wondering if the pretty blonde still lives at the Towers.

Piper

"YOU LOOK LIKE A WITCH!" my sister bellows, flinging a hand toward my hair. "What were you *thinking*?"

I touch my once-blond curls, now a rich espresso. Until today, I had virgin hair. "I don't know. I wasn't thinking, I guess."

"That's the very essence of your problem, Piper. You *never* think."

"I just...I needed a change."

"A *change*?" she repeats, exasperated.

"Yeah. And I don't understand why you care."

"Because I'm in charge!" She takes a slug from the glass of wine she poured upon seeing my hair. She indulges when she's had a rough day or when I've done something to piss her off, though she never allows herself more than two glasses. She's a machine that way.

We're in the kitchen, where she ambushed me when I walked

through the door. *You're late. Your bathroom's not clean. You didn't drop the mail in the box. What in the* world *did you do to your hair?* And now: "You're supposed to consult me before making big life decisions."

"Give me a break. It's hair dye. I didn't sign up to colonize Mars."

"How much did it cost?"

"For the color and a trim? Like, a hundred and fifty. You know, before tip."

She expels a breath that lifts her bangs—blond bangs. She's fifteen years older than me, which puts her at thirty-two. She looks twenty-five. She acts eighty-nine. She thinks she's God's gift to guardianship. "I hope you're kidding."

"I used my first paycheck."

"Excellent. Money well spent." Another swig of wine. "Your poor, poor savings account. I swear, Piper, do you ever consider consequences?"

I appraise my hair in the microwave's reflective door, then shrug. "I like it."

"Good, 'cause you're not spending more money to fix it. Live with it until it grows out."

"Fine." With false brightness, I ask, "How was your day?"

She groans. "Awful. The residents of this complex are killing me slowly. And now..." She points at my head, shaking hers. "Now this."

"You know, you could practice some decorum. Try this: *Piper, your hair looks nice.*"

18

"It doesn't."

Only Tati can make my blood pressure skyrocket this way. God, she's the worst. "What have the residents done now?"

"What *haven't* they done? Leaky toilets, late rent, dog shit in the courtyard. This is a luxury apartment complex, yet the people who live here act like barbarians." She gives me a sinister look. "You more than any other."

"You're impossible."

"And you're a constant headache."

I flash her my most saccharine smile. "The feeling's mutual."

I take a can of seltzer from the fridge, then turn for the hallway leading to my room. Before rounding the corner, I glance over my shoulder. Tati stands with her back to me, palms flat on the counter, head bent. She looks downtrodden. Managing Sugar Bay Luxury Towers isn't exactly her dream job, and the demands and complaints and excuses of the people who live here wear on her.

Still, she infuriates me with her constant criticism.

More than that, the snarky comments she made about my hair hurt my feelings. Which is why I can't resist saying, "I met your washed-up frat bro this morning."

She whirls around. Her cool blue eyes, same as mine, are intense. "What?"

"The guy you shacked up with last night? I ran into him this morning. In the kitchen."

She nails a fist to her hip. "I told him to stay in my room."

"Then he's not a good listener. An unfortunate start to my day,

19

and probably why I forgot to drop off the mail. It was distracting, finding a strange man in the apartment."

"He's not strange."

"He's not your type."

"You don't know anything about my type, Piper Nixon."

"Point is, you're so busy damning my flaws, you forget you're not perfect."

"You're wrong," she says, squaring her shoulders. "I'm painfully aware of my flaws. The difference between you and me is that I try to fix my mistakes. You revel in yours."

She never even *tries* to hear me.

"Thanks for the feedback. I'm off to my room now to revel in its messiness, my witch hair, and my barren bank account."

She fires a retort at my retreating back. "I wish you'd grow up."

"I will," I shout, "when you learn to keep your boy toys out of common areas!"

For the second time today, Tati drives me to slam a door.

Henry

DURING THE TIME IT TOOK to roll into my dad's apartment, take the grand tour, and dump my bags in the room that's mine for the summer, Dad asked me about grabbing food at Blitz Brews approximately 1,229 times. So that's where we've landed.

The sports bar is cool, I'll give him that. The floor and ceiling are dark-stained wood, the barstools are black iron, and old wine barrels have been fashioned into high-top tables. Booths ring the perimeter, and there are at least a dozen mounted TVs broadcasting baseball, golf, and deep-sea fishing. The shelves behind the bar are stocked with more booze than I've ever seen—a rainbow of neon liquor.

Dad whacks my shoulder. "Badass, huh?"

"Yeah, it is."

I like seeing him this way—gratified by this business he dreamed up, launched, and fostered. Back in Spokane, he worked in finance. He never seemed unhappy, but when he talked about his job, his eyes didn't flicker with pride the way they're doing now.

He leads me to the bar and introduces me to Mateo, bartender and shift manager, who has shaggy black hair and sleeves of ink. While my dad ducks into his office, Mateo describes the day he was hired while switching one of the TVs from ESPN2 to ESPN3, mixing a pair of pink cocktails, and cashing out a tab.

"Davis is a great boss," he says, putting a glass of soda in front of me. "He lets me work nights and weekends so I can take classes during the day."

"What are you studying?" I've known what I want to do after high school for as long as I can remember, but I'm always curious about other peoples' choices.

"Hospitality and tourism. I'm at Northwest Florida State." He grabs a rag and wipes down the bar; he hasn't stopped moving since Dad introduced us. "Bartending is a hell of a lot better than bussing tables or working at one of the family-centric tourist traps in this town. I spend my shifts chatting with customers and watching sports. Not a bad gig."

Dad reappears, checking in with servers, shooting the shit with customers, gulping up attention like a video game avatar powering up. When he makes his way back to the bar, he asks Mateo for an IPA, then leads me to a vacant booth. While we wait for food—chicken wings and a giant soft pretzel with beer cheese—he lists a bunch of activities he wants us to do together this summer: golfing and snorkeling and fishing and beach

22

volleyball. "We can rent dune buggies and take them out on the sand. And there's a place a few miles from here that has trails for riding horses—I've been wanting to check it out." He grins. "We're gonna have a blast."

Jesus H.

Back home, I spend a lot of time on my own. I have friends I see at school and buddies I see on the mountain during the winter. I have a text thread with Silas and Ricky, two guys I've been running cross-country with since middle school, but for the most part we just drop in training tips, run times, and expectations for upcoming meets. And of course there was Whitney. But mostly, I like flying solo. It's daunting, all the together time Dad's got penciled in. His intentions are good—he's glowing as he goes on and on and on—but he's overcompensating.

I fake enthusiasm as we finish our drinks.

Pushing the empty glasses to the table's edge, Dad flags down a server, a redhead whose name tag says LANA, and asks for another beer. "Bring one for Henry too."

My eyebrows rise almost as high as Lana's. I hold up a hand. "I'm okay."

"Come on," Dad says. "Throw one back with me. We're celebrating your arrival."

"Yeah, I'll just have another soda."

He gives Lana a *Can you believe this kid?* look, then winks at me. "It's cool, Henry."

Lana's waiting, amused. Dad's pushing. And I'm embarrassed. I'm not about to *throw one back* with my father.

23

"No thanks, *Davis*." I smile at Lana. "I'm good with soda."

She heads for the bar, probably glad to escape.

Dad leans in. Quietly, he says, "What difference will one beer make?"

"To your liquor license? You tell me."

He huffs. "Like you don't drink with your friends in Spokane."

"I don't."

"When I was your age—"

"When you were my age, you weren't dreaming about four years at West Point. If I go down for underage drinking, I'll have to kiss my future goodbye."

He gives a dry laugh. "That's dramatic."

"No, it isn't." The couple sitting nearest our booth turns to look. I'm not interested in having it out with my dad in front of an audience, but I'm not about to let a thirty-six-year-old man pressure me into boozing. I lower my voice. "I don't want to drink. Especially not with you—*my father*."

Lana returns, placing his beer and my soda on the table. Once she's moved on, Dad takes a pull from his glass and, more reticent now, says, "If my old man had offered me a drink when I was in high school, there's not a chance in hell I would've turned it down."

He was wild in high school. And college. I wasn't conceived by way of sensible choices and responsible behavior. "No shit," I say, indulging him.

He smiles, chagrined. "I have a lot of respect for you, Henry. You know that, right?"

24

Cool Davis is kind of a douche, but I like my dad when he's like this: open, earnest, real.

"I'm serious, buddy," he goes on. "You've got convictions. The convictions of a monk, but still."

I crack a smile. "I know what I want, that's all."

"Your mom's done a good job bringing you up. You're a lucky kid." His expression goes so wistful, I'm worried he's about to tear up. His reputation as bar owner and monster truck driver and IPA connoisseur is headed for the shitter if he doesn't pull himself together.

"Yeah, I am," I say, trying to help him regain his footing. "My mom rocks, and I get to spend the next couple months with my dad, hanging out at his kick-ass sports bar."

He sniffs, then laughs, then downs what's left of his beer.

Lana brings food, and we manage to get through the meal without any more weirdness.

Maybe I'll survive this summer after all.

Piper

THE BEST THING ABOUT SUGAR Bay Luxury Towers is the pool.

It sits in the courtyard between the east and west towers, and it's huge and extravagant and rarely in use, especially this late at night. With the exception of Sugar Bay Marine Conservation Park, it's my favorite hideaway.

I've brought a handful of cotton balls, nail polish remover, and a bottle of polish with me. Tati hates when I give myself manicures in the apartment because she *feels like she's going to asphyxiate*, so I've taken to doing my nails poolside. It's kind of nice, particularly after we've argued. The fresh air helps purge her anal-retentive negativity from my system.

I'm sitting on the paved deck with my legs dangling in the cool water, stripping my nails of their baby-pink polish, when a boy around my age intrudes on my solitude. He chooses a chair across the pool from where I'm sitting, one beneath a tall solar-powered lamppost. He glances my way for half a second before opening the book he's brought.

Interesting. When I was blond, I held guys' unabashed attention.

My curiosity is piqued, but I go on painting my nails with two coats of teal polish, allowing myself an occasional peek. He's got his nose buried deep in that book, a massive tome with a title I can't make out. His hair is wavy and chestnut, his brows thick, his jaw square. He's wearing a white T-shirt with black athletic shorts and Pumas. He squints as he reads in the crap light, carving a horizontal line of concentration across his forehead.

My nails have dried just enough when he glances up, his gaze connecting with mine.

I look away. Then back again.

Smooth, Piper.

He raises his hand in a wave, the corners of his mouth lifting slightly.

Holy balls—his smile is familiar.

A memory blinks into my head: my first kiss was with a tall chestnut-haired boy.

Except, this boy can't be *that* boy.

I wave back, feeling silly for entertaining the idea that a ghost from my past has suddenly reappeared. I feel even sillier when a gust of warm wind lifts my half dozen spare cotton balls and drops them into the pool.

I scowl at the mess. I could leave them, but littering sucks.

Sighing, I haul myself up to grab a net, careful not to ding my manicure. Stewing about my argument with Tati and my run-in with Gabi and what a bummer this day has been—minus my hair, which I really do love—I carefully fish all but one of the cotton balls from the pool. It's the last, bobbing close to the edge and requiring no real effort, that takes me under.

It's the boy's fault. As I'm crouching, reaching into the water with decent balance and a capable hand, he catches my eye again. I grow flustered, wobbly.

I yelp, shattering the pool's placid surface with my flailing body.

Thank god my phone's upstairs on my bed, not in my pocket.

I've plummeted into only a few feet of water, but I stay under for several seconds, scolding myself for the squeal I let out as I fell, worrying the splash I created was enormous, hoping I'm not screwing up my manicure and my fresh hair color with this unfortunate dip, and praying—*praying*—that when I surface, the boy will have disappeared into the night.

He has not.

He's standing on the deck, right above me.

He's doubled over with laughter.

He regains his composure long enough to reach out a hand.

What a gentleman.

Honestly, I'm reluctant to accept his help, but let's be real: I could use it.

I let him assist as I drag myself out of the pool, the traitorous cotton ball in my fist. When I'm on dry land, he lets me go so I can wipe the stream of water from my eyes. He only has a tenuous handle on his laughter when he asks, "Are you okay?"

"I'm fine," I say, mortified, studying my feet and the puddle expanding around them.

I shake it off—the embarrassment and the water—and with feigned confidence that borders on insolence, I look up.

It *is* him.

It's been three years; he's gained six inches and a solid fifty pounds, and his hair is shorter—no more boy-band shag. His once-round face is now strong lines and sharp angles, a dignified cleft marking his chin. His braces are gone, leaving his teeth so perfect I can't even be mad that he's laughing in my face.

Henry.

All grown up.

That night returns in a rush: Tati screeching with disappointment over a failed summer school test, followed by crushing loneliness and grief, which I hadn't yet learned to compartmentalize. I retreated to the pool and sat at the water's edge, sobbing with a hysteria that scared me. A boy came out of nowhere. He sat down next to me, sinking his feet into the pool, putting a paperback copy of *The Outsiders* on the deck beside him. He didn't try to console me; for the longest time, he didn't talk at all. But he was there, a comforting presence who knew nothing and asked for nothing and expected nothing.

Eventually, he spoke, a soliloquy about how saltwater pools aren't really different from chlorine pools because, thanks to this process called electrolysis, the salt transforms naturally into

29

chlorine. It was so utterly random that I was distracted from my tears and unexpectedly charmed.

We hung out until dawn—the first of many times I'd stay out past curfew—walking along the beach, exhausting subjects not important enough to recall. I didn't tell him about my dead parents or my mean sister or the world geography class she'd insisted I retake over the summer even though I'd passed with a C+ the first time around. He didn't tell me anything personal either, though he talked almost constantly about the tide and the constellations and the novel he was reading.

He was the brightest person I'd ever met.

Just before sunrise, under a lavender sky, we shared a kiss that felt like a beginning.

I was sure it was. So sure that I didn't ask for his last name, phone number, email address, or apartment number. I knew I'd see him again later at the pool.

I did not. Not that night, or the one after, or the one after that.

For weeks, I was heartbroken.

And then I wasn't.

He'd been what I'd needed that night: a comrade, a comfort, a kiss. He became the boy to whom I compared all others.

Henry has put a lid on his laughter, but now I'm giddy thanks to his reappearance, this boy I've spent the last three years romanticizing. I shock myself by catching a fit of giggles so intense that I'm short of breath by the time they subside.

"Hell of an entry," he says, grinning. "Ten points for the splash alone."

He's taller than me by several inches and has the physique of someone who cares about fitness. Three years ago, he was all limbs. He's got his book tucked under his arm, which is in keeping with my memory.

"I've been practicing, obviously," I say with a blasé shrug. I toss the offending cotton ball into the pile I've made of its friends, then check my nails. Miraculously, my manicure has survived. Hopefully my witch hair will too, if I give it a good rinse when I get upstairs. "I haven't laughed that hard in forever," I admit.

Lately, I haven't laughed much at all.

"Me neither," he says in a melancholy tone that hints at tough times.

Where did you disappear to? I think, gazing up at him.

His voice is lighter when he says, "Thanks for the show."

"Thanks for setting it in motion."

He extends a hand again, this time like *Nice to meet you.* I lose a breath to disappointment—he doesn't remember. But why would he? I was a blip on the radar of his life. A sad girl, a sweet kiss, an abridged romance. I bet he's met hundreds— *thousands*—of people between then and now. I bet he's captivated them all.

The truth of it is that I idealized a stranger, let one night become of astronomical importance in my mind. I wove an entire fantasy from the threads of a boy I knew for a few hours.

But now, here he is.

His hand is still outstretched, and the vibe between us is becoming awkward.

31

I can play this off. We'll simply meet again, for the first time.

I slide my palm into his.

You're a stranger to him, I remind myself.

Except now he's holding on to my hand like a lost friend found.

He says, "How've you been, Piper?"

Henry

"YOU REMEMBER," SHE SAYS ON an exhale.

I smile. "How could I forget?"

She pulls her hand free of mine; I've been clinging to her for-fucking-ever.

Get a grip, Henry.

"It's been a long time," she says.

"I guess," I reply, shrugging like a small but significant piece of my history didn't just fall from the sky—and into a swimming pool.

She looks a lot like I remember, except her curls used to be like corn silk, and now they're mahogany dark. "I've been wondering if you still lived at the Towers."

She blinks. "Have you?"

"Well…yeah." I scuff the sole of my shoe against the deck, the back of my neck going hot. That was a weird thing to admit.

"I still live here," she confirms. "I'll likely die here."

"It's crazy to run into you again." It's another asinine statement, but damn if she doesn't have me flustered.

She looks up at the stars, and I wonder if she's thinking about the night we met.

I sure as shit am.

She lowers her eyes to meet mine, narrowing them. "You disappeared. I thought I'd see you the next day. Or the following week. Or at least before *now*."

"I wish I'd said something—goodbye, for starters." I point to the east tower. "My dad lives up there. The last time you and I saw each other, I'd come to hang out with him for a week. I left the morning after we met. I should've told you, but it all seemed kind of..."

"Surreal?" she supplies.

I smile. "Yeah."

"And now you're here for another visit?"

"First in three years. I got into town a few hours ago."

"Well. Welcome back."

"Thanks," I say. And then, unsure what's supposed to come next, I let my gaze drop. Her cutoffs are dripping water down her legs. She's still wearing the blue T-shirt—the one she had on earlier when I spotted her in the parking lot. SUGAR BAY MARINE CONSERVATION PARK, it says. Tiny illustrated turtles dot the *i*'s. Her nails are blue green, similar to the color of the water in the illuminated pool.

She says, "I live in the west tower. But I hang out down here a lot."

34

She heads for a nearby lounge chair, then sinks onto it, gesturing to the one beside it. I sit, a little woozy suddenly, because holy shit, I've just plugged back into a conversation that disconnected three years ago.

The pool area's as nice as I remember—swept pavement, neat lines of chairs, lampposts that emit a soft glow—and so quiet I hear waves crashing down on the beach. The stars over the ocean are bright and innumerable. I get why she likes it here.

Piper.

I can't believe I'm sitting next to her after all this time.

Life is fucking weird.

A breeze rustles the palms. The air's warm, but she's soaking wet. "Are you cold?"

"Are you kidding?" she says. "The water felt good."

"Oh, so the swan dive was intentional?"

"Clearly."

"It's strange, though, right? That it's so warm in the middle of the night?"

"Not strange for Florida. Where do you live?"

"Spokane."

"Washington?" When I nod, she asks, "Does it really rain all the time?"

"Nah. You're thinking of Western Washington. Spokane's on the east side of the state. There's a mountain range that runs north-south, the Cascades, and it traps most of the precipitation that comes off the Pacific, which means the eastern part of the state is arid. The winters are cold and the summers are hot, unlike Western Washington, which is mostly mild and—" I cut myself off; her eyes are glazing over. "Sorry. Boring."

She flashes a teasing grin. "No, *fascinating*. How long are you in Sugar Bay this time?"

I set my book, *The Art of Command*, on the empty chair beside mine. "All summer."

"Why do you say that like it's a prison sentence?"

It feels disloyal to talk shit about my dad while he's upstairs sleeping off the quartet of IPAs he drank at dinner. I shake my head, remembering his suggestion that I call him Davis, his invitation to down a beer. "My dad's…a lot."

"A lot," she echoes. "I get it."

She's wearing a pearl in each earlobe, but her right ear also has a trail of tiny silver hoops traveling its helix. They're new. New to me, anyway.

I remember her tears when we first met, her insistence that whatever had caused them wasn't worth rehashing. Her assurance that she'd be fine, and could we just talk about something else? She'd calmed down, and I'd let it go because back then I was clueless about how to nudge the truth from a girl.

I don't let it go now. "Is your family maddening too?"

"Quite." She hesitates, inspecting the nail polish on her left hand. "You know how I said I hang out here a lot?"

"Yeah. Because your parents get on your case?"

"Because it's the perfect escape," she says, telling me nothing at all.

I smile. "Except now I know where to find you."

36

She huffs. "Like I'm worried. After tonight, you'll disappear for another three years."

I let my head rest against the back of the chair, angled so I can study the hills and valleys of her profile. Her oil-slick hair and straight nose are striking. The smattering of freckles across her cheeks is adorable. Her lips are full and glossy; it's hard to believe I kissed her once. My teeth were bracketed in braces back then. Must've been terrible for her.

"Chances are," I say, "you'll see me again."

She laughs, skeptical. "Your track record's shit. Excuse me if I don't get my hopes up."

While I fumble for a response, something in the distance catches her attention. I follow her gaze toward the west tower, where a featureless woman, backlit against the light of the lobby window, is waving in our direction. "Piper!" she shouts. "Home. Now!"

Piper pops up out of her chair, shaking her head.

"Your mom?" I guess.

"My warden. I've gotta go."

"I'll look for you next time I'm out here."

"Sure," she says, though it's clear she doubts there'll be a next time. She collects her cotton balls and polish, then heads for the west tower, where the woman has ducked inside.

Just before she steps through the gate, she turns back to call, "Hey, Henry? Seriously, though…it wouldn't suck to see you again."

Piper

THE NIGHT HENRY AND I first met, he told me about how his eighth-grade honors biology class spent two weeks dissecting fetal pigs for their final project and how interesting it'd been to see the inner workings of a mammal's anatomy.

"Gross," I said, adjusting my position on the pool deck. "Are you, like, a serial killer in training?"

My question must've startled him because he stammered, "I...uh...no? I am a huge nerd, though. I named my pig Old Major. You know, from *Animal Farm*?"

"Haven't read it."

"You should. He was cool. A lot cooler than the characters my classmates used for name inspiration. There were a lot of Wilburs and Miss Piggies in that lab."

I laughed. "I bet it smelled terrible."

"Oh, god, yeah. Have you had to dissect anything?"

"My biology class cut up cow eyeballs, but I refused." Threw real fit, I did. Gabi joined my protest in solidarity. Our teacher ended up giving us drawings of an eyeball to label for 80 percent credit. Tati shamed me for accepting a lesser grade, but Maggie and Byron, Gabi's parents, applauded their daughter for taking a stand.

"You refused?" Henry repeated, incredulous, like he was personally affronted. "Why?"

"Well, it's disgusting, for starters. And inhumane."

"Are you a vegetarian?"

"No."

"Then it's not inhumane. If you eat burgers, dissecting an eyeball in the name of science isn't a big deal."

"That's...one way to look at it," I said, reluctant to admit that he had a point. "No pun intended."

He smiled, and I almost swooned, like the ladies in the romance novels I snuck from my sister's bookshelves. I believed what he'd said about being a huge nerd, but he also had a sense of humor. After the screaming match I'd had with Tati, it was refreshing to be with someone who didn't take himself too seriously.

"This is the weirdest conversation I've ever had," I said, my voice raspy thanks to my earlier sob-fest.

He shrugged. "Are your parents expecting you home soon?"

"Definitely not."

I could tell my response raised some questions, but to his credit, he didn't pry. "You feel like taking a walk down the beach?"

39

I get lost in the memory as the elevator carries me up to the apartment, where my sister is undoubtedly waiting, simmering with annoyance at the late hour and the male company I was keeping down at the pool.

While Tati's interruption was unfortunate, how lucky that I chose to stay at the Towers tonight rather than visiting my other happy place, the Marine Conservation Park.

For the last few years, every couple of months or so, I've snuck in well past closing, late enough to bypass the rent-a-cop who makes nightly rounds. Through trial and error, I've learned the easiest entry point and memorized which paths are out of range of the security cameras. Turtle would disapprove, I'm sure, and Tati would ground me for a thousand years if she found out I was going so far down the beach in the dark—not to mention entering private property without permission—but the Marine Conservation Park is as grounding as it is sentimental. When I'm really missing my parents, or reeling from an argument with my sister, or feeling more lost than usual, thirty minutes spent watching the sea turtles or the rays swim gentle circles in their pools is enough to make me feel like I'm back on solid ground.

But had I indulged in a park escape tonight, I would've missed Henry.

It's as if our reunion was written in the stars.

Henry

WHITNEY 3:46 P.M.

Text me when you land.

7:39 P.M.

Did you make it?

9:22 P.M.

Hello?!

11:08 P.M.

You're leaving me to wonder if you died in a fiery crash?

1:22 A.M.

You suck.

2:20 A.M.

Henry. Could you just let me know you're okay?

2:48 A.M.

I texted your mom. She told me you arrived. Thanks a lot.

Shit, I think when I read those time stamps. I saw that she'd texted last night when I got back to Dad's, but I didn't open the thread because I'd just spent a drama-free hour with a girl, and it was so rejuvenating that I didn't feel like taking a step backward.

But it was a dick move, making Whit worry.

I check to be sure it's not the ass crack of dawn in Spokane, then shoot her a text.

HENRY 10:27 A.M.

Sorry! Yeah, I made it.

10:33 A.M.

Whit, I'm sorry. I'm here. I'm good.

WHITNEY 11:02 A.M.

I'm so glad.

The sarcasm saturating those three little words is mind-blowing.

I head out for a quick beach run. By the time I've gotten home, guzzled water, and cleaned myself up, Dad's shouting that it's time to head out. We've got a tee time at a very nice local golf course, the Emerald Outlook. Tiger Woods plays there when he vacations in Sugar Bay, according to Dad, who whoops me even though what he's drinking is a lot stronger than my Gatorade. He's not very humble about his victory, either.

When we get back to the Towers, I stand beneath the cold spray of the shower, hoping to soothe the sunburn I earned on the course. Afterward, I swipe a hand over the foggy mirror to find that my face is thoroughly charred. Fantastic.

I slather on aloe I find in the medicine cabinet, then throw on shorts and a T-shirt before grabbing a bottle of water from the kitchen. I hole up in my room, thinking about how skiing with Dad is a thousand times better than golfing with Dad. Why'd he have to move all the way to Florida?

My phone buzzes with a text: Whitney again. I still feel bad about cold-shouldering her last night, so I fire off a response.

WHITNEY 4:29 P.M.
How's Sugar Bay?

HENRY 4:30 P.M.
Okay. You good?

WHITNEY 4:33 P.M.
Fine.

HENRY 4:35 P.M.
You sure?

WHITNEY 4:36 P.M.
Yep.

I don't know how to reply, or if I even should. I came to Florida to put space between us. I feel shitty about leaving her to

43

sift through the mess we made together, but I can't let her anchor herself to me again.

Back in March, before spring break, before everything *really* went to hell, I sat my mom down and told her Whitney and I had broken up. She was shocked. She loves Whit, and she loves Whit's family.

"You two were so happy," she said, taking my hand in both of hers. We were at the table in our tiny kitchen. She'd just gotten off a shift and hadn't yet changed out of her scrubs.

"*Were* being the operative word," I said.

"Oh, Henry. I'm sorry."

I pulled free of her grasp, putting a mug of steaming tea in her hands instead. I love my mom a lot, but her sympathy wasn't helping.

"Are you okay?" she asked.

"I'm fine."

I wasn't. I was a walking contradiction. Sad but thankful. Relieved but pissed. Free but somehow still obligated.

WHITNEY 4:40 P.M.

Your mom misses you.

HENRY 4:42 P.M.

I've barely been gone a day.

WHITNEY 4:43 P.M.

I miss you.

4:57 P.M.

Henry?

HENRY 5:00 P.M.

Yeah—sorry. I'm with my dad. You know how it is.

WHITNEY 5:01 P.M.

Not really. Let me know when you've got time to talk.

She doesn't text again after that. I open our thread a dozen times over the course of the night, trying to figure out how to fix this for her. If I should. If I *can*.

I don't reengage.

After Dad leaves for the restaurant, I dial Mom. She answers with, "Whitney texted."

"I know. Sorry. I texted her back."

"Henry."

"Mom. What am I supposed to do?"

She sighs. She's at work. The sounds of the NICU are unmistakable. "I don't know. It's a fine line you're walking."

"Yeah."

She says my name again, less admonishingly. "I'm sorry for what you're going through. I'm sorry Whitney's become a source of discord."

I run a hand over my sun-fried face, which prickles and aches. Mom doesn't know every detail leading up to what happened this spring, but she knows the important stuff.

"It's my fault as much as it's hers," I say.

"It's not anyone's fault, honey. It just is."

"I wish it'd go away. I wish I could forget that any of it ever happened." I sound bitter, though I'm not sure I have a right to the emotion.

"It's part of who you are now. Grow from it. Don't let it drag you down."

I sit with that for a minute, hoping that one day her advice will tunnel from my head to my heart. "I'll try. Thanks, Mom."

"You're welcome. Now, tell me how your dad is."

"He's good. Same as always."

"How's the sports bar?"

"Really cool, actually." I don't mention Dad's request that I call him Davis or his suggestion that I have a beer with him. Mom mixes the occasional Seven and Seven after a tough shift, but she'd drown in the stuff before she offered it to me.

"What's his apartment like?"

"It's okay," I say, downplaying how nice the Towers are. Mom's never cared much about lavishness, and we've never been able to afford it anyway. I'm not gonna make her feel less than by describing Dad's leather sofa and state-of-the-art home theater system. "He fixed up the spare room for me. Bought a quilt and a dresser and everything."

"Does that mean you're never coming back?" she asks, her tone teasing.

"No way." Dad's place is great, and running into Piper last

night didn't suck, but Spokane's home. "He's trying hard," I tell Mom. "Like, too hard."

"That's his way. He can be a pain in the neck, but his heart's in the right place. Give him a chance, okay? He loves you."

"I know," I admit, though I had my doubts on the golf course. Seemed like the kind of torture you'd inflict on your worst enemy.

"I've got to get back to work, Henry. But I miss you. You're my whole heart."

She tells me that a lot.

I know it's the truth.

Piper

I DON'T SEE TATI BEFORE work on Wednesday morning, but she texts me a list of chores before my lunch break. It's like she's the wicked not-stepsister and I'm Cinderella. Except I don't have birds or mice to bolster my mood.

After my shift at the park, I walk back to the Towers, hoping Tati's still in her lobby office with a stack of complaints or applications or invoices—whatever she does on the day-to-day. I'm in luck; our apartment's empty. I blow off my sister's to-do list and make a quick change into a black bikini she calls *not nearly modest enough*, topping it with a light sundress that does double duty as a cover-up. Then I go to the beach, where I spend what's left of the afternoon with my worn-out copy of *Delphina of the Starlit Sea*, the first story in a blockbuster fantasy trilogy about a mermaid princess fighting for her rightful crown. It's my favorite series of all time. I reread it every year; this time around it's bringing me even more comfort than usual, because this summer blows.

Freshman year, Gabi and I spent a lot of time on this stretch of sand, camped out on the padded loungers, sipping seltzer, listening to new pop and old country, and trading books. We adore fantasy, and we both *love* Delphina. She's into true crime as well, and I haven't met a frothy romance I don't like, so we never had a shortage of stories to read. We'd take turns keeping watch for Tati, and when we'd spot her marching onto the hot sand, heels in hand, mouth pulled into a perpetual frown, Gabi and I would jet into the surf, pretending not to hear her shouts. Around five, we'd retreat to our respective homes, shower off the salt, and grace our families with our presence at dinner, then sneak out again after dark.

That's around the time that Hudson and Jayden started to join us. Sometimes Hudson's cousin Anna and her best friend, Michaela, came too, because they're in our grade and Hudson's too nice to leave anyone out. We had innocent fun: night swims and games of Thirty-One, betting quarters and laughing a lot.

Mitchel Damon moved to Sugar Bay at the beginning of sophomore year. He joined the wrestling team and became fast friends with the guys. The following summer, he started coming to our nighttime get-togethers. That was when gambling with spare change became a thing of the past. Damon advocated for skinny-dipping in the Gulf, games of I Never, and generously spiked drinks. Jayden's brother was twenty-four and didn't have a problem with providing alcohol to minors, so the guys began

49

showing up with wine coolers, Malibu, cheap beer, and Fireball. Our exclusive gatherings became parties, but as far as Gabi and I were concerned, everyone else was part of the backdrop.

It had been her and me since we were nine, when she moved to Sugar Bay with her parents and younger brother, Tyson. I was as much of a loner back then as I am now, happy watching movies with my mom, snorkeling with my dad, or paging through the ocean-centric library my parents proudly curated for me. Back then, I thought Tati was the sun and the moon, but she had moved to Boston, and I cherished having our parents' undivided attention.

The kids in my class didn't get me. I was mature for my age (though Tati refuses to believe that was ever the case) and quiet until I started blathering about subjects I cared about, like marine biology and the Delphina trilogy. I wasn't bullied, probably because I'd socked Jason Elliot in third grade. He'd called me a tramp, a word he couldn't define but took great pleasure in tossing around when our teacher wasn't listening. After that, no one gave me shit.

Gabi Moore joined us in November of fourth grade and was assigned the only empty seat in the classroom, which was next to me. After she'd loaded her supplies into the cubby under her desk, she noticed the paperback peeking out of mine—the first book in The Spiderwick Chronicles. "I liked that one a lot," she said. "Have you read the others?"

"Not yet, but I'm going to. Have you read *Delphina of the Starlit Sea*?"

She grinned. "I have—I love it! *Delphina and the Coral Crown* is my favorite."

"That's my favorite of the movies, but the first book is my favorite of the novels." Because my parents had originally read it to me, a chapter or two a night, snuggled up on the couch.

Gabi sighed happily. "I've seen the movies more times than I can count."

"Me too! We should marathon them together sometime."

We did that very weekend, laying the foundation of our friendship.

God, I miss her.

It's after five when my stomach protests its emptiness. I throw my cover-up on over my suit, pack my towel and book, and walk down the shore to the stretch of restaurants that draw tourists. Usually I steer clear of them, but coconut shrimp sounds amazing, and I don't feel like dealing with my sister.

I pick a sports bar, Blitz Brews. It's been around a few years, though I've never been inside because I have no use for sports or bars. Tati's eaten here, though, and she mentioned that it's good. The hostess greets me, pulls a menu from her podium, and walks me toward a line of booths along a wall of windows.

Adjusting my bag on my shoulder, I do a double take as I pass Henry, who I haven't seen since my belly flop into the pool. He's hunkered down at the end of the bar, face sunburned as hell, 100 percent engrossed in the book he was poring over before my impromptu swim.

He's as amusingly dorky as my rose-tinted memory of him,

51

and now he's hot too. It was nice to hang out with someone who doesn't know about my tragedy of a backstory or my recent screw-ups. I consider saying hi, but I'm guessing he's meeting his dad. Probably for the best; my imagination's done a number on him over the years, shaping him into a romantic hero instead of a teenage boy. It's probably wise not to clue him in to how bonkers the inner workings of my brain can be.

I take a seat several booths away, then peruse the menu, stealing glances at Henry every so often. He's seriously fried. Has no one handed him a bottle of sunscreen since his return to Florida? He doesn't look up as a waiter breezes by him and stops in front of me.

He's the hunky windsurfer type, dressed in khaki shorts and a collared shirt with BLITZ BREWS embroidered where a polo horse might otherwise be. His name tag reads CLAY. Tati would say he's too old for me, but he's probably only halfway through a bachelor's degree. I ask for coconut shrimp with fries and sweet tea with lemon. He nods, flashing me a catalogue-worthy smile before hustling toward the kitchen.

I'm taking inspiration from bookworm Henry and pulling my paperback from my bag when there's a commotion near the entrance. I look up to find the source of the noise.

Damon.

My heart plummets.

He's with Jayden and Hudson, guys I've known most of my life, guys I called friends up until the night everything fell apart. Before, Gabi and I were the sun of our own solar system,

52

a sparkling supernova the boys orbited with enthusiasm. Now that I've been cast out, I'm not sure what they think of me.

Not that I want Damon to think of me—not now, not ever.

The hostess who seated me gestures for them to follow her. Though he's only known Hudson and Jayden for a couple years, Damon's the ringleader of their trio. He makes seating requests and shouts questions about which TV will air the Tampa Bay Rays game. By the time they've settled a few tables away from me, in front of the TV they've deemed best, I'm pretty sure I've successfully hidden behind my book, despite the dismal odds.

"Holy shit—Piper!" Hudson says, his voice carrying across the restaurant. Of the three boys, I like him most. He's got a younger sister and a nice mom and a higher standard for manners than most of the guys I know, especially the wrestling guys. Right now, though, I hate him for calling attention to me. Because now Jayden and Damon are looking at me too, as is Henry, his expression caught somewhere between delight and surprise.

I force my distress down as Jayden calls out a hello. Damon says nothing, though his stare sends a tremor through me, rattling my facade of composure.

"Your hair looks awesome," Hudson says, waving me over. "Come sit with us."

I loop a dark curl behind my ear, then tuck in like a sea snail, rounding my spine, dropping my chin. Pointing to my book, I shrug like, *Little ol' me, reading alone at dinnertime.*

My pass garners affable boos, plus a dickish eye roll from Damon.

53

Jayden and Hudson move on to their menus, but Damon isn't done. He snares my gaze and holds it hostage. My face goes hot, and my palms turn clammy. A lot of what happened at Gabi's party is a boozy blur, but despite what she thinks she saw, I remember this: I felt worthless, powerless, *afraid* when I was alone with Damon. It's the same now, even in a busy sports bar with Hudson, Jayden, Henry, and a whole waitstaff within shouting distance.

His stare grazes my mouth before falling to my neck, my shoulders, my sternum, bared by my flimsy sundress.

Goose bumps fan out over my skin.

He takes off his dingy white baseball hat, stained with a ring of sweat. He runs a hand through his flaxen hair, then repositions the hat backward, giving me full view of his face. He licks his lips and then, in a voice that projects, says, "I liked you better blond."

I focus on the words printed in my book, which are starting to swim.

He won't quit. "You look hot in that bikini, though."

I look up and say, loudly and without thought, "Fuck you, Damon."

"You wish," he says, punctuated by a filthy hand gesture.

God. What does Gabi see in him?

People are looking at me like I'm a willing participant in this spectacle, though nothing could be further from the truth. I'm mortified and a nanosecond from crawling under the table when Jayden, bless him, throws an elbow into Damon's shoulder. "Dude, don't be an ass."

His admonishing is in good fun, all *Ha ha, boys will be boys*. He and Hudson are truly decent, but they're as clueless as Gabi when it comes to who Damon really is. Mostly they just enjoy railing on each other. Still, I send him a quick nod of thanks before nose-diving back into my book. Tears prick my eyes, and there's a mango-size lump in my throat, but I will *not* cry. Not here. Not in front of Damon.

A shadow falls over my table. I look up, expecting Clay and a plate of crispy coconut shrimp. I find Henry, holding his big-ass book and a half-drained glass of soda.

He slides in beside me, close enough that I feel the heat of his arm against mine. His body language allows for the assumption that we're together—maybe that's the point—and if that'll shut up Damon, great.

"Friends of yours?" he asks, nodding toward the guys.

"Define *friends*," I say dryly.

Raucous laughter explodes from their table. It's probably not aimed at me, but it feels personal. My flush deepens. I bet I'm as red as Henry's sunburned cheeks.

He's staring Damon down, and he looks *pissed*, like one more word out of this new adversary will have him shattering his glass in a Hulk-like fist. Damon's an all-district wrestler, but he's lean and only an inch or two taller than me. A tiger shark to Henry's great white.

I wonder if he's intimidated.

Damon looks away first.

Coward.

Henry swigs his soda then bangs the glass down on the table-top, seemingly disgusted by this idiot who harasses girls in family establishments.

I'm a little intimidated myself.

But when he looks back at me, his face clears. He shifts a little, like he's just become aware of how close we're sitting. In the space of a heartbeat, he's returned to the Henry I'm acquainted with: sweet, mindful, a little awkward.

"That guy's a tool," he tells me. "I apologize on behalf of my gender."

"Unnecessary, but thank you."

"You go to school with him?"

"Unfortunately."

"Does he always treat you like that?"

"It's a recent development."

"It's bullshit."

"Yeah. Tell me about it."

He gives me a reserved smile. "I didn't mean to butt in. You clearly had it handled. It just looked like you could use some backup."

Dog-earing the page I last read, I set my book on the tabletop. Henry puts his near it and asks, "Got a thing for mermaids?"

"Totally," I say, glad we've wordlessly agreed to pretend Damon doesn't exist. I rest a reverent hand on *Delphina of the Starlit Sea*'s worn cover; her black-blue hair swirls in the water around her, and her lilac tail is curled coyly. I'll never be ashamed of Delphina and her underwater world. "Mermaids are the best."

56

"I'll take your word for it," Henry says.

"You've never read the Delphina trilogy?"

"No."

"But you've seen the movies, right?"

"Nope."

"How is that possible? They're a freaking phenomenon." I narrow my eyes. "Are you one of those guys who thinks mermaids are only for girls?"

"Not even a little bit. I haven't read the Percy Jackson books or *The Lion, the Witch, and the Wardrobe* either. Fantasy's just not my thing."

"Fantasy can be anyone's thing."

He allows that. "Then I guess I'm not interested in reading about little kids."

It takes true effort to reel in my exasperation. It irks me when people act as though books about children can't have meaningful themes. Even Henry, unwitting star of my fantasies, isn't immune to my fierce defense of my favorite books. "Delphina's not a little kid. She's fourteen when the trilogy starts and our age at the end of the third book. By then, this land dweller who comes from nothing has saved the sea, found true love, and become the ruler of a kingdom of merfolk. She's a *hero*."

Henry smirks, amused. "If you say so."

I pick up my book and hug it to my chest, shielding it from his indifference. "You sound like my sister."

His eyes twinkle—he's obviously flattered. "Yeah?"

I level him with a glower. "That's *not* a compliment."

57

Henry

PIPER LOOKS LIKE SHE WANTS to tear my arm off, then use it to beat me over the head.

I'm saved by Clay, the server working our section. Mateo introduced me to him when I came in earlier. He goes to FSU but is renting a condo in Sugar Bay for the summer with a bunch of friends. He gives me a nod, drops off a plate of shrimp and fries, tops off Piper's iced tea, then takes off for another table.

Piper pushes her meal toward me. "I'll share, but only because this is enough shrimp to feed an army. I'm not rewarding your holier-than-thou literary attitude." She puts on a mocking tone. *"Fantasy's not my thing."*

I laugh, marveling at this paradox of a girl who reads kids' books and lobs f-bombs across restaurants. I'm supposed to eat with my dad later, but he's out in Pensacola at a restaurant supply store. Not long before I noticed Piper was here, he texted to tell me he's held up in traffic. I'm starving, and weak when it comes to fried food.

We let my apparent shit taste in books go in favor of attacking Piper's meal. The girl can put away some coconut shrimp. She pauses when she notices me dunking fries in tartar sauce. "Ew," she says.

"What'd you mean, *ew*?"

"Fries are meant to be eaten with ketchup."

"You have a lot of opinions," I tell her, tossing a tartar-dipped fry into my mouth.

She grimaces. "It's weird, is all."

"Don't knock it till you try it." I hold a saucy fry out to her.

"Pass."

She sips her iced tea, which has a half dozen squeezed lemon wedges floating in it. Her dark curls are coiled in a knot, and there are black bikini strings tied around her neck. Her dress is a very sheer field of flowers, and there's a dusting of white sand across her suntanned shoulders, like someone sprinkled sugar over her skin.

"Come from the beach?" I ask.

"Yep. I worked this morning. And now here I am, dining with a stranger."

"Hey, you can't criticize my literary *and* culinary tastes, then call me a stranger."

She grins, giving me a shrug like, *Touché*, and Jesus, her smile is contagious. "That shirt you were wearing the other night, the blue one—that's where you work?"

"Sugar Bay Marine Conservation Park." Her expression goes dreamy, like there's no better place in the world. "We rehab animals and educate the public. Lots of tourists visit."

"Should I check it out?"

"Totally. Come when I'm working, and I'll show you the best exhibits." She plucks a shrimp from the plate, chewing while she gives me a once-over. "Your face is scorched," she observes, as if I haven't noticed that I'm seared like a tuna steak.

I put a hand on the back of my neck—also burnt. "My dad and I golfed eighteen holes yesterday. He kicked my ass."

"Where'd you play? The surface of the sun?"

"Close. The Emerald Outlook. Do you know it?"

"No. I don't like golf."

"Neither do I."

She gives me an inquisitive look. "Then why'd you go?"

"My dad was fired up about it. We don't get to hang out a lot with him living all the way out here. I feel like I owe him some father-son time."

"You're a good human," she declares, like sacrificial golf is all it takes. "Except you're not supposed to put your dermis at risk to please others. SPF next time?"

"For sure. Lesson learned."

Her phone chimes from the depths of her bag. She digs it out and gives it a cursory glance. She frowns, then rifles through her bag again, unearthing a ten and a twenty. Tossing them on the table, she stands. "I've got to go. Do me a solid and make sure the check gets paid?"

I slide her money back toward her. "Don't worry about it."

"Henry. Just because I let you come to my rescue earlier doesn't mean you need to get all chivalrous on me now."

"I wouldn't think of it. The thing is, my dad owns this place. He's actually really into chivalry"— I pronounce the word in the same grossed-out tone she used—"and he'd kill me if I let a girl pay for coconut shrimp."

She pushes her book into her bag, then her cash. "All this time, I've been sitting with the owner's kid? Thank your dad for me. And thank you for hanging out."

I stand to let her out of the booth. She hauls her bag onto her sandy shoulder and flashes me a grin that makes my stomach somersault.

I squash the feeling, the attraction.

I've got no business falling for this girl. Not after what happened with Whitney.

My mouth is a lap ahead of my brain, though, because it's already tossing out an invitation. "I'm thinking about heading to the pool later. I've got to get through a meal with my dad, but I'm gonna need a swim after. You should come down. Around nine?"

She's quiet long enough to have me second-guessing my suggestion. But then another smile crinkles the corners of her eyes, and my regrets fly out the window.

"Yeah," she says. "I'll try to make it."

61

Piper

THAT FIRST NIGHT WE MET, as we walked away from the pool and the sadness I'd spilled all over the place, Henry asked about my favorite food (white rice with tons of butter and salt and pepper) and my favorite movie (*The Wizard of Oz*—I used to watch it with my sister, before) and my favorite song (Queen's "Somebody to Love" because my parents used to blast it through the house while they were cooking or cleaning).

"What about you?" I asked as we navigated the moonlit beach.

"I like folksy stuff. Watchhouse, the Avett Brothers, the Enliveners."

"Oh, me too! My best friend and I saw the Enliveners in May—they were amazing."

Gabi's mom, Maggie, had driven us to Atlanta for a music festival, and we'd had the *best* time. She'd hung back, letting us pretend to be on our own, as if we were older and more mature than our fourteen years. We'd worn halter tops and shredded jeans and hoop earrings that grazed our shoulders. We'd sung and danced. We'd drunk fresh-squeezed lemonade and pretended not to know what was going on when Maggie tugged us away from a group of college kids who were getting blazed on a blanket close to ours. Later, in a hotel room fancier than anyplace I'd ever stayed before, the three of us donned plush bathrobes and ordered slices of seven-layer chocolate cake.

I was about to tell Henry all of this when movement up ahead caught my eye.

"Hang on." I stopped to squint into the distance.

"What is it?" he asked, following my gaze.

"I think…" I took a few steps away from the water, toward the dune grass. I peered into the darkness, trying to make sense of the shape in the sand. And then, keeping my voice soft despite my excitement, I said, "Yes! There's a turtle up ahead. She's nesting."

"Wait, really? Like, a sea turtle?"

"Yeah. From here, she looks like a loggerhead."

"Can we go closer?"

"Maybe a little. We don't want to scare her. No phone flashlights, okay? She'll get disoriented."

We shuffled forward, making sure to give the mama turtle—who was definitely a loggerhead—plenty of space. We watched, fascinated, as she flapped her flippers in the sand, digging a body pit and a chamber in which to lay her eggs—probably about a hundred of them. When she was done, she buried and camouflaged the nest, then lumbered to the gulf, where a placid wave helped her glide into the dark water.

"That was the absolute coolest," Henry said once she'd disappeared. "I mean, *wow*. Have you ever seen anything like that before?"

"A couple of times, with my parents." When I began to get interested in marine life, my mom and dad started bringing me to the shore after dark, toting beach chairs, midnight snacks, and turtle-safe flashlights. "Once we saw hatchlings making their way into the ocean. They were so cute and tiny, scuttling down to the surf."

"But how did they know where to go? I mean, instinct, I guess, but how do they figure out where the water is?"

"They move toward light. The moon reflecting off the water is usually the brightest thing out here at night."

"Whoa. Nature is crazy-cool."

I smiled; my thoughts exactly. "What's really amazing is that when the turtles are ready to lay eggs of their own—like, twenty or thirty years later—they almost always return to the same beach where they hatched."

He lifted his brows, impressed. "How do you know all this stuff?"

My parents were super smart about ocean animals, and I want to be just like them was the truest answer. But it was also the most personal. I wasn't ready to go there.

64

I started walking away from the turtle's nest, bare feet sinking into the cool sand. Henry stayed by my side.

"I grew up near the beach." I nodded toward the book under his arm. "And I like to read, like you. Also, I love sea turtles. If I had to choose, I'd say they're my favorite animal. What's yours?" I asked, trying to throw him off the trail of my gloomy family life.

"Ostriches," he replied without hesitation.

I couldn't help but laugh. "Really?"

"Yeah. They can run twenty-plus miles at an average speed of thirty miles per hour. That means they could run a full marathon in forty-five minutes, theoretically. Incredible."

"Yikes. They look prehistoric."

"Birds are more closely related to dinosaurs than any other living animal, so that checks out. And yeah, they're creepy, but no more so than a turkey or a chicken."

"True," I said, shuddering at the memory of the blue-headed wild turkey I'd encountered the summer before while hiking with Gabi and her family.

We trekked out of the deeper sand, closer to the waves. There was plenty of room to walk without getting wet, but Henry took the spot closest to the water, a considerate act that didn't escape my notice.

We'd only known each other a couple of hours, but I liked him. He was kind. He was funny. He liked animals, even ugly animals. Our musical tastes aligned. He was smart, full of interesting trivia that was hilariously useless. He asked me questions,

65

like he thought *I* was smart. Like my opinions and experiences were valuable.

I couldn't imagine him laughing at me, or belittling me, or rolling his eyes at me, as my sister had taken to doing. Talking to him unearthed my confidence. Being with him made me feel secure.

I was hooked.

Henry

AFTER PIPER LEAVES BLITZ BREWS, I pull out my phone to send a run update to Silas and Ricky, only to find that Whitney's been texting. I think about ignoring her messages, but I'm not a monster. We've been through a lot together, but she's survived infinitely more as an individual. It's not in me to ghost her.

WHITNEY 6:23 P.M.

It's been a day.

6:26 P.M.

I feel awful.

6:27 P.M.

My head's a mess and my heart feels too full. Like it's going to leak sadness into my chest.

I'd call her melodramatic, but I get what she means. Sometimes it feels impossible to deal with the despondence that's crashed over me in waves during the last few months. It's got to be even worse for her.

HENRY 6:32 P.M.
I wish there was something I could do.

WHITNEY 6:34 P.M.
You could have stayed.

HENRY 6:36 P.M.
Us being in the same city wouldn't change what happened.

WHITNEY 6:39 P.M.
It'd make it easier to deal.

HENRY 6:42 P.M.
Whit, I'm sorry.

WHITNEY 6:44 P.M.
Me too. Can't wait until you come back.

What I haven't told her—what I can't make myself tell her—is that even if I flew back to Spokane tomorrow, I wouldn't want to be with her.

WHITNEY 6:45 P.M.

I know it got hard at the end, but it'd be different now. Better.

6:47 P.M.

Don't you love me anymore?

I'm trying to rally the courage to say no—the hardest truth I've ever needed to tell—when my dad slides in across the table from me.

"That took forever—my bad. Ready to eat?"

I nod and send off one more text.

HENRY 6:47 P.M.

My dad's here. Talk later.

"Is that the girl?" Dad asks, nodding toward my phone.

What happened with Whitney had me on my ass for weeks. Of course Mom told Dad. That's what co-parents are supposed to do, I guess: discuss their kids, trade notes, report challenges. But I wish she hadn't. It was bad enough rehashing it with her. I can't do it again with him.

"She's *a* girl," I tell him.

He nods, mouth sinking into a frown. "I'm real sorry about what happened, buddy. Tough stuff."

"It's all good now."

It's definitely not, but I get the feeling Dad's as reluctant as I am to walk across the hot coals of my incinerated relationship. Playing it off benefits him as much as me.

"Glad to hear it," he says, flagging down Clay. "I'm ready for a burger. How 'bout you?"

Shit—I love how he favors easy conversation over emotional outpourings. Sometimes I wish Mom would take one out of his playbook.

I owe him another round of golf.

"Yeah," I say. "Burgers sound good."

Piper

TATI'S TEXT WAS DRAMATIC AS usual, insisting I leave Blitz Brews immediately and run by Publix for a carton of almond milk because I selfishly drank the last of it this morning. I knock out the errand, then head for the Towers, waffling about whether to take Henry up on his invitation to meet at the pool.

It sounds suspiciously like a date, which I'm not into. I love me some torrid fictional romance, but I've never had a boyfriend. I've never wanted one. Tati's succession of failed love affairs has taught me that relationships follow a certain pattern: new love euphoria, flaws inevitably coming to light, increasingly intense bickering, heart-shattering end. And then there's the way Gabi has gone all heart-eyes for Damon, that filthy loser.

I'd rather be single forever.

But Henry *is* fun to talk to. Also, the way he shut down

Damon at Blitz Brews... I didn't hate feeling looked after, if only for a few minutes.

After Tati goes into her room for the night, I put on a fresh suit—a cherry-printed bandeau top and red high-waisted bottoms—then cover it with cutoffs and a tank. Slipping on my favorite Reefs, I peer into the mirror over my dresser. My curls, windblown and salt steeped, are beyond help, so I leave them in their knot. I take five seconds to swipe vanilla gloss over my lips, then tiptoe into the hallway.

All's quiet in my sister's room. It seems that nagging me about almond milk, then bitching when I bought oat milk *instead* of almond milk, has extinguished her fire for the night. I sneak past her door, then pull a beach towel from the linen closet and stuff it into my bag. I'm within arm's reach of freedom when she steps into the hallway.

"Where are you going?" she asks, not very nicely.

"To the pool."

Her gaze narrows. "I've heard that before."

The night of Gabi's party, I said I was going to the pool too. Only instead of a towel, I was toting two bottles of Pinot and one of peach Schnapps, all stolen from my sister, wrapped in T-shirts to keep them from clanking. I didn't go to the Towers pool, but I did go swimming at Gabi's. Tati was *livid* when I was dropped off in the middle of the night by none other than her then-boyfriend, Officer Adam Lopez. While out on patrol, he'd spotted me making a serpentine trek down the sidewalk near the Marine Conservation Park. My drunken brain had insisted that

72

now was the time to sneak in for some curative time with my favorite sea animals, but because I was a stumbling, bumbling mess, I drew the attention of a cop.

The most unfortunate cop.

By the time he drove me to the Towers and escorted me upstairs, I was sobbing.

Tati didn't care that I was borderline hysterical. She didn't care that I threw up until dawn. She didn't care that it wasn't my fault—not all of it, anyway.

"No, I really am," I say now, pulling down the strap of my tank to show her my suit.

She sighs, wary. "Why? It's after nine. It's dark."

"Fresh air," I lie. The truth—because a boy asked me to—won't go over well.

"What's in the bag?"

I bite back the *You're not my mother* retort that lives permanently on the tip of my tongue and hold my bag open so she can examine its contents.

When she's done, she steps back and crosses her arms. "You're not going to be accompanied home by a police officer, are you?"

"*No*, Tati."

"You have an hour," she says with a resolute nod. "If you're not back by ten thirty, I'm coming to get you."

Because she has nothing better to do.

I turn for the door. "Whatever. Have fun up here by yourself."

73

Henry's poolside when I arrive.

He's left a towel, his book, and his shirt on a chair near where he's sitting on the deck, legs dangling in the illuminated water. He waves as I approach, and whoa. I've had him pegged as an adorkable intellectual, which I still think is true, but he definitely has a thing for the gym too. It strikes me as comically unjust that this boy was granted brains, muscles, thick hair, *and* etiquette. What was left for the other boys once Henry received his attributes?

Maybe he's the reason Damon lacks any good qualities.

I drop my bag on the chair beside his stuff. I leave my clothes on, feeling a little shy about hanging with Mr. Washboard Abs in my bikini, and take a seat on the deck. I leave a chasm of space between us, wishing I didn't feel this new compulsion to keep boys at a distance.

"I was starting to wonder if you were gonna show," he says.

I splash water over my knees. "My keeper wasn't keen on me coming down."

"Ah. My dad's still at work, or he would've hassled me too."

"He's overprotective?"

Henry gives a derisive laugh. "More like he wants to hang out all the time. When I was showering earlier, he burst into the bathroom to tell me *Field of Dreams* was on TV. Let a guy rinse the shampoo out of his hair before you start hounding him about a movie that's older than he is, you know?"

I resist the urge to tell him how lucky he is, that he should never take his parents' care for granted. Not that Tati doesn't care about me. She cares that my GPA remains above average. She cares that I don't end up a teen mom or with a criminal record. She cares that I become a responsible, productive Floridian because I'm a reflection of her. Because she took on a parental role she never asked for. Because she refuses to fail.

She doesn't care like a mom or a dad would.

But this is one of those *grass is always greener* situations. Maybe if Henry knew how I live—perpetually pestered about the importance of good grades and my bank balance and my future—he'd think, *Yes, please.* I sure as shit wouldn't turn my nose up at watching a movie with my dad.

The way he regards me makes me worry that my usually dormant grief has revealed itself. Very aware of how intimate this conversation is about to become, I say, "Your dad must love you a lot to try so hard."

Henry grasps the back of his reddened neck, watching the water lap against the tiled pool wall. "Yeah. I just wish he'd tone it down a little. I want to *want* to be here, you know?"

His deep brown eyes lift to meet mine. The air is warm, infused with ocean salt and the lingering scent of tropical tanning lotion. It scares me a little, how much I like being around this boy who gives me space without asking why I need it.

I smile. "Yeah, I know. I want you to want to be here too."

Henry

I SLIP INTO THE POOL because the eye contact suddenly feels too intense.

My memories of Piper from three years ago are wholesome. Her blond curls. Her freckles. How she talked about loggerheads like she'd been studying sea turtles all her life. Her sarcasm made me laugh. Our kiss was transcendent. But mostly we floundered our way through the night. She joked almost constantly, and I talked way too much, but being with her was easy because—for me, at least—expectations were nonexistent.

Fate's laughing in my face now. I like her dark curls even better, she's still wryly funny, and I'd be lying if I said I haven't thought about what it'd be like to kiss her again.

I duck under the water, cooling my sunburned face, trying to pinpoint what I said to make our conversation go sideways.

Because her expression went gloomy for a minute, and I don't want to be the sort of guy who makes her sad.

I bitched about my dad.

She suggested I appreciate how good I've got it.

I resurface, shaking the water out of my eyes, and kick to where she's sitting. "You coming in?"

I pretend not to watch while she peels off her tank and steps out of her shorts. She moves down the deck to where the water's deeper, then launches into a dive that's a hell of a lot more graceful than her entry the other night. She swims toward me, hair flowing behind her. When she surfaces, she looks like a real-life mermaid.

"Thank you for coming to sit with me earlier," she says. "At the restaurant."

"I knew you had fried food on the way."

She smiles. "You did crush my coconut shrimp."

"Yeah, happy to be of service."

"Whatever the reason, it was nice to have company."

I push my hands through my wet hair. I like joking with her—she seems to welcome levity—but I have to ask: "What was going on with those guys?"

"Nothing. It's inconsequential."

Didn't seem inconsequential. She kept her cool, but there was frustration in the set of her shoulders, embarrassment in the flush that scaled her neck. Pushing her to explain seems like undercutting her agency, though. I refuse to be anything like that dick at Blitz Brews.

I try for a different kind of backstory. "What about your family? Do I get to hear about them?"

"Probably not."

"I told you about my whackadoodle dad."

A corner of her mouth lifts. "Whackadoodle?"

I nod. "An adjective I borrowed from my mom. It means *downright batshit, but amusingly so.* You can find it in the dictionary alongside a picture of Davis Walker."

She laughs, leaning back to dip her hair into the water, smoothing it as she straightens again. She's taken out the pearl earrings she was wearing the other night, but the trail of hoops remains.

"You want to hear about my family, Henry Walker?" She gazes up at the dark sky, like she's deciding whether I've earned the right. She must decide I have, because she says, "I've lived with my older sister since I was ten. That's when my mom and dad died—a drunk driver blew through a stop sign and smashed into their car while they were visiting Tampa."

"Holy shit, Piper. God, I'm so sorry."

She shrugs, water rippling around her shoulders. Mine must be a platitude she's heard a thousand times.

"Tati became my legal guardian. She quit the interior design job she'd just gotten in Boston and moved back to Sugar Bay, a town she spent her adolescence itching to leave. She's been playing reluctant pseudo-parent ever since."

I ought to be punched in the nuts for disparaging my dad's efforts the way I did.

78

"Jesus—I can't even imagine."

"It was a long time ago. I mean, it absolutely sucks, but I've come to terms with it."

Is it possible to come to terms with a loss that huge?

What happened with Whitney cut me deep. It still hurts when I let myself think about it for longer than two seconds. But both my parents, gone forever? It's incomprehensible. I want to ask Piper how she carries on because sometimes, when I get caught up in my head, it's a struggle to keep my shit together.

Instead, I ask, "What's your sister like?"

"Tati's...a force."

"I'm imagining a tornado."

She winces. "Or a hurricane, yeah."

"Is she mean to you?"

She cups a hand and sends a playful splash of water into my face. "Not like you're thinking. She's just on my case all the time. About everything. You saw her the other night, waving me upstairs like I'll end up a convict if I stay out past midnight. And before you try to defend her, I know. She's trying to fill the role of two parents. She wants me to be safe. She loves me. All true. The problem is, aside from her job and a couple of high school friends who live in Pensacola now, she's got nothing going on. She has nowhere to funnel all her type A tenacity. So she rides my ass. Constantly."

A light bulb flickers on in my head. Piper's sister tries too hard. My dad tries too hard. They're each overly focused on the

79

teenager in their life, but if they had somewhere else to direct that energy, someone to run interference...

What if Dad and Piper's sister—Tati—meet? What if they have stuff in common, other than the fact that they're both responsible for a seventeen-year-old they don't understand? What if Dad likes Tati, and Tati likes Dad?

They'll start hanging out. They'll keep each other busy. They'll make each other happy.

And then I might get to go on a run or read or study for the SATs without Dad yammering about how it's called *summer break* for a reason. Piper would make out well too—she'd get a reprieve from Hurricane Tati.

"How old's your sister?" I ask.

"Thirty-two. Why? Trying to find yourself a sugar mama?"

"Ha ha," I deadpan. "She's single?"

Piper nods. "Newly."

"My dad's thirty-six. Also single."

Her eyes flash with understanding. "Wait—are you thinking what I *think* you're thinking?"

"Maybe." I smile conspiratorially.

She considers, twisting a curl around her finger. "A setup... I'm not opposed. Not yet, anyway. What does your dad look like? Because Tati's hot."

If Piper and her sister resemble each other at all, then yeah, that's likely true. Good thing Dad's not a troll. In the last few days, I've noticed plenty of women giving him a second look. I bet he and Tati are playing in the same league.

"He looks kind of like me," I say. "But, you know…old."

Piper laughs, angling her head to study my face. "So, not hideous."

"Definitely not hideous."

"What's he like? Other than the golf thing."

"He's into having fun. Likes to go out. Likes to meet new people. Extroverted." Piper's mouth is sinking into a frown. Her sister's not super social, then. I reroute. "But he's smart too. And driven. He owns a successful business."

"So I've seen. Tati's been to your dad's restaurant, actually; her glowing review was why I went in earlier. But no one's ever accused her of being a party animal. Other than sporadic dates and an occasional girls' night with friends she's had since grade school, she rarely goes out."

"That's not a bad thing, necessarily. They might balance each other."

She nods, but haughtily, like I'm in for a surprise where her sister's concerned. Still, she asks, "What's your plan?"

"I guess we need to figure out a way for them to meet."

"It has to seem organic, though. Tati will be pissed if she realizes I'm meddling."

"For sure. Totally organic. What if they actually hit it off?"

She smiles, mirroring my enthusiasm. "What if they have a romance?"

"They'll be busy. Dating. Courting. Whatever people in their thirties call it. Then they'll stop caring so much about what you and I are up to."

"Henry, I think you're on to something."

"I think *we're* on to something."

She twirls, laughing, sending a fountain of water droplets into the air.

I grin. If Tati's a hurricane, then Piper's a sun-shower, bright and rejuvenating. I feel pretty damn lucky to bear witness.

Piper

THE NEXT DAY, I HEAD to the park for a morning of cleaning tanks and feeding animals and assisting guests. It's hot and sticky outside, but Turtle smiles approvingly when he sees me sweeping the path leading to the tidal touch pools, which is all the encouragement I need.

It's been a while since I've come here alone after closing. The pool at the Towers has proven to be a pretty effective escape lately, and I'm getting my fill of the park during work hours, which is a lot less risky. Still, I decided to check in on the rays and the sea turtles during my break; I miss my quiet nights with them.

I spend the better part of my shift thinking about Henry. Late last night, I searched for him online. I found a trove of information concerning Henry Walker, a retired NBA player born in the eighties, but it wasn't until I launched into a real deep dive that

I came across my Henry in a few local news articles about his cross-country achievements. I don't know what sort of information I was hoping for, but long-distance running isn't very juicy.

Hunting for him on socials was a bust. No Facebook (not surprising—Tati's the only weirdo I know who uses Facebook) and no Snapchat (also unsurprising—Henry doesn't seem like the type). He has an Instagram account, but it's private. All I can see is his profile photo (George Washington's illustrated face—unhelpful). He's posted three photos, follows eighteen people, and has seventy-six followers.

I was tempted to raise his follower count to seventy-seven, but then he'd know about my virtual stalking.

I have *some* pride.

I keep thinking about his suggestion that we set up his dad with my sister. Henry is cute and smart, which means his dad likely is too, if there's truth to that adage about apples falling from trees. Tati would approve of Henry, which means she's sure to like his father.

This is *so* going to work.

Except when I get home from the park, Tati's in a mood.

"Work stuff," she snaps when I inquire during dinner.

Once, a few years back, I asked her why she didn't ditch her apartment management job and go back to interior design. The reasons were varied and delivered in an exasperated tone, but the gist was that her position at the Towers gives us a lovely yet affordable place to live, results in reliable twice-monthly paychecks, and doesn't require her to waste time hunting for a position at a design firm, building a client list, or working her way up from the bottom all over again.

"Adulthood requires sacrifices," she told me, like she was the only one who'd lost out.

Now, she lets her angst out in a barrage of complaints: my beach bag tracked sand into the laundry closet, I left my breakfast dishes in the sink, and my room's *still* a mess. "Have you started drafting admissions essays?"

"Not yet." She's nudged me about getting a jump on this task about twelve hundred times. She wants me to go to college in-state—no farther than Tallahassee, which is only two hours from home. She wants me to get a business degree. She wants me to be practical and boring.

"You never do what I ask," she grumbles, tucking into her stir-fry.

Before dinner, she found printouts about Hawai'i Pacific University's marine biology program on my desk and predictably lost her mind. "Hawaii's almost five thousand miles away!" she squawked, crumpling the paperwork.

Those miles have a lot to do with why I find Hawaii appealing. When I tried to tell Tati all the other reasons Hawaii interests me, she literally put her foot down, hard, on the floor. "Absolutely not."

She says she wants me to go to college locally because she'll miss me if I'm far away, and because she wants to be sure I'm safe and cared for, and because out-of-state tuition is sky-high. I believe her—I do. But I often wonder if there's more to it.

She didn't get to chase her dream.

Why should I?

As I slip out of the apartment after dinner, I make myself a promise: I'm going to leave Florida after high school. I'm not sure where I'll go—maybe a university, maybe community college, or maybe I'll spend a year working various jobs to get a feel for different career paths. Whatever the case, I need a break from the Sunshine State.

One more year, I think, passing the pool. *And then, freedom.*

But a different sort of freedom could come even sooner, if Henry and I can figure out a way to nudge his dad and my sister into a relationship.

He's all smiles when he swings the door open. His dad's apartment is a mirror image of ours, but while Tati is meticulous about cleanliness, Henry's dad appears to give zero shits. The living room isn't dirty, per se, but it's cluttered with sports equipment and flip-flops and restaurant supply catalogs. The sofa pillows are all over the place. A huge TV spans most of one wall. There are half a dozen remotes on the coffee table, along with a stack of *Sports Illustrated* magazines and an empty water bottle.

"It smells weird in here, doesn't it?" Henry asks while I take it all in.

I sniff the air. "I don't think so."

"Kind of, though? Like...dude?"

Laughing, I say, "*You're* a dude. You're supposed to be impervious to the stench."

"So there's a stench?"

86

"Not even a little bit." I inhale again. "All I smell is French fries."

He grins and leads the way to the dining room.

"I made us a snack," he says, gesturing toward the table.

It's set with paper plates and bottles of soda. There's a platter of perfectly golden fries in the center, plus a supersize jar of tartar sauce and a bottle of ketchup—the latter, I suspect, a kindness to me.

"All that's missing is candlesticks."

"My dad's fresh out," Henry says, pulling out a chair for me.

I sit, then help myself to a generous serving of fries. He does the same, then spoons a dollop of tartar sauce onto my plate.

"Really?" I ask.

"Just try it."

I do, reluctantly.

It's kind of good.

"I'll refrain from saying I told you so," he says, wearing the smuggest expression.

I laugh and throw back a few more—the stir-fry Tati served was less than delicious; in our home, nutrition trumps flavor—while taking stock of my surroundings. Table, chairs, buffet. Not one piece of artwork on the walls. No fresh flowers or knickknacks or personal touches. Henry's dad could use some help in the home decor department. I try to picture Tati—smooth hair, flawless skin, signature red lips, courtesy of MAC's Ruby Woo—in this space. She wouldn't quite fit, a rose among daisies.

At the far end of the table sits a laptop, two thick SAT prep books, and clear pouch packed with pens and highlighters.

"Your dad's gearing up for the test?" I say.

Henry smiles. "He's not really the studious sort."

"You seem to be."

He shrugs. "I like knowing stuff."

"Me too. But it's summertime. Why not relax a little?"

"I can't afford to relax. I'm applying to the U.S. Military Academy—West Point."

"Is that different from applying to other schools?"

"Yeah, it's more involved. Like, I had to write to my state's congressional reps and senators to request a nomination. Applicants have to pass a medical exam and a Candidate Fitness Assessment. There are interviews. Plus, there's the usual stuff like transcripts and SATs and a personal statement."

"Whoa. Was your dad in the military?"

He snorts out a laugh. "My dad barely made it through high school, and he partied his way through college. My pop went to West Point—my mom's dad. He was a colonel when he retired around the time I was born. He was a big part of my life when I was growing up. He passed a few years back."

"It's cool that you want to follow in his footsteps."

His eyes flash with pride; it's clear he has a lot of love for his grandfather. "For sure. West Point's competitive, but the Army's the only thing I've ever wanted to do." He waves at the prep books. "That's why I've got to spend this summer nerding out."

"The Army." I try to imagine having such a regimented,

transient lifestyle. Tati would approve of the discipline, but she definitely wouldn't be okay with me moving far away or stepping into dangerous situations. "What do your parents think about you joining the military?"

"They're cool with it. My mom grew up an army brat, so she gets it more than most. My dad doesn't give a shit what I do," he says, rolling his eyes, "so long as I'm having fun."

"Is it weird that I already like your parents?"

He laughs. "Nah. They're likable people. What about you? Post–high school goals?"

I wipe my hands on a paper napkin. "*Goal* is such a serious word. Mine are more…dreams. And they're not Tati-approved, so probably nothing will come of them."

"She doesn't really have a say, though."

"Oh, but Henry, you haven't met her."

He muses on that, his brows knitting together. I wonder if he's having second thoughts about setting my sister up with his dad. I've made Tati sound like an utter drag.

"What are they," he asks, "these dreams of yours?"

Sometimes I wonder if my aspirations sound silly, like the longings of a little kid who's just visited Sea World. But marine biology is the only future I've ever wanted.

Henry leans in. Softly, he says, "Piper, tell me."

God, he disarms me. More than that, it's nice to have a meaningful conversation. Since my falling out with Gabi, I've existed in a world of one.

"Marine biology," I say. "I want to work with marine animals."

He smiles. "Like you do now."

"Yeah, but professionally. With a head full of knowledge about what it takes to help them thrive in their natural environment." I fold my hands on the tabletop. "My parents met at the University of New England. My mom studied aquaculture and aquarium sciences, and my dad majored in marine affairs—so, conservation. I wish I could do something similar. Money's an issue, though. Degrees aren't free."

When she sold our childhood home, Tati divided the profit between my parents' funeral costs and legal expenses, which she vaguely explained as being related to her accepting guardianship, then invested what was left in a 529 college savings plan for me. So there *is* money. But given how much out-of-state tuition and living expenses cost, that account will dwindle quickly if I leave Florida.

"I get it, trust me," Henry says. "But there are scholarships. Grants. Loans."

"Yeah, there are. And if I go to college, I'll probably have to apply for all three. My biggest roadblock is Tati. She wants me to do something practical. Something that'll earn me money and accolades. A career that requires power suits, not wet suits."

"Uh, with all due respect, who cares what Tati wants? It's your life."

True. But what I'd never say aloud is this: My sister gave up everything to take care of me. She left Boston, a city she adored, and all of the friends she'd made there. She abandoned a hard-won interior design internship and a boyfriend who had no

90

interest in moving to Florida or helping to raise a kid he didn't know. She sold our beloved childhood home to crawl out of debt. She took a lower management position at a beachside apartment complex because entry-level design jobs are hard to come by in resort towns. She abandoned her dream of owning her own design firm and chased promotions within the property development company that owns the Towers so we could continue to live here. We fight like an old married couple, but in the tenderest part of my heart, I'm thankful for Tati.

Also, I feel indebted, like I owe her a white-collar career and a prosperous future. The life she hasn't been able to have because of me.

"Tell me to shut up if I'm overstepping," Henry says, "but I think you should give marine biology a shot. It's your passion, your legacy. At least explore your options."

"I have a little." And then I tell him about Hawai'i Pacific University. The more I talk, the more my excitement grows. "I'd love to live on an island," I say. "Or in Oregon or South Carolina or in the Northeast, like my parents. I want to leave Florida. I want to see more. I want—"

I want room to figure out who I am apart from my sister is what I'm about to say, but before I can get the words out, the front door opens. From my seat at the dining table, I watch a man with tousled brown hair and a plaid button-down—a man who looks a lot like *The Hangover*–era Bradley Cooper—step into the foyer.

My mouth falls open.

Tati's recent hookup.

91

Before I can work out what he's doing here in the apartment that belongs to Henry's father, Henry greets him.

"Hey, Dad. We saved you some fries."

Henry

"THANKS, BUDDY," DAD SAYS, STANDING motionless in the entryway, staring at Piper.

I clear my throat.

He reanimates.

He leaves his canvas satchel—cooler than a briefcase, he says—on the floor. I guess I'll put it away later, like I put away the coffee mug he used this morning, along with the jar of hair putty he left on the kitchen counter.

I don't even know what hair putty does.

Usually, my dad bounces around like a kid who's slurped down a giant Mountain Dew, but tonight he's subdued. He cruises over the table, takes a napkin, and piles leftover fries on it. Then his gaze returns to Piper. He looks at her like he recognizes her. Hell, maybe he does. They've both lived at the Towers for the last several years, and Sugar Bay is small. It's not far-fetched that they might've run into one another before tonight. But if he knows her, why doesn't he say so?

She boldly returns his stare.

What the fuck is going on?

It's not like my dad's being creepy. He's not checking her out—I'd *die*—but he's being really freaking weird. Is he so shocked that I've invited a girl over?

"Dad," I say, breaking the silence.

He wades out of his trance, giving his head a little shake. God, can he ever just be normal?

"This is Piper," I say. "She lives in the west tower. Piper, my dad, Davis."

He gets his shit together enough to extend his hand in her direction. "Nice to meet you."

"Likewise," Piper says with a cool nod.

The second she drops his hand, Dad steps back. I've never seen him so uncomfortable. If Piper's mood hadn't taken a nosedive in the two minutes since he rolled in, I'd find this all kind of hilarious. I've told her enough about him—his name, where he works, that he's a single dude living here, at the same complex she lives at. If she knew him, she would've made the connection, right?

Dad leaves the dining room for the kitchen, where he opens the fridge and pulls out a beer. He pops the top with the opener that, far as I can tell, lives on the countertop near the sink, always at the ready. Clutching the bottle neck, fries in his other hand, he says, "I'll leave you two to…whatever it is you're doing."

He shifts his gaze toward my SAT prep books, then gives me a disapproving look. Jesus—he thinks I invited Piper over to study. He's probably wondering how he helped produce such a grind of a kid, but by some miracle, he keeps whatever's going on in his head to himself. He skirts the perimeter of the dining room, heading toward the hall. But before he jets, he turns back to ask me, "Fishing tomorrow?"

I shoot Piper a *Help me* look, but she's too fascinated by her chipping nail polish to notice.

Defector.

"Okay," I tell him, only to ensure that he leaves the room.

I wait until he disappears to toss a fry at Piper. "Now I've got to spend another day baking in the sun, this time on the open water. Your sister likes to fish, right?"

I get a sympathy laugh, but then she's on her feet. "I'm going to get going."

I scramble out of my chair. "Wait. Really?"

She checks the time on her phone, practically running for the door. "Tati will freak if I'm not home soon."

"But we didn't talk about—"

"Yeah," she says with a hand on the knob. "The more I think about it, the less I like the setup idea. It's not going to work."

Before I have the chance to try and convince her that *yes*, of course it'll work, she's marching into the hallway.

Piper

HE FOLLOWS ME INTO THE corridor, and for a paralyzing second, I think he's going to take hold of my arm. In a flash, I'm transported to that night at Gabi's when Damon grabbed my arm, and my muscles tie themselves into knots, anticipating a touch that—thank god—never comes.

"What happened?" Henry asks as we stride parallel paths toward the elevator.

I shake out my hands; my fingertips are tingling.

You are not with Damon.

You are not in danger.

"I told you, it's late."

Henry eyes me, skepticism blatant. "But everything was fine until—"

I push the elevator button. My body has started to relax, catching on to what my brain has always known: Henry's not a threat. Still, my mind is racing. Maybe because I never imagined I'd see Davis again. Maybe because his brief history with Tati is going to mess up Henry's truly excellent setup plan. Maybe because, once again, life is completely out of my control.

"You should go back to your dad's," I say, because telling him *Your dad and my sister already hooked up* is just too awkward.

The elevator arrives with a ding. Its doors slide open.

"I'd rather walk you across the courtyard," he says.

His voice is calming, imploring. Like it was the night we met, when he helped me stop crying, when he left me feeling sun-warmed, like a shell nestled in sand.

He came back.

Three years later, he came back.

I step into the elevator. And then I extend a hand to hold the door. "Okay."

It's a silent ride to the ground floor. I'm embarrassed about sprinting out of the Walkers' apartment, about how oddly I acted in the hallway. And that's after I fell into the pool, shouted obscenities through Blitz Brews, and laid bare the sob story that is my past.

Honestly, I can't believe this boy still wants to share space with me.

As we pass through the courtyard, I raise a question I'm not entirely sure I want answered. "How weird do you think I am?"

He replies without deliberation. "Exceptionally weird. But I'm weird too, so it's cool."

I smile. "My sister knows your dad."

97

"Really? How?"

"I don't know. They're just…acquainted."

He steps ahead of me and opens the door of the west tower. The lobby is cooler than the night outside, and my overheated face welcomes the artificially chilled air. I pause in front of the elevator's silver doors, not wanting to be stuck in a small box while discussing what had to have been a casual smash between my sister and his dad.

Henry's side-eye has become intense. "Acquainted how?"

I cringe.

He makes the leap. "Oh."

"The day you got into town—that morning—your dad was at our apartment. It was early. He was drinking our coffee."

He tilts his head, amused. "How *dare* he?"

I grin despite myself. "He'd obviously slept over. Which is fine. Whatever. They're adults. Tati's responsible to a fault. I'm sure they were safe and—are you laughing at me?"

He is. He's cracking up.

"You think this is funny?!"

"No. *No,*" he says, fighting for composure. When he can't manage it, he gives in to laughter. "Actually, yeah. It is funny. It's fucking hysterical. Here we are trying to set them up, and they're already boning."

"They're not *boning.*"

He's still snickering. Watching him doubled over, nose pink with sunburn, makes me laugh too.

He's right. This *is* funny.

"I'm pretty sure it was only the one time," I say once my giggles have subsided. "Tati was embarrassed when I called her out."

"Embarrassed? But my dad's the stud of the Towers. Just ask him."

I give him a sympathetic smile. How are he and Davis even related?

Okay, but I *can* appreciate their physical resemblance: wavy hair, cleft chins, tall frames, broad shoulders. The way they smile with charming self-deprecation. But their personalities seem to be an absolute contradiction.

"I'm glad he came home when he did," I tell Henry, who's leaning against the wall, gazing down at me. "Who knows when we would've connected the dots otherwise? Can you imagine if we'd set them up not knowing they'd already shared a bed?" I glance at my phone, and yeah, it's getting late. I press the elevator button; Tati's going to go apeshit if I don't walk into the apartment in the next two minutes. "Looks like my sister will be in my face all summer. And you'd better invest in some sunblock, my friend."

"Hang on," Henry says. "Tati and Davis have hung out before—that means they've got chemistry. All they need now is a nudge into something more."

"That feels…icky," I say, watching the elevator's illuminated numbers count down.

Tati doesn't have a history of long, fulfilling relationships. Now that I've had some time to think more critically about orchestrating a setup, I'm realizing it's a dicey idea. She and Davis know each

99

other; if they wanted to date, they would. Plus, if Henry and I interfere, pushing them into something serious, and then Tati breaks it off with Davis (or, more likely, Davis breaks it off with her), things could become uncomfortable between Henry and me.

The affection I've started to feel for him is delicate and exciting. I'm reluctant to jeopardize it.

There's a lot at stake.

"What if Tati thinks your dad's a jerk?" I ask. "What if your dad thinks Tati is a snob? We have no business sticking our noses into whatever they've already got going on."

"I disagree," Henry says.

I laugh. "Clearly. But trust me, if Tati found out I interfered with her love life, she'd be pissed."

The elevator arrives. I step inside. Even though I'd like to see this conversation through, I'm picturing my sister upstairs, glaring at her watch while she taps an agitated toe.

Henry follows me, and as the doors close, he says, "Not if things between her and my dad work out. They might be perfect for each other. In that case, she'll be grateful."

"She's never grateful. Best-case scenario, they have a good few months before things fall apart. Tati doesn't handle breakups well, and guess who gets to deal with her in the aftermath? Plus, after they inevitably crash and burn, things will be weird between you and me. That would suck. I like eating French fries with you."

I survive by keeping my feelings close. By keeping others at a distance. Gabi's the only person I've ever opened up to, and all that got me was a ruined reputation and a summer without a social life. So it unnerves me to admit that last part. The French fry part.

The elevator slows to a stop. Henry says, "I like eating French fries with you too."

We're different in a lot of ways, he and I, but there's amity when we hang out. It was there between us three years ago, and it's here tonight. I meet his eyes and offer a smile that's not silly or sarcastic, but sincere.

His return is a gift. I'm not about to gamble it on Tati and Davis.

It's not until we've reached my apartment door that he speaks again. "Okay. Let's forget about your sister and my dad. Tomorrow, I'll try to survive a day on the open ocean, and you try not to set Tati off."

"And we'll meet up for fries or swimming or something soon," I tell him.

He pulls his phone from his pocket and passes it to me. I key in my number and then watch him walk back to the elevator. Before he steps inside, he graces me with the most winsome smile, confirmation that we're doing the right thing by abandoning the setup idea.

Losing my new friend's just not worth the risk.

As the elevator begins its descent, I unlock the apartment door and creep inside.

Tati is perched on the sofa, eyes firing laser beams of disappointment.

"You're late."

Henry

MY DAD PAID FOR AN excursion out on the Gulf on a thirty-foot charter boat that we're sharing with a captain and two crew members, plus four twentysomethings who're whooping it up bachelor party–style. We shove off at the ass crack of dawn. I have to forgo my run, but I'm trying not to be a downer because maybe this will be fun.

Dad's pumped. As we motor away from shore, he bounds around the boat with a can of charter-provided Coors, toasting Josh, the groom-to-be, who's vacationing from Jersey with his friends. Ten minutes in, the bachelor party guys already worship Dad. The crew, a freakishly tan brother-sister pair called Matthew and Marissa, do too. He invites everyone onboard to Blitz Brews later. He seems to collect people like the Pied Piper.

If I didn't look so much like Davis Walker, I'd question my paternity.

The weather's nice today, though it's always nice in Sugar Bay. The sky's a vivid blue, and the gulf is calm, glittering in the sunlight. I slather on sunscreen and listen as Matthew and Marissa explain about rods and reels. I Googled *gulf fishing* last night, partly because I couldn't sleep and partly because I didn't want to look like a dumbass today, but it becomes clear pretty quick that we're on a party boat that lets you leave with fish, not *Deadliest Catch*.

The crew's doing all the work, but the sun's relentless and I'm still roasting. Halfway through the morning, when Dad stops flirting with Marissa long enough to toss me a beer, I consider cracking it open.

I end up passing it to Todd, Josh's best man, who's on the bench beside me. He opens the can with a metallic pop. After a long pull, he states the obvious: "Dude. Your dad's a trip."

Davis is across the deck, shotgunning a beer. It's, like, nine o'clock.

Todd jabs me with his tanning-oil-covered elbow. "You're a lucky kid."

I let out a disbelieving laugh, flipping my baseball hat from backward to forward so my face doesn't end up twice baked. And so I don't have to watch my father guzzle foam.

"Seriously," Todd says. "I was twenty-four before my dad had a beer with me. Pretty sure yours would hold a funnel for you."

I don't want to talk about my dad or how much it bugs me that Todd's right.

He points toward his friends, who've gathered around to egg

Davis on. "Josh and me grew up on the same block. He's the first of our crew to buy a girl a ring. You got yourself a girl?"

I think of Piper before I think of Whitney, which is fucked.

The boat dips over a wave. I feel removed, like I'm watching an alternate version of myself muddle through a conversation with this stranger. The disconnect is superior to being present, though. When I'm in my head, guilt gnaws at me.

"No," I tell Todd. "No girl. Not anymore."

"Sorry, kid," he says, peering at me through water-spotted sunglasses. "What happened?"

He seems like a cool guy, though he's got an outline of the state of New Jersey tattooed on his biceps, a dubious choice. "It ended," I tell him. "Ran its course."

He nods with authority. "Probably for the best. Have fun while you've got the chance."

"Yeah, I'm not the best at having fun."

He laughs, holding up the beer I handed him. "I sensed that about you."

Have fun. Chill. Relax.

I've heard variations of *don't be such a stick in the mud* more times than I can count. From Ricky and Silas and other buddies back in Spokane. From both of my parents and my grandma. From my pop too, when he was alive, which always gave me pause, considering how many personality traits I inherited from him.

God, Henry, loosen up, Whitney used to say.

We started going out last September, at the beginning of junior

104

year. I see now, thanks to the ass-kicking clarity of hindsight, that she was out of my league. She reigns about twelve steps up the social ladder from where I sit comfortably as a varsity cross-country runner, National Honor Society member, and recreational skier. Whitney's a dancer and a debater, a butterfly of a girl who attracts attention just by being.

We'd known each other most our lives, but when we were matched as partners for a chemistry project, she took a liking to me. Maybe it was because I was better at labs than she was. Maybe it was because her mom, a nurse and a close friend of my mom's, already approved of me. Maybe she genuinely liked me. I was definitely into her.

By Halloween, she was blowing off her friends to hang out at my house, where we'd spend Mom's long shifts making out. For Christmas, she gave me candles she'd made herself. They were poured into glass beakers and smelled like pine, and I loved that she'd put so much thought and time into my present. But by the time New Year's Eve rolled around, our romance was losing steam. Whitney had grown tired of hanging out at my house. She wanted to have more fun, drink more boxed wine, and party with the friends she'd been neglecting. She wanted me to ditch studying and skip runs so we could do things my mom—obliviously smitten with my girlfriend—would've shit bricks over. Classes ditched to ski at Schweitzer Mountain, nights in motel rooms neither of us could afford, beers guzzled in Whit's friends' dingy garages.

I should've ended it long before I did, but there was such

familiarity between us. There was also the complication of our mothers, our relationship's most enthusiastic cheerleaders.

I should've muted the bullshit and listened to my gut.

Todd rejoins Josh and the rest of the groomsmen, so I haul myself off the bench to help Marissa and Matthew maintain the lines. The fish are biting, and while I know enough to be sure I don't give a shit about deep-sea fishing, I feel like I should participate so my dad gets his money's worth.

Not that he's paying attention. Josh and the groomsmen are shotgunning beers of their own now, making a mess all over the deck. Dad's encouraging them with hoots and foot stomps. His top-siders are speckled with froth.

Jesus H. I'm onboard the SS *Frat Party*.

I drive home. Thanks to the huge lunch we had on the water, Dad has sobered up. Mostly. Still, he's not into taking chances behind the wheel—an exception to his usual throw-caution-to-the-wind attitude that I respect.

"Let's grill the fish this weekend," he says as I guide the Ram away from the marina. We've got a cooler of them secured in the truck bed, gutted and cleaned by the crew. Not a bad deal, especially for Dad and the bachelors, who did jack-all when it came to reeling them in.

"I guess," I say.

Dad turns in his seat, giving me a once-over. "What's up, buddy?"

106

"Just tired."

"But you had fun, right?"

I might've, if you hadn't spent the whole time partying with strangers.

He looks so damn earnest. So hopeful. Telling him the truth would be like sending a kid's balloon into the wind.

"Yeah," I say. "It was cool."

He grins. "You wouldn't be so wiped if you hadn't stayed out late with your new girl."

I tighten my grip on the steering wheel. It's the first time he's brought up Piper, and of course he's being patriarchal about it. "She's not *mine*. We're friends."

He chuckles. "In my experience, friendships have a way of becoming more."

Were he and Tati friends before they hooked up?

Of course he knows Piper's sister. There's one woman in all of Sugar Bay who I've got roundabout access to, one woman who might distract Davis long enough to let me enjoy a full night's sleep and a morning run and a fucking breath, and he's already bedded her.

We're almost back to the Towers when he reaches into the glove box. I'm watching the road, so it isn't until he chucks something small into my lap that I realize it's a package of condoms.

"Have some fun," he says. "But for Christ's sake, be safe."

I fire a glare in his direction.

Then I shut him out for the rest of the day.

107

Piper

TATI'S TAKING THE AFTERNOON OFF for her biannual teeth cleaning. She never misses dental appointments. She never pays bills late or forgets to get her Volvo's oil changed. She's the most disciplined individual I know.

I get home from work not long after she gets home from the dentist. She's in a foul mood. Apparently, she had to skip lunch because there was a catastrophe with one of the hot water heaters in the east tower. Thanks to her fluoride application, she can't eat anything for another hour.

Lucky me.

She drags me to Publix, a grocery run I'm hoping will bank me enough sister points to get me out of the next chore on her list. When I was a kid, before Tati moved to Boston, she'd bring me to the store for donuts and Dr Pepper and Cheetos. Today, we fill the buggy by circling the perimeter. She's always going on about how the aisles are stocked with processed foods that are trash for our bodies. She's probably right. Still, I slip in Nutter Butters, a box of Lucky Charms, and a six-pack of Red Bull.

All in all, it's an uneventful trip, until we're on our way out.

Gabi's on her way in with her mom and her twelve-year-old brother, Tyson.

I avoid eye contact like a boss, hoping they'll go about their business.

They don't, because Tati and her big-ass mouth call out hello.

Maggie grins and waves. She's stunning, one of a few Black models to grace the pages of J.Crew catalogs back in the nineties. And she's so nice. She gives Gabi a nudge like, *Go say hi!*

Tati has no idea that Gabi and I aren't talking. Maggie must not either, because she cheerfully bags lemons while her daughter makes a slow shuffle toward us.

"Gabi, hi!" Tati says, pulling her into an embrace. Despite our history of (innocent) troublemaking, she loves Gabi, who gets stellar grades and plays piano concertos for packed halls. Tati has legit accused me of being a negative influence on my best friend. Like I'm capable of forcing Gabi to do anything she doesn't want to do. Until the Damon incident, she was a willing conspirator in whatever mischief was on the docket. When we were younger, that meant pranking my sister or sneaking out to toilet paper the houses of boys who'd left us jaded. Later it became secret joyrides in Maggie's BMW or wine guzzled behind my locked bedroom door.

Gabi's gaze skims my newly darkened hair. I hate myself for

109

wondering if she likes it. Maggie's putting a bunch of bananas in her cart, and Tyson is poking avocados, looking bored. He can be a pain sometimes, but he's the closest thing I've ever had to a brother. And Maggie treats me more like a daughter than Tati ever has. I want to run through the produce section and hug them both.

I resist because holy balls, Gabi looks like she's about to breathe fire.

"I haven't seen you since summer break started," Tati says to her. "What's been keeping you so busy?"

"Piano," Gabi tells her. "Same as always."

She's been taking lessons since she was four and teaching them since last year. When we were twelve, her dad used the word *virtuoso* after a recital at the Saenger Theatre in Pensacola, which earned an epic eye roll from his daughter. Gabi never boasts about her talent. For her, playing is the same as breathing: instinctive and sustaining.

My sister smiles. "Next time you and Piper are at our place, be sure to say hello."

How dense is she?

Gabi and I still haven't acknowledged each other. How has Tati missed the disgust that's thickened the air? And why hasn't she asked *me* where Gabi's been lately? She could have at any time. Instead, she's chosen to interrogate my former best friend while our frozen whole-wheat waffles thaw.

"Oh, Piper and I don't hang out anymore," Gabi says.

If I could disappear through the floor, I would. At least then

I wouldn't have to watch my sister's expression cloud with confusion.

She looks from Gabi to me, then back again. "I don't understand."

Try to keep up, Tati.

"We're not friends anymore," Gabi says flatly. "Piper didn't tell you?"

My sister glowers. "No. She did not."

"Okay," I say, giving Tati a push toward the exit. "Let's talk in the car."

She moves reluctantly toward the automatic doors. Just a few more feet and—

"She kissed my boyfriend," Gabi calls, halting Tati in her tracks.

Gabi's not a timid girl, but she's diplomatic. It's not like her to cause a scene in the neighborhood market, but now that Maggie and Tyson have disappeared down the baking aisle, she's dropped her shield and picked up a sword.

Tati walks back to her. "When?"

"A couple of weeks ago. At my house. In my *room*."

My stomach churns. Hell would be preferable to this.

Tati sputters. "Why would she do that?"

"She was drunk," Gabi says, like, *Isn't she always?* "Damon said she was all over him."

"Piper," Tati chides, shaking her head.

I'm barely holding back a cascade of tears, but I can't *not* speak up. "That isn't what happened," I say.

111

Gabi's gaze clashes with mine. "You're calling Damon a liar?"

"Yes," I say, squaring up to her.

Gabi's bullshit detector is well calibrated. She values authenticity and despises deception, and she's stubborn as hell. But last year, she fell for Mitchel Damon, bad boy punk to her piano prodigy perfection. He's loud and vulgar, a redneck and an asshole. Maggie and Byron hate him. But isn't that the draw? He satiates Gabi's defiant streak.

"What Damon told you? That is not how it went down."

She crosses her arms. "Whatever, Piper."

"It's *not*. If you'd let me explain—"

Shaking her head, she says, "I don't need your explanations—not this time. I saw you with him. I've never felt so betrayed—"

Enough!

I turn and walk out of Publix.

Gabi and I hit a rough spot a few months back, over spring break. I missed her biggest recital of the season to hook up with a tourist whose name has already slipped my mind. The fight was my fault; I selfishly put a boy before her and lied to cover my ass, telling her Tati wouldn't let me go to the recital. Tati shot holes through my story not two days later, and Gabi confronted me. When I came clean, it was heart-wrenchingly obvious that she was more disappointed by my dishonesty than the fact that I'd missed the recital. I swore I'd never do anything to make her doubt me again.

By the time she walked in on Damon and me at that party, I had already surrendered. She'd missed my confusion, his

112

maneuvering, my bartering, his hushing. She didn't hear me trying to plead my way out of that bedroom. She didn't see me grappling with him, someone who was quicker and stronger and much more sober than me.

She took his word over mine.

Why wouldn't she? I'd lied before.

———

I've been waiting on the sweltering asphalt for almost ten minutes when Tati comes out of the supermarket, shoving the buggy with wrathful purpose. She loads the groceries into the trunk, not bothering to unlock the passenger door, ensuring that I'm cooked through by the time she's done.

"How could you take her side?" I ask when we're both in the Volvo. I jam my seat belt into its slot. My rage-fueled crying ran its course before she emerged from the store, but my indignation hasn't gone anywhere.

"Well, Piper. Let's review the night in question. You drank illegally, and you left Gabi's house alone in the middle of the night. Adam found you wandering more than a mile down the beach, wasted. He drove you home in his squad car—while on duty—and then, if you'll recall, he broke up with me while you puked all over the bathroom, which I later had to clean. Why would I take your side when you habitually make terrible choices?"

God, is she right?

113

Am I to blame for what happened with Damon?

If I'd been more responsible, I might not have found myself alone with him. If I hadn't had so much to drink, he might not have singled me out. I wasn't in the right headspace to reason with him, to effectively say no, to fight him off. There was little chance I'd be able to reliably recount what he did later, and he knew it.

Does responsibility lie with me or him?

Him.

Jayden and Hudson knew I was drunk. Jayden mixed most of my drinks, and Hudson helped me out of the pool. Neither of them lured me to a private room. Neither of them put their hands on me.

Damon is a predator.

So why is guilt whispering accusations in my ear?

Because I make terrible choices, like my sister said.

I wait for her to pull onto the main drag before I say, quietly, "I wish you wouldn't assume I'm always at fault."

"But you so often are! Do you need examples of your most foolish decisions? Let's start with last year, when you drove my car without permission. *Before* you got your license."

"I was with Gabi," I counter, "who *was* a licensed driver. And we only drove in the parking lot of the Towers. She was teaching me how to parallel park!"

Tati thumps her hand against the steering wheel like a judge banging a gavel. "Illegal! What about sophomore year, when you were caught cheating on your history midterm?"

"*I* wasn't cheating. I knew that study guide front and back."

That semester, Jayden was in danger of failing U.S. history, which was going to get him booted from the wrestling team. I'd only wanted to help him secure a C, a grade just good enough to keep him on the mat. I positioned my paper so he could sneak a peek or two. In retrospect, I probably should've kept my answers to myself. Jayden and I both got zeros on that test, and he didn't get to wrestle for the rest of the season. "I was trying to help a friend," I tell Tati, my voice small.

"You were *cheating.*"

The way she spits out that word makes me sound like a delinquent, not a girl trying to boost a buddy.

"Let's get back to what happened last month at Gabi's," she continues. "You kissed your best friend's boyfriend, which is so unbelievably wrong I can't even wrap my head around it. Then you came home drunk at *seventeen.* It's one thing to screw up every once in a while, but I wish that just once, you'd take responsibility for the mistakes you make."

"I don't need to! You're always around to throw them in my face."

She *pffts*, like I'm *so* ridiculous. "You destroyed your best friendship—your *only* friendship. Do you honestly feel good about that?"

"If you want the truth, I haven't felt good for a long time. You have no idea what happened between Damon and me, but instead of asking, instead of checking in to make sure I'm okay, you're taking Gabi's story at face value. You're taking her side over mine."

"Okay." Tati flips on her turn signal. The Towers and salvation are in sight. "Why did Gabi walk in on you with her boyfriend?"

I could tell my sister everything. Yes, I stole her booze and lied about where I was going. I got bombed and dove into the pool half naked for the pure exhibitionist fun of it. Stupid, stupid, stupid choices. But being with Damon?

Not a choice.

How can I describe those moments I spent with him?

His cold hands.

My tunneling vision.

His stale breath.

My dry heaves.

His sharp words.

My terror.

I can't.

All I see is the look Tati wore that night after Officer Lopez— *Adam*—hauled me into his cruiser and drove me home. After he told her I was lucky he'd brought me to her instead of to the station. After he told her things were over between them, that he couldn't be with a woman whose "ward" was a budding criminal.

She was devastated.

But she bounced back *real* quick, getting down and dirty with Davis Walker.

As she pulls into her spot at the Towers, her expression is one of superiority; she doesn't look like a big sister who will stand by me.

Still, she says, "Tell me. What happened that night?"

116

She doesn't want the truth. She wants to be right.

And I can be as heartless as she is.

"I kissed him," I tell her. "Just like Gabi said."

Henry

I WAIT A FEW DAYS before putting Piper's number to use.

She doesn't want to set up my dad and her sister, and that's cool. But I haven't had a second away from Davis since our fishing excursion. He's talked me into hanging out at the beach, followed me into the Towers' gym, treated me to a matinee of a new spy thriller, and dragged me to Blitz Brews the last couple of nights, where he left me at the bar while he walked the floor, spewing merriment all over his patrons.

I like Mateo—he keeps the conversation and soda coming. But I don't want to spend all summer bellied up to a bar, watching an acquaintance pull beers and mix mai tais.

Last night, I got sucked into another of Whitney's tearful text vortexes. When I told her I had to get to bed, she called my mom, who was cramming for a test. Mom, in turn, called me.

"Handle your business, Henry," she said firmly, but with

sympathy. "If you want her to leave you alone, you have to say those words to her. Otherwise, you're stringing her along." Then she told me I was her whole heart and that she had to get back to studying.

I *do* want Whitney to leave me alone. I want that more than anything. And I get what my mom means about leading her on. Still, saying *Don't contact me ever again* to a girl who's hanging on by a fraying thread feels wildly cruel. I ended up texting Silas, who's in the same social circle as Whitney and is the more sensitive of my running buddies. I asked him to check in on her.

Take her to get coffee or something? She's having a hell of a time. She could use a friend.

He replied quickly and asked for no explanation, which is probably why he and I get along so well: No problem, dude.

I give up on sleep just before sunrise, haul my ass out of bed, and run four miles down the beach and four miles back. Afterward, I take a cold shower because Florida is hot as shit even before the sun's fully up. I'm not being particularly quiet, but there are no signs of life from Dad's room. Peering through the doorway, I find him sprawled out on his mattress, mouth open as he breathes raspily.

I text Piper: Want to grab breakfast?

It takes her a minute to respond, time I spend hoping Davis doesn't roll out of bed before I can bail.

Then: Okay.

A few minutes later, I'm knocking on the door to her place.

She answers, wearing a dress that's the same blue as her eyes. Its straps are thin and its hem is high. I'm into it.

119

"Let's go," she hisses, grabbing my arm and giving it a tug.

I stagger forward as a voice calls, "Piper! Hang on!"

She groans, turning back reluctantly.

A woman steps into the hallway. Her hair's blond, and she's wearing dressy pants and a silky blouse that's buttoned up to her throat. It's Saturday morning, so that's kind of weird. She's got a dusting of freckles across her nose, like Piper.

This must be Tati.

"Where do you think you're going?" she asks.

"Breakfast," Piper says.

"You've cleaned your room?"

"I'll do it when I get back."

"What about your essays?"

"What about them?"

Tati's mouth becomes a thin line. "Have you reached out to Gabi?"

"No."

"You need to. Today."

"I will *not*," Piper says, fists clenched at her sides.

"Piper—"

She's shrinking, a lot like she did that night at the Blitz Brews when the dipshit in the dirty hat harassed her. She must have an internal well of audacity, though, because she lifts her chin and says, "Gabi can go to hell."

"When will you—" Tati starts, her voice laced with exasperation. She drops suddenly off when she notices me. "Who's this?" she asks, tipping her chin in my direction.

120

Piper sighs. "Henry. He's visiting his dad, who lives in the east tower. He's polite and responsible, and we're going to get breakfast, as I said. Henry, this is my sister, Tati. You know, the one I told you about?" She says this last part with gleeful malice, like Tati ought to be worried.

I step forward to shake her hand. "Nice to meet you."

"You too," she says with coolness that makes my balls shrivel. I assume she's made the connection: *Henry* plus *visiting his dad* plus *east tower* equals Davis Walker.

I pull my hand away. "Ready?" I ask Piper. "I made a reservation."

"Definitely." She hustles down the hall. Over her shoulder, she calls, "Be back later."

"You've got work to do this afternoon!" her sister retorts.

"Don't I always?" Piper mutters.

While we wait for the elevator, I glance back at Tati, who's still in the hall, fists glued to her hips. My dad can be a clown, what with the beer shotgunning and condom dispensing, but his brand of frustrating seems less soul-sucking than hers.

When we're behind the elevator's doors, Piper brightens. "A reservation? Really?"

"Nah. I just wanted to get us out of there."

"Nice. I think she knows who your dad is."

"Yeah, I got that vibe. Also, I'm polite and responsible?"

"Totally," she says. "And you're my knight in shining armor. Because wow, I needed a rescue."

Piper suggests Clementine's, a shop with acai bowls and smoothies and donuts that smell amazing. The place is swarming with people. We wait in line, then make our picks—chocolate-glazed and rainbow-sprinkled donuts—plus a Sunrise Acai Bowl that Piper swears will change my life. We take our food outside to a group of crowded picnic tables. A family's vacating one, and we snag it, sitting side by side because the umbrella shades only half the table.

Piper scoops blended acai, granola, and a banana slice onto a spoon. "I can't believe acai bowls aren't huge in Spokane," she says, holding it out to me.

"Maybe they are," I say, taking the spoon. "I'm not all that adventurous about food." *For good reason*, I think, looking down at what she's given me. The mashed-up acai—a berry, she explained while we waited in line—is bright purple. I can't remember the last time I ate something purple. But she's looking on expectantly, so I shovel the spoon into my mouth.

It's good.

"Right?!" she says, like she's in my head.

I laugh, scooping up another bite while she loads a spoon of her own with mango and chocolate shavings. I want to ask her about the girl Tati mentioned back at the Towers—Gabi, who deserves either an apology or a trip to hell—but Piper's in such a good mood that I opt to keep things light.

"So," I say. "Your sister's blond."

122

She arches an eyebrow. "I used to be too, remember?"

"Vaguely." Fourteen-year-old me thought her light hair was cute, but now that it's a brown so rich her eyes appear almost hypnotically blue, it's hard to recall her any other way.

"I had it colored the day you came back," she tells me. "Tati was outraged."

"Why?"

"She thinks it's too dark. Too dramatic. *Witch* was the word she used."

"That's bullshit. I like it."

She pauses, spoon halfway to her mouth, eyes locked on mine. "Thank you."

"You're welcome." I split our chocolate-glazed donut with a plastic knife, then demolish half before saying, "Your sister... pretty type A?"

Piper rolls her eyes. "I tried to tell you. She's impossible."

"Has she always been?"

"No. She was intense before my parents passed, but she was also really fun. When she lived in Boston, she invited me to visit her for a week. Our parents weren't into the idea at first, but she pushed and, like always, she got her way. It was summertime, and we went to New York City for a few days. We saw Central Park and the Statue of Liberty, and went to *Wicked* on Broadway. She bought me frozen hot chocolate at Serendipity and an American Girl doll at the flagship store." I must not appear suitably impressed because she pokes me with her elbow. "American Girls are a big deal when you're nine."

123

"I'm sure."

"She became a dictator when she was forced to raise me."

I don't know why I feel like I need to make a case for Tati, but "It's probably been hard on her" falls out of my mouth. Piper's eyes go wide with offense, and goddamn it, I wish I could take it back.

"Yeah. Sucks for her, getting a whole twenty-five years with our parents while I got a measly ten. Poor Tati."

I rub the back of my neck, feeling like a chump. "I shouldn't have said that. It was stupid—I don't even know what I'm talking about."

She polishes off a final scoop of acai before meeting my eyes. "People always defend Tati. She's made a thousand sacrifices, she didn't ask for this life, raising teenagers is hard...all fair points. But I didn't ask for this life either. I lost my parents *and* my big sister."

I pass her the other half of the chocolate donut. A peace offering.

She accepts. "So, I've met your dad... What's your mom like?"

"She's cool."

Piper frowns. "I need more than that."

I think for a minute, trying to figure out how to describe my mom in only a few sentences when she's spent my whole life filling innumerable roles.

"She works crazy hard," I begin. "She loves nursing, but she chooses her shifts based on my cross-country schedule so she can cheer me on at meets. She treats me to ice cream at this shop in Spokane, Sweet Peaks, after grades are posted each semester. She taught me to ski when I was five, specifically so my dad could take me to the slopes on the weekends; she wanted us to have something in common so we could bond, I guess. And she walks after dinner every night. She likes when I come along. So even if things are hectic, we count on that time together, you know?"

"Not really," Piper says, but not sadly. "How long was she married to your dad?"

"Uh, zero days. They were set up by friends for one of my dad's fraternity pledge dances and had a fling. They're nothing alike—Davis can be a pain in the ass—but they get along okay for my sake."

"It's nice that you decided to spend the summer here even though you and your dad aren't super close."

"That's kind of the point, though. To get to know him better while giving my mom space to rock her master's program. Plus, Sugar Bay doesn't suck."

It's true—I like Sugar Bay, and I want to have a better relationship with my dad, and my mom's glad to have extra time to focus on school. But I left out a big part of the story.

The biggest part of the story.

Piper studies my face, like she senses I'm not being entirely forthcoming. I should tell her about Whitney. There's no reason not to. The longer I hold off on mentioning her, the shadier I feel and the heavier the secret becomes. But talking about the worst month of my life on a perfect Saturday morning...

I can't do it.

125

Instead, I tell Piper more about cross-county, the responsibilities I'll have as captain during my senior season, and Silas and Ricky, teammates who make what might otherwise be a lonely sport a lot of fun. I tell her about the fishing excursion I took with my dad. I tell her about my nights at Blitz Brews and the staff members I'm really starting to like. I crack her up telling her how Davis almost broke his neck trying to outpace me on a treadmill in the gym yesterday.

She brushes donut sprinkles from the picnic table's weathered surface. "Do you think you'll make it through a whole summer with him?"

I flash back to Davis partying on the fishing boat. Snickering as he threw condoms my way. Forcing small talk yesterday while he puffed and wheezed in the gym. Popping a beer when he got home from Blitz Brews last night, then a few more after that. More often than not, it's me who points out that it's time for a meal, who cleans up the apartment, who suggests that it might be time for bed. I genuinely love my dad, but he's exhausting. Since arriving in Sugar Bay, I've felt more like his parent than his kid.

I sigh. "I don't know if I'm gonna make it through another week with him."

Piper

HENRY IS NOBLE, GIVING UP the summer before his senior year, time with his friends and his mom, familiarity and stability in the city where he's lived his whole life. And all to hang out in Florida with his father, who makes him nutty.

"You're a good person," I declare.

He swallows, smoothing a hand over his hair. A rebel lock falls over his forehead. It's an imperfection I find hopelessly endearing. "Yeah, I try," he says.

"I want to help you."

I'm not sure when I made this decision. Maybe the other day, after Tati embarrassed me at the grocery store. Maybe this morning, when Henry fibbed about making a reservation just to help me shake my sister. Or maybe just moments ago, when he spoke so sweetly about his mom. But I do—I want to help him.

"Help me how?" he asks.

"I want to make this summer better for you."

He smiles uncertainly.

"Let's set them up—your dad and my sister. If you still want to. I understand if you've changed your mind after meeting Tati, though. Seems cruel to subject Davis to her again, now that I'm thinking about it."

He laughs. "Don't change your mind because you pity me."

"I'm not that altruistic," I assure him. "I'll get something in return."

"Right. Liberation."

"Yeah, but also you. If Tati and Davis are busy with each other, then you and I can keep hanging out. If you want. I mean, *I* think that'd be fun. Maybe you haven't noticed, but I'm not exactly swarmed by friends."

God, Piper. Word vomit much?

Henry's totally cool. "Yeah, what's up with that, local girl?"

I use a finger to swipe a bit of leftover chocolate glaze from my otherwise empty plate. It's uncomfortable to admit that my companion count hovers somewhere around one—*him*. But whatever. I'm in a friendship drought. It happens.

"Local girl doesn't equal popular girl," I say, faking nonchalance. "Something happened a few weeks ago. It's not worth delving into, but the abridged version is that my best friend is pissed at me."

"This is the Gabi your sister mentioned earlier?"

"Yep."

128

"What about the ass monkey who was at my dad's restaurant? Was he involved?"

I fan my face—is the sun blistering hot, or is it humiliation that's toasting me? "You're annoyingly perceptive."

"And you're aggravatingly elusive."

I laugh despite myself. "I'll take that as a compliment."

"Seriously, though." He's smiling, but his tone is solemn. "I've got questions."

"I believe it. But we have something more important to talk about: Tati and Davis."

Henry

A FEW DAYS LATER, I'M perched on a barstool at Blitz Brews, like I've been nearly every night since I arrived in Sugar Bay. Dad's in Owner Mode, which is a welcome reprieve from Party Mode and Buddy Mode and Competitive Middle-Aged Athlete Mode.

This morning we snorkeled, which wasn't terrible. Afterward, on our way back to the truck, we passed a group of college kids in FSU gear playing beach volleyball. Dad butted in, asking if we could join, then bump-set-spiked his way to lunchtime. I bust my ass in the gym and can run five miles in well under forty minutes (U.S. Army Ranger standard), but the only time I've ever played volleyball was in middle school PE, and that was in a gym, not on sand.

I'm sore as shit.

Mateo's working, which makes the wait bearable. I'm on my

second soda, and he's telling me about Lana, the server who watched my dad and me argue about beer my first night in town. Apparently, she and Mateo went out for six months, then broke up when she fell for some girl who lives in her building. This was at Christmastime. He's still bummed.

I don't blame him. Whitney and I split in early March, and I still feel the hurt of it. It's not that I miss her, but more so the idea of her. I've mentioned her to Mateo, but as if she was a passing interest. She was not. I don't half-ass things. I can't care just a little bit.

Which is why it's better I'm alone.

Except I've been doing a lot of thinking about Piper.

I glance toward the entrance again. She should be here by now. Seems illogical to jump straight to the conclusion that she's not gonna show, but I'm starting to worry.

Dad comes out of his office, ruffling my hair as he walks by. He joins Mateo behind the bar and tells me, "Hot chicks, ten o'clock."

I tame my hair and track his gaze to a table of women sitting across the restaurant. They're in their late twenties, probably, and laughing loudly. Fancy drinks abound. I roll my eyes because shit, Davis is obnoxious.

"Did you get dinner?" he asks me.

"Yeah. Bacon burger."

"You haven't ordered the same thing twice, have you?"

"Nope. I'm going to experience the full menu." Before I came to Florida, I survived on chicken strips and fries, peanut butter sandwiches, and the creamy noodle casseroles my mom makes. I hate celery and white chocolate and soft cheeses and wheat bread. The thought of consuming a piece of raw onion makes me want to hurl. But since my venture into the world of acai bowls, I've been trying to branch out. So what if exploring the menu of a restaurant my dad owns, one filled with foods that are mostly quintessential American cuisine, isn't fraught with danger? Feels like something.

"What's your favorite so far?" Dad asks.

"Probably the coconut shrimp."

"Same! The sirloin chili's amazing too. So's the grouper. Try one of those tomorrow."

He snags a fry from the few left on my plate, dunks it in tartar sauce, then pulls himself a beer. He ducks back into his office, glass in hand.

Shaking my head, I scan the lobby again and—fucking finally—Piper's checking in with April, the hostess on duty. Tati's behind her, looking jittery as all hell. Her gaze jumps around the lobby, the dining room, the bar. She's gripping the strap of her bag like it's a rappeler's rope and she's dangling from a sheer cliff.

She definitely knows this is Davis's place.

Piper looks totally at ease. She's wearing a short denim skirt and a tight black tank, and her dark curls are pulled into a high ponytail.

Our eyes meet across the busy restaurant, and she grins.

Piper

IT WAS TOUCH AND GO, getting Tati to Blitz Brews.

As soon as she got home from work, I spouted a carefully crafted lie about getting started on my college admission essays. While she seemed pleased, she didn't jump at the chance to reward me. She's never been the positive reinforcement type—not with me or herself. As she often reminds me, she doesn't have the time or the money to indulge. She's got to stay focused and keep a roof over our heads.

Okay, Tati.

I insisted on dinner out, guilted her into it with the phrase I use sparingly and judiciously—*Mom and Dad would have taken me.* Then I offered to drive because I'd strategically waited until she'd had a glass of wine to suggest leaving home.

When I pull her Volvo into the parking lot of Blitz Brews, she has an absolute fit.

"What's the big deal?" I say as I shift into park. "I want seafood."

"I'd rather have Italian."

"That's stupid." I open the door and step into the balmy night. "It's hot. I'm not eating heavy pasta when fresh fish is an option." I walk toward the restaurant with her keys in hand. Obstinate as she is, I don't think she'll opt to broil in the car while I eat red snapper in an air-conditioned sports bar.

Behind me, a car door slams.

"Wait up!" she calls.

———

I see Henry before he sees me.

He's sitting at the bar, talking to his dad.

My heart manages a swoop of excitement before I bully it back into submission.

He's in jeans and a gray T-shirt, and his hair is disheveled in its usual way. His sunburn has become a tan, and it's doing him all kinds of favors.

I'm looking at him not like a hot guy, I realize, but like a hot guy with potential.

A flurry of nerves kicks up in my stomach.

Henry's my buddy, my neighbor, my partner in crime.

He's not a prospect.

And anyway, tonight isn't about him or the undeniable exhilaration I feel when I think about being with him. Tonight's about Tati and Davis.

I speak to the hostess while my sister squirms beside me. It's strange, acting as the adult in our duo, but I manage, requesting a table because those are closer to the bar than the booths circling the restaurant's perimeter. "For four," I whisper while Tati's distracted, digging around in her purse for her trusty Ruby Woo.

We have to wait a few minutes. The longer we stand in the lobby, the more my sister resembles a caged and very agitated tiger. I elbow her as she rocks from foot to foot and take immense pleasure in saying, "Holy balls, Tati. Stand still already."

"I'm trying," she mutters, opening a compact to apply her lipstick.

Oh my god, this is the *best*.

I sneak another peek at Henry, who's guzzling soda. He looks nervous. But then his eyes collide with mine and spark with light. I smile. His whole face comes alive.

It's a heady feeling, wielding the power to animate someone so vividly.

"Let's go," Tati snaps, pushing me forward, shattering the trance I've fallen into.

The hostess has taken off, weaving through the crowded tables. I follow. My sister trails close behind, like she's using me as a buffer.

As soon as we're seated, my name rings out.

I make sure to widen my eyes and drop my jaw. Henry's walking toward us, wearing the same *What on earth are you doing here?* expression I'm feigning.

"Hey," he says. "Here for dinner?"

"Yep. You remember Tati?"

He gives my sister a nod. "It's wild running into you guys here."

"Oh?" I smile up at him. "Why's that?"

"This is my dad's restaurant." Subtly, he winks at me. He's a cute winker, not a smarmy winker. Of course he is.

My stomach's flitting around again, same as when he grinned at me a few minutes ago.

God—I'm attracted to Henry.

I mean, I've been attracted to a dreamy, idealized version of Henry for the last three years, but that was meaningless, because that Henry was just a fantasy. *This* Henry, this flesh-and-blood, studious boy who wants to go to West Point and likes to dip his fries in tartar sauce and thinks he's too good to read the Delphina trilogy? He's real, and he's standing right in front of me, smiling like he's been waiting all night to set eyes on me.

I'm not sure I have a type, but if I have an *anti*-type, it's Henry Walker.

And yet...

He turns to Tati. "My dad opened Blitz Brews a few years ago."

"How nice for him," my sister says, voice tight.

A beat of silence passes before I remember the script and gesture to the chair beside mine. "Henry, you should join us."

"Oh, I don't want to intrude."

"You wouldn't be. Right, Tati?" I frown at my sister and call, "Hello—Earth to Tati?"

She's scanning the restaurant like a lifeguard scanning the beach.

I say her name again, sharp with impatience.

"Oh!" she says with a nervous laugh. "What?"

I roll my eyes. "I was telling Henry he should join us."

"And I said no thanks. Third wheel and all." He's good—hitting the beats we discussed right on cue, his tone light, his vibe virtuous. "Actually, though," he says, touching his chin. "My dad's here. I could go get him. Then there'd be four of us."

"I don't think—" Tati starts.

I beat her to the punch. "Yes! Go get him!"

Henry motors away, giving Tati no time to manufacture an argument.

She fidgets.

I sip my ice water.

Henry returns with his dad.

The astonishment that splashes over Davis's face is pure comedy.

"Dad," Henry says, "you remember Piper? This is her sister, Tati."

They stare at one another, wearing matching expressions of stupefaction. I sense that they'd like to pretend this is their first encounter, except Tati knows I've met Davis, and Davis, of course, remembers me. There's no way to create a convincing *nice to meet you* narrative.

"Davis," Tati says in the same intrigued but wary way someone might say *viper*.

"Nice to see you again, Tati."

"Hang on," Henry says with contrived—though convincing—disbelief. "You two know each other?"

"We're acquainted," Tati says.

I grin. "Small world."

"Sure is," Davis says, making eyes at my sister.

Tati glares at me. She's on to our plan.

Oh well.

"You guys really should sit," I say. "You know, since we're all friendly." I push the chair next to me out, and Henry slides into it, leaving his dad to round the table and take the seat beside Tati.

We're silent for a few minutes, scrutinizing our menus, until a server drops by to take our orders. Davis and Henry have already had dinner, apparently, so they choose desserts, and Davis asks for a beer. I begrudgingly agree to share a crab cake sandwich with my calorie-conscious sister. I'd prefer my own entree, as I'd like to eat my feelings; so far, this setup isn't going great. Our table is a melancholy island in the otherwise exuberant ocean of the sports bar. But Henry seems unflustered, so I try to chill.

"Haven't heard from you in a while," Davis says, twisting in his seat to look at Tati.

"Yes, well. I haven't had a lot to say."

"Funny. That wasn't the case last time we were together."

Whoa—I've never seen a man contradict my sister. They usually fall all over themselves to win her good graces.

She's got no response, so he must have a point.

"Where'd you guys meet?" Henry asks.

Davis smiles wistfully. "The beach. We were both out for a walk. Ended up walking together."

"Piper and I met at the pool," Henry volunteers. "Twice. This last time, she fell in."

"Had she been drinking?" my sister asks.

He's caught off guard. "I, uh, don't think—"

"*No*," I interject. "Jeez, Tati."

"If she was with my boy," Davis says, "she wasn't getting into any trouble. He's the most responsible kid on the planet."

"I'd take responsible over reckless any day," Tati says.

A reckless drunk—how wonderful to know that's how she sees me.

"I don't know," Davis says after a swig of beer. "Sometimes responsible gets boring. I'd like to see Henry live a little. Make some mischief once in a while."

Tati huffs. "And I'd like Piper to stop seeking mischief out."

I find myself leaning closer to Henry, my ally in this agony. He smells soapy and crisp. For a second, I let myself imagine what it'd be like to cocoon under his arm. The phantom sensations—warmth, safety, comfort—surprise me. I haven't felt the urge to touch anyone or be touched since before that night with Damon. When I'm with Henry, though, I don't feel on edge. If I were to ask him to slow down or back off or leave altogether, I'm confident he would.

Across the table, Tati's shoulders are starting to relax, even as she goes on about what a piece of work I am. Davis appears amused.

I elbow Henry and mutter like a ventriloquist, "What is happening?"

"They're connecting," he says close to my ear.

"Yeah, by talking shit about *me*."

He shrugs. "And me. The boring one."

"She's so impulsive," Tati's telling Davis. "So careless. And dishonest!"

I'm tempted to defend myself, but I did lie about my college essays earlier, so I'm not operating with the cleanest track record. I might be *sort of* impulsive and *a bit* careless and a *little* dishonest sometimes. So what?

"He's got his whole future planned out," Davis says, waving a hand toward Henry. "He gets up every morning to run. He's *never* without a book."

Tati laughs—laughs! "Hey, now. I like to read."

"No shit. I've seen the library you call a living room. And what's so wrong with a little impulsiveness anyway?" he asks, nodding in my direction. "Adventure's hard to find when you're married to a blueprint."

Well. Davis might be okay.

I'm no body language expert, but Tati must think so too. She's swiveled her chair toward him and is inclining her shoulders in his direction. She looks at him like he's preaching gospel, which is crazy because she disagrees with literally everything he's saying.

Davis seems positively entranced by my sister.

"Speaking of blueprints," he says, "what've you got going on later this week?"

"Oh, gosh. I'd have to check my day planner."

For a second, I think Tati's being serious. But her eyes are sparkling, and her mouth is quirked into a smile aimed right at Davis, and I realize that—holy shit—she's teasing him. *Flirting* with him.

"Yeah, I've seen your day planner," he says, matching her grin. "Work, work, work. I assume you're free evenings and weekends?"

"I *might* be," Tati says. "Depending on what you have in mind."

Davis stretches an arm over the back of her chair. He's not touching her—not being handsy or too forward—but there's something suave about his posture. Tati's fixated on him as he says, "How about we go someplace nice? Someplace fancy."

Henry leans toward me and whispers, "How hungry are you?"

"Pretty hungry."

"Cool. Let's get out of here, and I'll buy you a burger somewhere else."

I glance back at Tati and Davis. If this were a rom-com, the next scene would be a montage of the rest of their evening, set to a peppy song. The two of them trading anecdotes about their teenagers, Tati sharing her crab cake, Davis feeding her bites of his mud pie. They'd laugh and flirt. His palm would migrate to the small of her back. Her hand would land on his leg. And then, when the moon is high, they'd head out to the beach, where they first met. They'd kiss, silhouetted by starlight.

"Yeah," I tell Henry. "Let's bail."

141

Henry

DAD COULDN'T GIVE A SHIT when I tell him Piper and I are leaving. Tati smiles, waving her sister off.

Piper gives me a flabbergasted look, dropping a ring of keys into Tati's purse.

Before we walk out of Blitz Brews, I glance over my shoulder. Tati's laughing at something Dad said, which is nuts—I rarely find the guy funny. He's lit up, like dinner with this woman is all he's been hoping for.

"Well," Piper says once we've made it outside. "That didn't bomb."

"Holy shit, no. I was all about setting them up, but I wasn't entirely sure it'd work."

"Same. Tati was *horrified* when we pulled up here. I thought she was going to choose the long walk back to the Towers over going inside."

"How awkward were those first few minutes, though?"

"Pain. Ful." She puts a hand on her stomach. "God, am I happy to be out of there. Now, about that burger."

———

We end up at the putt-putt course, where Piper promptly inhales the burger I pick up at the snack bar. She tucks away an order of tater tots and a root beer too. When she's finished, she tosses her trash and rubs her hands together. "Okay. Let's get our golf on."

We acquire clubs and balls. She chooses purple for herself and green for me. "Because yours will blend into the turf, and then I'll win," she says, like this is a theory she's tested.

"Don't underestimate my skills. People like me excel at putt-putt. It's something about the immense focus needed, combined with the fact that putt-putt doesn't require you to communicate with others. Don't get cocky, is all I'm saying."

She goes first, managing two strokes on a par three.

Damn.

She plucks her ball from the hole, perches on a nearby bench, crossing her ankles like royalty, and says, "Your turn, sucker."

Takes me four strokes.

The game continues. She keeps overachieving. I keep under-performing. I meant what I said about putt-putt—I'm usually decent. I even held my own on an actual golf course with Dad yesterday. But Piper's crushing me and being terrifically arrogant about it. I can't explain why, but I kind of like having my ass

143

handed to me by this girl.

"You grew up in a resort town," I remind her as we walk to the thirteenth hole. "You've been putt-putting your whole life."

"Hardly. I've only been here a few times."

"Tati brought you to whack balls through the mouths of gigantic pirate heads?"

"Definitely not. My dad and I came when I was little. He was a good golfer and an awesome teacher. I've been here with a couple of unimaginative dates too."

"Hey, now. Putt-putt was your idea."

She gives me a mild smile. "Who said this was a date?"

She's got a point. Being with her is so easy, I let myself get caught up in the moment. We came here to escape Davis and Tati and Blitz Brews, not launch a romance of our own.

"Not me," I say, spinning my ball on the palm of my hand.

She arches a brow like she's disappointed in my response. Like maybe she wanted me to try and convince her that yeah, this *is* a date, and not a bad one.

"Do you think Davis and Tati are still together?" she asks.

"Hopefully. Do you think they're still talking shit about us?"

"Probably." She sets her ball in the tee box, lines up, and takes a smooth swing. The ball rolls toward the flag, coming to rest six inches from the hole. She taps it in, then beams. While I set up, she says, "It's hilarious that what bugs Tati most about me are traits your dad apparently has too."

"*Impulsive and careless*, she said, right? I guess that's Dad sometimes, yeah."

144

"And you're apparently responsible to the point of being boring. That's Tati, unequivocally."

I whack my ball with a lot less success than Piper. "Opposites attract," I reason with a shrug.

I expect her to give me another of those shit-eating grins, but her expression goes solemn. "Do you really believe that?"

Her eyes are the prettiest blue.

She's trapped me with her gaze, and she's messing with my head. Because suddenly, I don't know what I believe. Whitney was my opposite in a lot of ways, and as a result, we clashed. By the end, I was weary and drifting. Were we attracted to each other? Fuck yes. The problem was that our attraction couldn't transcend a shit ton of conflict.

When I came to Sugar Bay, emotionally beaten down, I was set on reclaiming my focus. I was going to concentrate on *me*. I was going to be careful and keep my heart safe, my future intact. I wasn't going to fly off course—not again.

I wasn't counting on reengaging with Piper.

"Know what I like about you?" she asks.

I mentally brace myself. "What?"

"Everything your dad gives you a hard time about. I think it's cool that you plan ahead. It's amazing that West Point's your goal, that you're busting your ass to get there. I like that you read books that look like they belong on the dusty shelves of a research library. I like that you're smart and attentive and mature. Being with you makes me feel—"

Her eyes go big, like her brain's just now catching up to her

145

mouth. She shakes her head, then pulls our scorecard from the pocket of her skirt, suddenly riveted by the numbers on it.

I need to know how that sentence was meant to end.

"Makes you feel what?"

Nothing.

"Come on, Piper. What were you going to say?"

Looking up and into my eyes, she says softly, "Safe. Being with you makes me feel safe."

Piper

I STOMP HENRY IN PUTT-PUTT.

He doesn't seem to care.

We walk back to the Towers. It's late, and the main drag's dead, save for a few tourist-laden rideshares. The sky is clear and blue- black, scattered with stars. As stir-crazy as I so often feel in this town, I'll miss its nights when I move to one of the faraway states I daydream about.

Tati loved Boston, with its green spaces and vibrant arts scene and universities, but she had to have been sad about leaving Sugar Bay. Waves crashing against white sand. Incomparable sunsets. Hole-in-the-wall cafés and custom T-shirt shops and an exciting influx of tourists come spring. Would she have visited if Mom and Dad were still alive, fulfilling the roles she's been forced to assume? Would she have come back to see me, her little sister, not her annoying charge?

"What're you thinking about?" Henry asks as we meander toward the Towers.

"The ass-whooping I just handed you."

"Ha ha," he deadpans. "For a girl who's celebrating, you look pretty pensive."

"It's nothing," I say, even though I'd like to tell him that I'm thinking of my parents, the stars and the ocean, my sister.

"Doesn't seem like nothing." His tone sounds almost indifferent, but I know this is how he demonstrates patience, and it works.

"I was thinking about Sugar Bay," I admit. "How as much as I want to leave one day, I'll miss it."

"It's a great town."

"Yeah. Full of memories."

He gives me a sweet smile. "I can't even imagine."

It's not until we're standing in front of my door in the west tower that he speaks again. He props his shoulder against the wall, and I match his posture, standing closer than I have in all the days since we reunited.

"Remember when we met? The first time?"

I blink, sleepy yet thrumming with energy. "Yes."

"You were crying."

Three years later, the memory makes me blush. "I remember."

"I didn't ask why."

"Because you were polite."

"Because I was chickenshit. I didn't want to send you running." He smiles wryly. "I don't think you'll run tonight."

This is getting deep, but he's right.

I shake my head; I'm not going anywhere.

"Then I'm gonna to ask. Were you crying because of your parents?"

I sift through my memories, trying to figure out how to explain that night in a way that'll make sense to Henry, a boy who's got a living mom and dad, two people who'd step into traffic for him. "Kind of. And because of my sister. She and I'd fought earlier that night, and I felt very alone. If Tati, who'd lost our parents too, couldn't understand what I was going through, then how could anyone? You know?"

He drops his voice to a whisper. "Yeah. I think I do."

"You've felt sadness like that?"

"Not in the same way, but sadness, yeah."

I smile up at him. "Turned out to be a good night, though. Being with you made the heavy stuff seem lighter. By the time we said goodbye, I felt a lot less alone."

"And then I vanished," he says, his low pitch betraying his regret.

"Well, yeah. That sucked. Except..." I hesitate, trying to decide how forthcoming I want to be. This moment feels special, like we're in a bubble of truth. Like there's no way I'll say the wrong thing. And so I forge ahead. "Except you never really vanished. I thought about you a lot afterward. That night turned out to be everything I needed. *You* were everything I needed."

He smiles with charming conceit. "You're referring to my mad kissing skills, aren't you?"

149

I lift a brow. "You were my first."

His smile becomes sincere. "You were my first too."

"I thought I was hallucinating when I saw you at the pool the second time."

"Jesus, same! I was sure you were a mirage."

He shuffles forward, extending a hand toward me. He leaves his palm open in the air between us, letting me choose whether we take things further.

Should we?

When he disappeared three years ago, I was inconsolable. That week was the first time I snuck onto Marine Conservation Park property after hours, an act of pure desperation. The pool no longer felt like a refuge, the childhood house I'd made a million memories in belonged to a new family, and there was a gaping hole in my heart, one that had been momentarily patched by a boy who'd then left without explanation. Yet another person whose presence I couldn't depend on. When I finally accepted that Henry was gone for real, I wanted nothing more than comfort, than to feel the unconditional love of my parents. The only place their spirits endured was the park. That night, I sat on the pavement beside their memorial medallion in the quiet darkness, weeping.

I'm confident that Henry won't vanish again, but I've got other concerns. Saying yes to more than friendship with him is entirely different from saying yes to a night of fun with a tourist boy or a tipsy kiss with one of the guys from my school. Saying yes to Henry involves trust and vulnerability.

Saying yes to Henry means handing over my heart.

Thanks to Damon, I know all about the wrong sort of boy. The sort of boy who takes, who demands, who hurts. Henry isn't that sort of boy.

I'd be crazy not to see where he and I can go together.

I slip my hand into his. It feels good—nowhere near as scary as I expected.

"That kiss," he says, swinging our linked hands between us. "How'd it measure up?"

"It's the kiss to which I've compared every one since."

He lets out a laugh so hearty I worry he'll disturb the neighbors.

"I mean it," I tell him. "Dry a girl's tears, make her swoon with talk of science and history and politics, spend forever at her side watching a turtle nest, then kiss her on the beach as the sun comes up? Perfect."

He tugs me gently toward him. His warmth encircles me, his eyes taking on a new vibrancy, brown flashing with starbursts of gold. My heart pounds, excitement and anticipation spinning into joy. This moment reminds me of sandy toes, a sherbet sunrise, a whirlwind night with Henry.

He wants to kiss me again. His expression broadcasts his longing.

Fear that has nothing to do with him lingers in my body, pinching at my muscles, scratching at the back of my neck. But tonight, fear is overshadowed by need. A need to know whether Henry and I can stir up the same electricity we created when we

151

were fourteen. Even more than that, a need to reclaim the control I used to have over my body, its impulses and its responses.

I take another step closer, laying my hand against his chest, atop his drumming heart.

He's a friend who doesn't look at me like I'm a disappointment or a challenge or a bother. He's nostalgia and newness, simultaneously a haven and an escape.

I want to kiss him too.

Henry

I TUCK A LOOSE COIL of hair behind her ear, moving slowly and deliberately.

I'd be an idiot not to have noticed the way she sometimes startles, the way she maintains physical distance. The way she's hesitant to touch. I don't remember her being like that three years ago, and speculating about why she's changed ignites a firestorm of anger in me.

She doesn't flinch. She doesn't move away. She doesn't lift her palm from where it rests against my sternum. She doesn't tug her hand free of mine.

I put everything I've got into decoding her expression, the pace of her breath.

"Are you okay?" I ask, because it seems crucial to be sure.

She smiles. "I think so."

"You'll tell me if that changes? If you're ever not okay?"

She lets out a breath and nods.

I gesture toward her apartment door. "Do you need to go in?"

"Probably. If Tati's home, she'll be waiting up."

"What if she's still with my dad?"

"Then we should start a matchmaking service because holy balls, we have a gift."

I laugh. Chemistry is what we have. She's got to feel it too. As frantically as my brain's shouting about how I should back off, keep my priorities in mind, remember what happened last time I went all-in on a girl, my skin's buzzing where it touches hers, and my muscles twitch with the need to pull her closer.

"We should do it again," I say.

Her eyes flash with curiosity. "Do what again?"

"Kiss." And then I scramble to backtrack. "I mean, if you want. Or not. But I want to. You should know that. So if the urge ever strikes, I'm"—my face is hot even before I finish making my witless admission—"a willing participant."

She gives my chest a playful shove. "You had better game when you were fourteen."

I take her teasing in stride. She's exactly right.

"I'm not here to run game. I'm here so you can out-putt-putt me and judge my condiment choices, then school me on *Delphina and the Talking Turtle in the Trench.*"

"That's *not* one of the titles—" she starts before realizing I'm messing with her. She drops her head back, laughing, setting loose the lock of hair I tamed a minute ago.

That's it—making Piper Nixon laugh is my new life's goal.

154

"Where do you come up with this stuff?" she asks.

I tap my temple. "There's a lot going on up here. You've barely scratched the surface."

"I'm starting to understand that."

She squeezes my hand, her gaze holding mine.

I'm a willing participant.

Jesus H. She must think I'm the world's biggest tool.

Or...not.

Okay, no, she doesn't, because holy shit—she's rising up onto her toes, leaning toward me, sweeping her tongue across her bottom lip.

A shiver of anticipation rolls through me.

Inches separate us, a single breath.

My eyes have just fallen closed when the sound of an unlocking dead bolt makes them fly open again. Piper pulls back, slipping her hand from mine as she whirls around.

The apartment door swings wide. Tati sticks her head into the hallway. "Oh, I thought I heard voices. Glad you made it home safe." She looks from Piper to me, then back again. She smiles. "I'll...leave you to it."

And then she disappears behind the closing door.

Piper swivels to face me, eyes dinner-plate round. "Who the hell was that?"

"That was your sister," I say, playing along, "who clearly spent an enjoyable evening with a very pleasant companion."

She snorts. "Are you, like, seventy-five?"

"Practically."

155

Now she laughs. "I should go in. Want to hang out tomorrow night?"

I grin. "I'll check my day planner."

Piper

DAMN TATI FOR INTERRUPTING!

She's not in the kitchen. She's not in her room either. I assume she's holed up in her bathroom, performing her twenty-six-step skin care routine, so I head for my room to try and unwind. My pulse is skipping in circles.

My sister's voice startles me as I pass the living room. "Piper?"

She's nestled into the couch's corner, wrapped in the wonky ocean-blue afghan my mom knitted during a foray into yarn and needles that lasted only one summer. She has a glass of wine in one hand, a novel in the other. Her hair's pulled into a messy knot, a rarity, and—most unexpected of all—her feet are propped up on the coffee table. The very coffee table she scolded me for leaving a water ring on last week.

"Come sit," she says.

Her amiability is unsettling. She must be toying with me.

Or she's possessed. Still, I park on the couch, slipping my feet beneath a loose corner of the afghan, and ask, "Everything okay?"

"All good. Seems your evening progressed nicely."

"I guess," I say, wondering how much she saw in the hall. Henry and I didn't make it as far as kissing, but almost. What Tati interrupted had to have looked intense.

"Henry seems nice."

"He is. He sucks at putt-putt, though."

She laughs, reminding me of the old Tati, the sister I knew before our parents' accident. She laughed all the time back then, from deep in her belly. She made others laugh—me especially— with witty observations and sharp sarcasm.

"How did your evening...progress?" I ask.

"It was nice." She looks smug, like *nice* is a vast understatement. "Davis isn't the washed-up frat bro you think he is."

"I'll take your word for it. You look..." *Relaxed. Radiant.* "Like you had a good time."

"I did. It was lucky we bumped into them, wasn't it?"

I smile innocently. "Very lucky." And then, to avoid accidentally setting her off, as I so often do, I say, "I'm going to bed. I've got to be at work early, and I'm beat."

"Night, Piper."

I pinch myself on the way to my room. That conversation— this whole night—feels like a dream I'm going to lurch out of any second.

I turn back to glance at my sister before closing my door. She sets her book down to pick up her phone. Her brows draw together in concentration before her expression eases into a broad smile. In all the years she's been my guardian, in all the years she's managed the Towers, I've never seen her regard her phone with anything but disdain.

She's texting Davis—she has to be.

I close my door with a quiet click, then fall backward onto my bed.

I grin up at the ceiling.

I'm *free*.

Henry

MY DAD'S IN THE APARTMENT when I get there, lounging on the couch in front of a baseball game that's broadcasting from the West Coast, brew in hand.

"What's up, buddy?" He lifts his bottle like he's toasting me.

"Not a lot, *buddy*. How was your night?"

"Damn good, my boy. Damn good."

I quell a shudder, ready for him to launch into a gag-inducing description of how sexy he thinks Tati is. Instead, he asks, "Where'd you run off to?"

"Putt-putt. Piper won."

He laughs, then takes a pull of his beer. He's swapped his street clothes for sweats and an old T-shirt. I like this version of him: laid back, trying, but not *too* hard. "What's she like?" he asks. "Other than wild, like Tati says."

I fall onto the couch. "She's cool."

"Smart as you?"

"Yep. Tough too."

"'Cause of what happened to her mom and dad?"

Tati's talked with him about her parents—interesting.

"I guess that probably has a lot to do with it," I say.

"You round the bases yet?"

Ahh, there's Davis.

"Jesus, Dad. Really?"

He downs what's left of his beer, then sets the empty on the coffee table. "Just curious. Should've known you're not one to kiss and tell."

"No, I'm not." Even if I was, I wouldn't tell *him*.

"Don't get pissy," he says, reaching across the couch to jostle my shoulder. "I was just making conversation. Keep your secrets if you want. Just know that I wanna talk if you do."

I wish I could talk to him about digging Sugar Bay but missing Spokane. About Piper and my conflicted feelings. Not that I'm conflicted about *her*. I like her a lot—that's easy—but I'm conflicted about pursuing something with her.

Opening up's just not in my DNA.

"I'm taking Tati to dinner tomorrow night," Dad tells me.

"I thought you and I were going bowling."

He sits up straighter. "Shit, Henry. I forgot. I'll reschedule. Tati'll understand."

"No, no." I temper a smile. "Go with her. You and I can bowl anytime."

"Really? Thanks, buddy." He relaxes into the couch again.

"You should do something with Piper. She's obviously taken a liking to you."

"Oh yeah? You gathered that in the seven minutes you've spent with us?"

He shrugs, shooting me a lazy smile. "You're my kid. What's not to like?"

Piper

I DREAM ABOUT HENRY AND our first kiss: two fourteen-year-olds with no experience and little to lose, who won't see each other again until we're seventeen, with plenty of experience and loads to lose.

In the morning, I try to convince myself that I've built it up, spent years fantasizing about a connection that was, in reality, rushed and immature. But I'm not sure that's the case. Our connection has survived time and separation. It doesn't feel rushed anymore, and I don't think it's immature.

Three years ago, I made the first move. After we watched the mama turtle, I reached for Henry's hand. His palm rested against mine, unmoving, as if the touch surprised him, as if he wasn't sure what to do about it. I gave him a chance to pull away, laugh it off, change our course. Instead, he laced his fingers through mine and held on.

He talked about snow skiing, something I'd only ever imagined doing. He talked about his friends, a couple of guys he ran cross-country with. He talked about his parents, but only in generalities: His mom liked to bake bread on Sunday mornings, and his dad, who'd once been his skiing buddy, was taking up golf. I didn't know they weren't married or that they lived thousands of miles apart. I didn't know that Henry's time in Florida had already run its course.

He took his cues from me. The way I avoided talk of my family, the way I spoke vaguely about friendships, the way I referenced school like I was an observer, not a registered student.

He gaped when I told him I'd never seen snow. "How is that possible?"

I shrugged. "We have frosty mornings every once in a while during the winter, but the sun melts it almost right away."

"Do you want to see snow?"

"I want to see a lot of things," I said softly.

All that time, he kept my hand in his. Kept my mind busy. Kept my tears at bay.

When the sun announced itself on the horizon, he said, "I've gotta get back."

We turned for the Towers.

I was grateful for this brown-eyed boy who'd come out of nowhere. We hadn't even parted ways yet, and I couldn't wait to see him again.

The beach was empty except for a few early joggers and a host of trawling seagulls, and he pulled me in. Shyness heated my face. I remember worrying that he could feel the fierce vibration of my heartbeat.

He looked deep into my eyes. "I'm glad I met you."

In retrospect, it was a goodbye.

Later, I called Gabi to gush about the rendezvous, which I'd inflated to romance-novel status. She *oohe*d and *aahe*d as I divulged every detail: the way Henry had leaned in; the way he'd pressed his lips to mine, an innocent kiss that became less so as it gained traction; the way he'd released my hands to find my waist, drawing me gently forward, until I wrapped my arms around him. I told her how it had felt as though static were popping and snapping in the air, the energy he and I had created together spilling over.

"Oh, my god, Piper!" she squealed. "I'm beyond jealous, but so, so happy for you. I can't wait to meet him!"

It wrecks me, knowing that she might never.

My first kiss with Henry was a string of moments that stayed with me. A kiss that started nervously and ended gratifyingly. Three years later, we're staring down adulthood. We've got hours of deep conversation behind us, and we rarely let a morning pass without texting. But last night, we let a follow-up kiss slip out of our grasp.

I can't wait to be with him again.

Shortly before sunset, we meet on the beach reserved for residents of the Towers. It's a gorgeous stretch of sand, rarely

165

used because most of the people who live on the property take the beach for granted. Not me. I'd live out here in a grass hut if my sister approved.

Henry's on one of the loungers with a book, *Dereliction of Duty*. There's a brown paper bag perched on the neighboring chair—dinner, I think.

He looks up as I cast a shadow over him, surprised one second, grinning the next. He ditches his book and moves the paper bag off the chair, gesturing for me to sit.

I do. "I thought we were going to get dinner out."

"I brought food instead," he says, giving the bag a poke.

"I'm intrigued." I nod at his book. "Should I have brought reading material?"

He smiles, his eyes reflecting the glowing sun. "Nope. I got here early because I thought it'd be busy. I had no idea we'd have the whole beach to ourselves."

I wave a hand at the pastel sky. "Most residents don't appreciate amazing sunsets or sugar sand or warm salt water or pods of dolphins."

"I think you just described paradise." He says this sincerely, except he's not appreciating paradise either—he's gazing at me.

"Sorry I'm late," I tell him. "Tati was a special sort of cyclone tonight."

"Bad mood?"

"The opposite. Have you seen *Sleeping Beauty*?"

"It's been a while."

"Well, she does a lot of skipping around in the forest, singing

166

dreamily, chitchatting with woodland creatures. Tati went full Princess Aurora while she was getting ready tonight. I was a woodland creature."

Henry laughs. "Davis was feeling himself too. He busted out what he called the 'good' cologne, and he must've changed his shirt six times."

"Tati borrowed one of my sundresses. One she told me exposed too much skin a couple of weeks ago. Go figure."

His gaze drops to my bare legs. The sundress I'm wearing exposes a lot of skin too, and the breeze flutters its chiffon. I sit very still, expecting his lingering attention to make me uncomfortable; I'm anticipating the sensation of a thousand spiders skittering over my skin, like when Damon closed Gabi's bedroom door, trapping me inside. It happened at Blitz Brews too, when he spewed that remark about what I was wearing.

I wait for that itchy tingle, ready to quash the shudder that'll almost certainly follow.

It never comes.

Henry realizes he's checking me out the moment I decide I don't mind.

"Sorry," he murmurs, turning his head to watch the slowly sinking sun.

"Don't be," I tell him. "You didn't do anything wrong."

I reach for him, letting my open hand hover in the space between our loungers. He shifts his gaze back to me, linking his fingers with mine.

"I made you uncomfortable."

My chest floods with warmth. He's so conscientious. So eager to make things right—to *do* right. I smile, giving his hand a reassuring squeeze.

"No you didn't, Henry. You never have."

Henry

IT WAS SMART, BRINGING DINNER. The beach, the sunset, the girl—I don't want to be anywhere but here. We drag our chairs close together, then make a picnic of the fried chicken and waffle fries and grapes I picked up at the grocery store.

"Good call on the finger foods," Piper says, wiping her hands on one of the napkins I grabbed last-minute. "Although you should've let me pitch in. I could've brought dessert."

I dig into the bottom of the bag and pull out two plastic-wrapped cookies.

She grins. "You thought of everything!"

I thought of her. Last night, before I fell asleep. This morning, during my run. This afternoon, while I was reading poolside, picking up food, getting ready for the beach.

It worries me, how constantly she's been on my mind.

It was the same when Whitney and I started going out. We

hung out all the time, and when we weren't together, we texted continuously. We shared our locations and checked in on each other way too often. On the rare occasions we weren't in contact, I got lost thinking about her. In those earliest months, my grades took a dip and my run times slowed; Silas and Ricky gave me shit about losing my edge. My mom became concerned. Still, she couldn't hide how happy she was that I was spending time with a fun, charismatic girl. Eventually, I got a handle on my schoolwork and improved my times. Whit was at our house more often than not. My friends warmed up to her. Mom declared us a great match. In the beginning, I thought we were too.

Is that how everyone falls—hard and fast, powerless to stop their descent?

But this won't be like last time. I won't lose myself. Piper won't ask me to.

"Chocolate chip and oatmeal raisin," I tell her, holding out the cookies. "Your pick."

"Chocolate chip. Obviously. Fruit has no place in a cookie."

She's so random and opinionated, open to delving deep into the most ridiculous topics. I like this about her, probably because I'm the same.

I give her a quizzical look. "Raisins are fruits?"

"They're dried grapes, smarty-pants."

"Yeah, but—"

"Wouldn't you call a prune a fruit?"

"I'd call a prune inedible. Anyway, that's a ballsy statement: *Fruit has no place in a cookie*. What about Fig Newtons?"

She wrinkles her nose. "Yeah. Gross."

I concede, inhaling my fruit-studded dessert, wracking my brain for an example of a delicious cookie that's got fruit in it. I'm struggling. Maybe she's on to something. But then, in the recesses of my memory, a light bulb flickers on. "My mom used to make these cookies at Christmastime. They were shortbread, I think, but she'd put a scoop of strawberry jam in the middle. They were fucking amazing."

"She doesn't make them anymore?"

"Not these last few years. Once I was in high school, she started taking holiday shifts at the hospital that no one else wanted. She figured she'd let the parents with little kids stay home on Thanksgiving and Christmas. So the cookie-baking fizzled. But I'm telling you, those strawberry shortbreads were the shit."

"Okay, point made. If your mom ever offers me a jam cookie, I'll try it."

"You won't regret it. Does Tati make Christmas cookies?"

"Ha! She makes lean meats and vitamin-rich vegetables, and that's about it. Gabi's mom makes dozens and dozens of holiday treats, though, starting the first day of December. Peanut butter bars and eggnog cookies and these rolled pecan cookies covered in powdered sugar. So good. I spend a couple of hours at their house every Christmas Eve. Gabi's parents make me feel like family."

She so seldom brings up Gabi, I want to keep her talking. "Do you guys get each other presents?"

She nods. "The first Christmas we were friends, in fourth

grade, we both got each other books by chance. We've done that every year since—a book swap. This year, though..." Her smile flattens. "I guess I won't need to go to the bookstore." She shakes her head, so gloomy now that my heart squeezes.

"I'll trade books with you," I offer.

Eyeing *Dereliction of Duty*, she makes a sour face. "I'm not sure our literary tastes mesh. I'll buy you *Delphina of the Starlit Sea* and grill you on every juicy chapter."

"Then I'll buy you something nonfiction and dense, like... *Undaunted Courage*." I blow out a reverential breath. "Lewis and Clark, man."

She laughs, then finishes her cookie, crumpling its wrapper and dropping it into the bag with the rest of our trash. "Do you know what Tati and your dad are up to tonight?"

"No idea. I ask him as few questions as possible. He takes any display of interest as an invitation to do or say something outrageously inappropriate, like throwing boxes of condoms at me or inquiring about which bases I've rounded."

Piper blanches. "With *me*?"

"Uh...yeah? Thing is, I honestly don't think he cares. He asks questions like that because he thinks that's how guys are supposed to talk to each other. Or maybe it's to get a rise out of me. He knows I'm not going there with him."

"But why would you? You haven't even hit the ball in three years."

I laugh, surprised by her boldness. "If I didn't know better, I'd think you were throwing down a challenge."

172

She scoots forward on her chair, resting her cool hands on my knees. The wind's making her curls unspool like streamers. She says, "Tati's timing last night was a bummer."

"I thought so too. It gave me time to think, though." I don't want to kill the mood because I like where this is going, but her eyes are bright and she's smiling warmly and I'd be a dick not to level with her. "Piper, you and me together…it's kind of complicated."

Her brow furrows. "Because of Tati and Davis?"

"Maybe. But also because I'm leaving in August. Is that something you're okay with—complications?"

"Are *you* okay with complications?"

I fold her hands into mine. "I think so, yeah. I like you. Like, a lot. But I need to be straight with you."

The sun's fallen below the horizon, but the sky still glows orange, pink, and purple. Piper's face is shadowed, making it impossible to read her expression.

"Okay," she says. "Then be straight with me."

I pull in a breath. "There's this girl back in Spokane. It's over between us—it has been for months. But we were together for a while, and it was brutal at the end. I'm still kind of banged up."

"Like, you still care about her?"

I pause, considering. "I guess I'll probably always care about her, to some degree. But not like I used to. It was intense between us. There's a lot of baggage. A fucking cargo ship full of baggage. But I don't want to be with her anymore, if that's what you're asking."

173

She purses her lips, thoughtful. "You're sure?"

"Yeah. Very sure."

"Okay."

"Okay?"

"Yes. Okay. I'm sorry you had bad breakup. But I'm glad you told me."

I roll my neck, letting my shoulders relax, only just realizing how tense this conversation has made me. I was ready for her to drill into me, demand details, project whatever past bullshit she's lugging around onto what she and I are building.

That's what Whitney would do.

But Piper's being very mature about the whole thing. Is this how relationships are supposed to go?

She smiles. "Henry, I like you too. I don't want you to keep parts of yourself walled off."

I smile, flooded with relief. "You're really cool, you know that?"

She shrugs endearingly. "Yeah, I do."

I lean in. "You want to go to first base with me?"

Laughing, she says, "I thought you'd never ask."

Piper

IT'S HAPPENING AGAIN.

Henry and me, kissing on the beach.

He releases my hands to skim his palms up my arms, across my shoulders, under my hair. I shiver despite the heat surging through me. He's very good at this. Attentive, with an underlying urgency that makes me want to crawl into his lap.

Instead, I revel in a rare release of control.

I believe he'll do right by me.

He draws back, eyes closed, forehead touching mine.

"That was better than last time," I whisper, basking in the afterglow.

He opens his eyes, mouth stretching into a smile. "I hope so."

"Had a lot of practice since then?"

"Enough. You?"

"Enough."

The truth is, I've had plenty of practice—throwaway, just-for-fun practice. I've kissed both Jayden and Hudson while bombed at parties, along with plenty of other Sugar Bay High boys who aren't worth remembering. And then there were the tourist kisses, spring break boys and summer boys, which have been some of the best because expectations—theirs and mine—were zilch.

After Henry disappeared three years ago, I quit assuming boys would stick around. I stopped presuming they owed me anything or that they ever wanted more than a few minutes of pleasure. I learned that real boys were nothing like book boys and convinced myself that if I expected disappointment, I would only feel a pinprick of hurt when it inevitably came.

I've been fooling myself.

Henry moves in again, and I meet him, rising to my knees, tugging him up with me. He loops his arms around my waist, pulling me against his chest. I spend half a second feeling caged, and like he has a sixth sense, he loosens his hold, dancing his fingertips up my spine. He seems to understand, somehow, how challenging it is for me to give myself over, how tough it is for me to relax. But then I'm melting into him, raking my hands through his hair, running my fingers over the slight scruff of his jaw. He groans, a low rumble in his throat.

I've trusted a scant few people in my seventeen years: my mom and dad, Tati sometimes, and Gabi, before.

Now Henry.

Eventually, we do the hard work of pulling apart. We're both winded and flushed.

"So, second base, then?" he asks, and I laugh.

"Maybe not out here."

He glances up at the Towers, gridded with windows through which anyone could look down on us. "You think my dad and your sister are still out?"

I check the time. "It's early. It'd be a bad sign if they weren't."

"You want to putt-putt again? Or go swimming?"

"We could go upstairs," I suggest. "Watch a movie. Or something."

He grins, catching on to what I mean by *or something*.

"Yeah," he says. "Let's do that."

Henry

WE GO TO HER PLACE. Tati's not there, thank god.

Piper pulls Netflix up on the living room TV, which is tiny compared to the monstrosity Davis has mounted in his living room, and flanked by loaded bookshelves. She picks a sitcom I've never seen, then gives me a questioning look.

I shrug—who gives a fuck?

She hits play, and then we ignore the first two episodes in favor of making out on the couch. It's possible I've died and ascended—being with her is that good.

A third episode's starting when we hear keys rattling in the hall. Hastily, we straighten, smoothing our clothing, laughing at each other's faraway expressions. We're sitting on the couch with a couple of inches as a buffer when Tati comes through the door, followed by my dad.

"Oh!" Tati says, like it never occurred to her that the apartment wouldn't be empty.

"Welcome home," Piper says cheekily.

Tati cruises into the living room. Dad trails her comfortably. I forgot he's been here before. They sit down in the pair of chairs across from the couch, and things get weird quick. What are we supposed to do? Rehash our respective dates? Trade anecdotes? Resume the show and hang out together, a strange quartet?

How's that gonna work, when I can still taste Piper's vanilla lip gloss?

"How was dinner?" Dad asks.

"Really nice," Piper says. She shines a smile on me, like I cooked her a seven-course meal instead of serving her greasy chicken out of a paper bag. I almost reach for her hand, but I'm reluctant to give my dad shit to tease me about later. "We ate on the beach. The sunset was unreal."

"We saw it through the window at Squid and Oyster," Tati says, naming the restaurant Dad told me is the swankiest in Sugar Bay. And then she tells him, "I prefer to eat indoors."

He nods, accepting this factoid like he's working on a Tati dossier.

"Anyway," Piper says, eying the pair of them, "it was nice of you to walk my sister upstairs, Davis."

"My pleasure." And then he gets the hint. "I should probably take off."

"Oh," Tati says. "Probably."

It doesn't seem like she wants him to go.

179

They came here to hook up, I realize, which is hilarious. Too bad they didn't choose Dad's place. They'd probably be a hell of a lot happier right now.

I know I would be.

"You coming, buddy?"

"Hang out a while longer," Piper says to me. She locks eyes with Tati, daring her sister to protest. She doesn't, which seems to surprise Piper.

"Yeah, I'll stick around."

"Not too late, though," Dad says. Normally, he doesn't give a shit what time I come in. I've stayed down at the pool until after midnight a couple of times, and he didn't utter a word.

He's wearing his Responsible Father hat for Tati's sake.

He pushes up out of his chair and heads for the front door. Tati follows. They turn their backs to us in the foyer, which is considerate because I don't care much about how they say good night, and now I can lean into Piper and whisper, "I wonder what base they would've landed on if we hadn't been here."

She snickers, then curls into my side, restarting the show.

Piper

I SLEEP IN THE NEXT day. It's a blessed Saturday, and I don't have to work. When I stumble into the kitchen late morning, I'm surprised to find Tati in silky floral pajamas, humming as she sips coffee and pages through a magazine. Sunlight streams in through the windows.

"What are you doing?"

She glances up. "Reading."

Most mornings, even weekends, she goes down to the gym, where she spends forty-five minutes on the stair climber, listening to a self-help book or a metaphor-laced opus or, sometimes, a romance.

"What's on your agenda today?" she asks when I sit down with a glass of orange juice.

You tell me, I want to say. Saturdays and Sundays are for chores and errands and personal improvement. Tati makes lists of tasks for herself and for me, and we don't quit until it's all knocked out.

And she wonders why I sneak out to tie one on.

Though not this summer. These days, escape looks different.

"I don't know," I say experimentally.

She nods, as if a free Saturday is and always has been acceptable.

"What's on *your* agenda?"

"I was thinking about going for a manicure."

I nearly choke on my juice. After rent, car insurance, investments, and groceries, there's not a lot of extra money left for fun things. I know because Tati tells me all the time, like when I ask for jeans from Abercrombie or suggest that it might be time I had a car of my own. Plus, my sister doesn't like professional manicures. She's never found a nail tech capable of doing the job as well as she does it herself.

She actually says stuff like that out loud.

She has bestowed upon me her best mani tips and tricks, though, so I can't shame her too harshly.

"That sounds nice," I tell her.

She smiles. "Do you want to come? My treat."

I inspect my nails. The teal polish I used the night I fell into the pool is long gone, and my cuticles could use some love. But do I want to spend upward of an hour with my sister in a nail salon?

"Okay," I say, because if she's trying, I should too. "Thanks."

She closes the magazine. "So, tell me about last night."

182

Never—not once since my first movie with Daniel Chen in eighth grade—has Tati inquired about one of my dates. Before Mom and Dad passed, she'd dish juicy tidbits about her nights on the town and ask me about the boys I crushed on at school, but since she morphed from sister to guardian, she hasn't asked about anything but my grades and my bank account and whatever irresponsible thing I've done most recently.

"It was just dinner," I say with a shrug.

"Henry seems like a responsible kid."

"I mean, yeah."

"He's not your usual type."

I fold my arms over my chest, defensive, though I've had the same thought. "You think he's too good for me?"

She blinks. "That's not what I said. It's just that with the exception of Gabi"—she pauses pointedly, apparently still salty about our friendship breakup—"he's not the sort of person you usually surround yourself with."

As if she even knows what sort of people I surround myself with. Other than Gabi, I don't invite people over. I've been friends with Hudson and Jayden and, tangentially, Anna and Michaela, since middle school, yet Tati's only met them briefly. I sure as shit haven't brought any of the vacationers I've casually connected with over to hang with my sister, especially not after one of those boys was the catalyst for the missed-recital fight Gabi and I had over spring break.

Tati assumes I spend time with riffraff because of a few *tiny* mishaps. Like, okay, January of junior year, Gabi and I helped

Hudson, Jayden, and Damon nick our rival high school's district wrestling championship cup—a harmless prank. It was as simple as the five of us ditching third period and driving to Sun Crest High School during their widely publicized pep rally. Gabi and I crept into the lobby, which was empty but echoing with chants coming from the gym. I picked the trophy case lock with a bent bobby pin, and Gabi grabbed the cup. Too easy. We raced back to the getaway car, where the boys were waiting, whooping about our triumph.

Our celebration was short-lived. An attendance clerk in the front office had spotted Gabi and me in the foyer, looked out at the bus lane, and jotted down Jayden's license plate number. Turns out it's not cool to trespass on the property of a school you don't attend. Not cool to swipe that school's stuff, either. By the time I got home that afternoon, high on the all-in-good-fun theft, Tati had been notified by my school's furious administration.

I received a two-day suspension and a somberly delivered *If you ever participate in anything like this again* threat.

My sister was enraged.

"I surround myself with decent people," I say now, sounding petulant even to myself.

Tati tucks a blond wisp of hair into her ponytail. "I'm not trying to pick a fight, Piper. I'm trying to tell you that I think Henry's good for you. I approve."

I don't need your approval! begs to be said.

It's true—I don't. But that's not what's bugging me. It's Henry. Rather, the points Tati just made about Henry. He *is* different

184

from other boys I've spent time with. Hudson and Jayden are tons of fun, and they've got big hearts, but they're troublemakers, and they're not exactly scholars. Henry, on the other hand, is going to graduate high school, rock higher education, and then serve our country. He has no tattoos, piercings, or scars earned by way of stupid stunts. He doesn't have a rap sheet of misdemeanors like vandalism or possession. And while that means he's a fantastic influence, blah, blah, blah, I'm worried about how being with *me* will impact *him*. College is hopefully in my future, and I've managed to dodge actual arrest, but I've made mistakes. Tati and Gabi will attest to that.

Am I going to mess up Henry's plans? Corrupt him? Turn him feral?

No. Not today. Today I'm going to do better. I'm going to be considerate. Peaceful. Kind. Today I'm going to be the sister Tati wishes for.

"Well," I say, keeping my tone pleasant, "thank you for your approval."

"Are you mad?"

"No."

"Piper."

"Tati," I return, dragging out the syllables.

She sighs. "I really don't want to argue."

"I don't either."

She looks skeptical, but she doesn't hassle me. "Go shower. We'll have a good time at the salon. No more talk about boys."

I do as she asks.

The whole point of setting up her and Davis was to help chill her out. Help her cheer up. Help us reclaim some semblance of a sister relationship rather than the custodian-captive dynamic we've been operating under for so many years.

It's working.

Who am I to scoff at success?

Henry

JUST ABOUT EVERY MORNING SINCE I've come to Sugar Bay, I've gone running. Pretty sure my dad would prefer that I skip my workouts, just roll out of bed, and get ready for whatever activity he's got planned. But my split times and my mental health require that I put in the miles.

When I get back to the apartment, winded and high on endorphins, I almost always find my dad in the kitchen, swilling coffee and demolishing cherry Pop-Tarts, leaving me to figure out a breakfast of my own. Today, though, he's gone out for donuts. When I come out of the bathroom, shaking out my shower-damp hair, he's on the couch watching *Legends of the Fall*, pastry box on the coffee table.

"Hey, buddy." He gestures toward the donuts. "Apple fritter or Boston cream?"

I snag a bottle of water from the fridge, then grab an apple fritter, zoning out in front of the movie until it ends. I watched it with Dad for the first time several years ago, back when he lived in Spokane. It's one of my favorites.

"So, what's going on today?" I ask when he shuts off the TV.

"Whatever you're up for."

I give him a *don't bullshit me* look.

He laughs. "Really. I'm gonna head to the restaurant in a few hours, but until then, we can do whatever you want. Or you can do your own thing." He leans in to jab me with his elbow, all *wink-wink nudge-nudge*. "Maybe you're hoping to see Piper?"

"Maybe," I say, like I'm not counting the minutes until we can hang out. "You and her sister hit it off, huh?"

Dad gives me a slick grin. "I'd say so." And then a shadow of concern falls over his face. "Does it bother you? The idea of me seeing a woman?"

"Why would it?"

"I don't know. 'Cause of your mom?"

"Dad, I'm not delusional. I've got no happily-ever-after fantasies about you and Mom."

He lets out a breath. "I didn't think so. Wanted to be sure, though."

Sometimes I forget that he's a real live adult. In moments like these, he feels like a *dad*. I don't hate it. "If you like Tati, see where it goes. I don't care."

He jostles my shoulder. "Don't know how I got so lucky with you, Henry."

"Yeah, well, I didn't make out so bad myself."

188

He grabs the remaining apple fritter and takes a bite. After chewing and swallowing noisily, he says, "Piper's not gonna mess you up like the last girl you went out with, is she?"

He took Whit and me out for dinner a couple of nights after Christmas, the last time he visited Spokane. We went to a nice steak house downtown by the river. He had a lot to drink, and we ended up bailing before dessert. I had to drive his rental back to Mom's, where he promptly passed out on her couch. She was pissed, but she let him sleep it off, grumbling while she filled a glass of water to leave out for him. Whitney seemed a little embarrassed, like it was her fault the conversation hadn't been sparkling enough to keep him from overdoing it.

I took her home, embarrassed myself.

"The last girl didn't mess me up," I tell Dad, though sometimes I wish I could heap blame on Whitney. Would it be a relief to aim all my anger and sadness at her instead of myself? For sure, but that'd be unfair. Whit wasn't any stupider or more negligent than I was.

"She sure as hell didn't do you any favors," Dad says.

I groan, dragging a hand down my face. "I don't want to talk about Whitney, okay? But no, Piper's not gonna mess me up."

"Your Mom told me—"

"Dad, seriously. Whitney and me...we're off-limits."

He nods. "I respect that. I've gotta tell you, though: I like Piper better."

I crack a smile. "On what grounds?"

"She seems fun, is all. I get the impression she's working on

189

giving her sister a few gray hairs, and that's how I was when I was your age. She's gonna be good for you."

His swift approval makes the donut I just demolished roil in my stomach. Do I belong with someone Davis endorses? Someone he *relates* to?

"You want to go down to the pool for a while?" he asks. "Bring one of those books of yours. We can hang out. Work on your tan."

"Yeah," I say, because that actually sounds like a good way to kill a few hours, not to mention quiet the whispers of doubt that are suddenly running laps through my head.

Piper

HENRY AND I GO TO a movie Saturday night, a date that includes popcorn and a long kiss good night. He compliments my manicure even before I point it out and asks what kind of candy I want without assuming I'll choose Twizzlers because they're fat-free.

I pick chocolate-covered almonds, and they're delectable.

I like this: the normalcy of an evening out with a boy. I like being treated as an equal, not a goalpost. I like coming home to a peaceful apartment where my sister isn't grilling me, or shouting at me, or calling me slothful.

The following morning, the Fourth of July, Davis suckers Henry into horseback riding and Tati drives to Pensacola to have brunch with a couple of high school friends, so I stay in, celebrating the empty apartment and the rare opportunity to do whatever what I want.

Which is nothing.

After lunch, I meet Henry down on the sand in my favorite suit, a royal-blue T-back bikini with cheeky bottoms that my sister absolutely hates. We read on loungers (me: *Delphina and the Siren's Secret*, the second and angstiest book of the trilogy; Henry: *Freedom Found*, the autobiography of a famous skier named Warren Miller). I ask him why he doesn't invest in an e-reader; he tells me he has one but that he shipped a box of nonfiction to his dad's before leaving Spokane because the feel of a physical book in his hands is far superior to an electricity-dependent device, a rationalization I can't argue with. We rub sunscreen into each other's shoulders and share cans of seltzer. When the sun gets too hot, we run down to splash in the surf, then buy a pair of snow cones from a beachside vendor.

That night, we skip the annual Independence Day poolside potluck hosted by the Towers' board of directors (a group of power-hungry senior citizens Tati is constantly butting heads with) in favor of finding a quiet spot on the beach to watch the fireworks that explode in colorful starbursts over the ocean.

It's the most perfect day.

When Monday morning rolls around, I'm refreshed and ready for my shift at the Marine Conservation Park. It passes without incident until my lunch break. I've just left Turtle's office, where he spent a few minutes checking in with me, asking if I'm ready for more responsibility—yes, definitely—when I spot Damon in his grimy baseball hat.

My pulse cranks into overdrive.

192

How *dare* he show up at this most sacred place, my home away from home?

He's with his brother, Cole, who's in middle school, and they're standing in line at the snack hut, where I was headed. They're roughhousing: Cole rises up on his toes to flick Damon's ear, and Damon hauls off and sucker punches Cole's arm.

God. As much as Tati and I fight, it's never as savage as this.

Heart hammering, I duck into the souvenir shop before Damon spots me. I hang out for a few minutes, letting Candice—a University of West Florida student who's spending her summer working the register—chatter about the facial she's going to get later. Unknowingly, she talks me off a very high ledge. I could hug her. Instead, I wave and step back outside, scanning my surroundings for that gross hat.

It's nowhere to be seen.

I fill my lungs to capacity, then exhale slowly.

I still have twenty minutes of my break left to burn, so I take my place in line at the snack hut, then order a sweet tea and a hot dog. I've pocketed my change and am drizzling mustard over my lunch when a low voice says my name.

I whirl around, my hot dog falling from my hand and somer-saulting to the pavement. Mustard splatters across my Vans.

Damon is standing in front of me.

"Whoops," he says.

I stoop down, dizzy, *sick*, and pick up the mess. I toss it into a nearby trash bin, then retrieve my sweet tea from the counter, careful not to spill because we don't do lids or straws

193

at the park. Feigning indifference, I meet Damon's gaze and say, "Excuse me."

He doesn't move.

His brother sits on a bench across the path, apparently bored. There's a snack hut bag and a pair of drinks beside him. Damon must've caught sight of me when I got in line and told Cole to stay with their food.

I try to step around him. He shuffles to the right, blocking my escape without drawing the attention of the dozens of people milling around.

There's a nasty gleam in his eye.

His father relocated the boys to Sugar Bay from Crestview, a small town near the Alabama border. I've never met the man, but I've heard he's scary. According to Gabi, Damon's parents' marriage was tumultuous. A year before the move, there was a physical altercation that left his mom hospitalized but unwilling to press charges against his dad. Instead, she cut ties and moved to Charlotte. I'd never judge a woman for seeking safety, but it's hard to make sense of a mother who flees a dangerous situation and leaves her children behind.

I used to feel bad for Damon.

I don't anymore.

"Where are you running off to?" he asks.

"I need to get to my post." I gesture to my T-shirt. "I'm at work."

"You can spare a minute. Haven't seen you in a while."

"I wonder why," I say caustically.

He drops the pleasant veneer, sliding a step closer. The hairs on my arms prickle as I try to convince myself that he won't touch me in front of witnesses.

"Talk to Gabi lately?" he asks.

"You know I haven't."

"She said she ran into you at Publix. She said you told her I was a liar."

Did he track me down to confront me about this? I wouldn't put it past him.

I clutch my sweet tea with both hands to keep from slapping the shit out of him.

His eyes roam across my face, from the beads of sweat collecting on my forehead to my bottom lip, snagged between my teeth. His smile spreads. "I didn't lie, Piper. I didn't have to. Gabi saw what she saw. She drew the most logical conclusion. All I had to do was agree with her."

"You're such an asshole." I hurl the accusation hard; it rings in my ears. The guests in listening range turn to stare. So do Travis and Adam, the guys working in the snack hut. Adam looks peeved by my unprofessionalism—as if *I'm* the problem—but Travis seems concerned.

I want to sink into the sidewalk.

I give Travis a nod to let him know I'm fine, though I'm very much *not* fine. Damon tips his chin at the guys like, *It's cool; we're pals,* then reaches out. I don't know if he aims to pat my arm or squeeze my shoulder or ram his fist into my biceps like he did to his brother, but I can't stomach the thought of him touching me, even for decorum's sake.

195

I spring back.

I let my cup fly.

Its contents splashes all over him in a shower of crushed ice and sticky sweet tea.

"Fuck!" he shouts, throwing his arms wide, glaring at his soaked shirt, then me.

The bystanders gawk, tittering with curiosity. Over on his bench, Cole snickers.

"Whoops," I say flatly.

Damon's foaming at the mouth, eyes clouded with fury. "You're a bitch. A *bitch*."

"So I've been told. There are shirts for sale in the gift shop, should you want to pick up something dry. And please, have a sunny day."

"God damn it, Piper—"

I spin around, escaping amid the sounds of low whistles and surprised cackles, the disordered racket of the strangers around us rehashing what they saw.

If you only knew, I think.

My chest hurts and my throat's swollen because I'm about to burst into tears. I duck into a nearby restroom, lock myself in a stall, and perch on the toilet, propping my elbows on my knees, letting my head fall into my hands. I try to get my breathing under control, to keep my tears beneath the surface, but the sight of my shoes, stained with yellow mustard, does me in.

I give myself two minutes to cry.

Two minutes to sink into self-pity.

Two minutes to exorcize it from my system.

Then I get up, leave the stall, and splash cool water on my face.

I look my reflection hard in the eye: *Get your shit together.*

I leave the restroom, then continue on to the sea lions' pool. It's their lunchtime, and even though I'm hungry, I've got to help prep their blend of squid, capelin, mackerel, pompano, and herring.

All the while, I think about a Thoreau quote I read in English class last year: *It's not what you look at that matters. It's what you see.*

Those people at the snack hut—the guests, Adam, Travis, and even Cole—saw Damon standing close to me, talking vehemently, making me unbearably uncomfortable. Or maybe they saw me fumbling my hot dog, responding with snark, assaulting a guest with sweet tea.

Perception is a fickle bitch.

I know what happened in Gabi's bedroom.

Damon does too, though he'll maintain his innocence to the grave.

Gabi observed a moment, and then—like Damon said—drew a conclusion. Because didn't I choose the attention of a boy over her a few months back? Haven't I spent the last few years drinking abundantly and hooking up casually?

She made a two-second observation, generated context, and decided I was guilty, just as everyone who witnessed today's confrontation will likely do.

It's what you see.

When it comes to Damon, I wish there was a way to change what Gabi sees.

Henry

I FIND PIPER AT THE pool on Monday night after a series of my texts go unanswered.

Her shoes are on the pool deck, splattered with bright yellow. She's sitting on a lounge chair, knees pulled up, arms wrapped around them. She's got a Delphina book on the chair beside her, its cover featuring a mermaid leaping out of the sea, purple tail arched against the moonlit sky.

She barely acknowledges me.

I take the chair next her, wishing I'd brought a book of my own. I can't figure her out—why she's so quiet, why she ignored my texts, why she didn't check to see if I wanted to come down to the pool with her.

"Am I bugging you?" I ask after a long silence. "Being here?"

She turns to look at me. "Not at all."

"What happened to your shoes?"

She glares at them. "I spilled mustard."

"Huh."

"Yeah. It's been a day."

"You want to tell me about it?"

She drops her head back against the chair, closing her eyes, freezing me out.

I stew in the silence, racking my brain for something I might've said or done to make her mad. Sometimes I don't realize when I've been insensitive, absent, or just a dumbass. It used to irritate Whitney when I'd go dark because I was thinking about an upcoming test or an approaching meet. Only after she'd call me out would it dawn on me that I needed to emerge from my mental burrow and communicate.

"Did I do something wrong?" I finally ask.

Piper's eyes pop open. She turns to face me, resting her bare feet on the ground, and sets her hand on my arm. "Henry, no. God. You must think I'm such a—"

I don't let her finish. "I think you've had a day. Like you said."

She grimaces. "Work sucked."

"Generally? Or did something happen?"

"Something happened," she admits with obvious reluctance. "Remember that first night at your dad's restaurant?"

"The coconut shrimp night."

She gives me a ghost of a smile. "The tartar sauce night. Those guys who were a few tables over from us? I ran into one of them at the park today."

"The biggest dick, or one of the lesser dicks?"

"The biggest dick. The other two—the lesser dicks—are okay. We're friends. Or we used to be. Damon isn't a friend. To make a long story very short, he sucks."

Anger sparks behind my ribs. I saw how he treated her that night, in front of his buddies and in a restaurant full of people. I didn't like it. I can only imagine how he acts when there isn't an audience to mitigate his asshattery.

"I wouldn't mind hearing the long story," I tell Piper.

She shakes her head, which doesn't surprise me. She has her secrets, just I have mine.

"He tried to dredge up a bunch of shit today, is all. Who does that?"

My teeth ache, I'm clenching my jaw with such force. I ease up enough to mutter, "Someone who wants to make you feel small."

She runs her hand over my arm, scrutinizing my expression. I concentrate on her touch because the wildfire blazing through me feels dangerous.

Who does he think he is, showing up at her job?

Who does he think he is, trying to dim her light?

She says, "You look mad."

"I am mad."

"Henry."

She says my name soothingly, without her usual bravado. She's soft-eyed and vulnerable in a way I've never seen. She doesn't need my fire. I pull in a breath and take her hand. I trace the peaks and valleys of her knuckles with my forefinger, awed by her soft skin. Her nails are sparkly silver.

"He's a dirtbag, Piper. Screw him for treating you like shit."

She gives me a conniving smile. "I dumped sweet tea on him."

"Good. Fuck that guy."

I tug on her hand until she leaves her chair for mine. She squishes in beside me, and I wrap my arms around her. My anger's dissolving now that she's tucked beneath my chin, her breathing paced with mine, and I can't deny the way my heart triples in size when I think about how I'm the guy she's chosen to trust.

Being with you makes me feel safe, she said the night we played putt-putt.

Being with her makes me feel lucky, like I've stumbled across a cool spring after a grueling desert run.

I kiss the crown of her head, and she buries her face in my T-shirt, hugging me hard.

We stay that way, quiet, late into the night.

Piper

TUESDAY MORNING, I WAKE UP very early. Still in my pajamas, I drag my laptop, barely touched since school let out for the summer, to my bed. Leaning against a nest of pillows, I fire it up and navigate to Google.

I think you should give marine biology a real shot, Henry told me that first night we hung out at his place. *At the very least, explore your options.*

I've thought about his words a lot the last couple of weeks. While I'm hanging out with him, while I'm lying on the beach under the hot summer sun, while I'm vegging out with Tati in the apartment. But mostly I think about it when I'm at the park. Henry was right: I'm living *my* life, not my sister's. No matter how indebted I am to her, no matter how obligated I feel to follow the life plan she's sketched out for me, I do have choices.

Why shouldn't marine biology be a path I consider seriously? It's what I'm most passionate about.

My mom and dad made it happen.

Why can't I?

Hawaii still calls to me, but I want to know what else is out there. I settle in to read up on the nation's top programs, located up and down both coastlines. I like what I learn about Duke, though their acceptance rate is dismal. UC Berkeley looks good too, but I'm not sold on the Bay Area's notoriously dreary weather. The College of Charleston would be ideal if it wasn't so close to Florida.

It's Stony Brook University on Long Island that really gets me excited—even more so than HPU. They offer a bachelor's degree in marine sciences and a master's in marine conservation and policy, areas of study similar to my parents'. Stony Brook's program offers tons of opportunities for research and internships, as well as lab and fieldwork. The cost of attending, after aid, is relatively reasonable. Plus, SBU is only a couple of hours by train to New York City, which I loved when Tati and I visited. And it's just a few more hours from Albany, where Grandpa and Grandma live. Though we don't have the closest relationship, I talk to them on the phone from time to time. Maybe I could get them to speak to Tati, to convince her that New York is a safe option—a *good* option. Maybe knowing that I'd be close to family would nudge my sister into letting me move north.

SBU happens to be close to West Point too.

But the program is competitive, more so than most programs

here in Florida. I'm going to have to keep my grades up through senior year, rock the SATs, and impress Turtle enough to earn an enthusiastic letter of recommendation to have any shot at being accepted, being considered for scholarships, and convincing Tati that I'm capable of living on my own so far away.

I close my computer, feeling hopeful.

My dream isn't so far out of reach after all.

I can do it.

Of course I can do it.

———

Just before my lunch break, Turtle calls me to his office.

"I heard there was trouble between you and a guest yesterday," he says after I've taken the seat across from him. His desk is cluttered with mail and travel coffee mugs and paperweights shaped like marine animals.

"Who told you that?"

"The boy you drenched with sweet tea reported the incident. Adam, who was working the snack hut, confirmed his story."

Adam, that little snitch. He probably made it sound like I poured my drink on Damon because of some bratty need for attention, not because I was scared out of my wits.

"Did you talk to Travis?" I ask.

"I did. He said it looked like the boy"—Turtle consults his notes—"Mitchel Damon, provoked you. But he didn't think the spilled tea was an accident."

205

I fold my hands, trying to figure out how to salvage this situation. The thought of Turtle disciplining me, of losing the chance at a letter of recommendation I only just realized I need, of losing my job…I can't stand it. Plus, telling Tati that I've been reprimanded, or worse, *fired*? She'd shit her pants.

But pretending to regret standing up to Damon doesn't sit well with me either.

"I'm sorry there was a disturbance, Turtle. I'm sorry I was a part of it. But I'm not sorry for defending myself. Mitchel Damon is a menace."

Turtle sighs, tenting his hands under his chin. "I like you, Piper. You know I do. I'm rooting for you to do well here. But I can't have a repeat of what happened yesterday."

"I understand. And that's why I think you should ban Damon from the park."

He chuckles. "I'm not sure I have cause to do that."

He might if I gave him the whole story.

I think about Henry's reaction to my retelling of yesterday's incident, his tight jaw and clenched fists and ruddy cheeks. I was able to ease his frustration, but what took its place might've been worse: pity.

I don't want people like Henry and Turtle—people I respect—to think I'm weak. I want to take care of myself. I want to prove that I'm responsible, strong, and capable.

"It won't happen again," I promise my boss.

"I'm glad. The park's reputation is important. The *park* is important—you know better than most. You're a hard worker.

I admire that. But I can't have irresponsible behavior soiling our good name, no matter the circumstances. Do you understand?"

I nod, then slink out of his office.

Weeks after our clash in Gabi's room, Damon's still screwing things up for me.

Henry

TIME FLIES BY.

Dad continues to see Tati almost every night. He lets me off the hook during the day more often than not, either because his dates make him too tired to plan outings or because he's got new priorities. Whatever the case, I'm here for it.

As often as Dad's been out with Tati, I've seen Piper more. Every night, it's a movie or the pool or putt-putt. On the mornings she doesn't have work, we go to Clementine's, then spend the hottest part of the afternoon on the sand, reading or napping under an umbrella, or in the surf.

In all the times we've been swimming together, she hasn't worn the same suit twice.

Yesterday, we cruised down to the pier and played carnival games, watched fishermen reel in grouper and red snapper, and ate our weight in cotton candy. When we passed a couple of guys jamming on guitars, their instrument cases full of glinting quarters and wrinkled bills, we paused to listen. They blew through a song by Tom Petty and one by the Plain White T's before launching into something slower, a song I recognized in the first few bars.

"This was my parents' song," I told Piper after one of the performers sang the first verse. "For the few months they were together, anyway."

She looked up at me, eyes bright, cheeks rosy. "I don't think I know it."

"It's old. Bob Dylan. 'Make You Feel My Love.'"

"We should dance."

"Nah, not to this one. It's cursed."

She laughed, lifting my hand, twirling beneath my arm. I could smell her rose-scented shampoo and the pink sugar on her breath. "I don't believe in curses. Come on, Henry. Dance with me."

It was the middle of the afternoon, and the pier was crowded. "I can't dance."

"Everyone can dance. Some of us just do it better than others."

No, but really—I can't dance. Dancing in public? In broad daylight?

No thanks.

She circled her arms around my neck and nestled her head against my chest. Her feet shifted back and forth, her hips and shoulders swaying to the music. The steady rhythm of her heart thrummed through me.

Like I had any choice but to shut down my nerves, kick my

self-consciousness to the curb, and follow her lead. Closing my eyes, I held her close.

Her sister calls her careless, but that's all wrong. She's care*free*, full of spirit and life.

When the song faded into its final note, the trance I'd fallen into broke. I opened my eyes to find that we'd attracted a crowd of fellow boardwalk dancers, a whole host of couples in Hawaiian shirts and halter tops and flip-flops holding one another beneath the midday sun.

Piper grinned up at me, and my heart, which had only just started sputtering back to life that night she fell into the pool, swelled with joy.

I found her again, at exactly the right time.

———

A few days later, Piper promises to leave a ticket for me at the Marine Conservation Park's will-call window, telling me to come around lunchtime so she'll be free to show me around. She meets me near the entrance in cutoffs, her blue work T-shirt, and a pair of gray Adidas. Her stained Vans must've been retired or trashed. Her hair's in a knot that sits atop her head, her legs are sun-browned, and her face is flushed. She's cute as hell, and I smile as I lean in to kiss her cheek.

"Do I stink like fish?" she asks, scrunching her nose.

"Nope." She does a little, but I don't give a shit because seeing her in her element cancels out her mermaid perfume.

"I've got thirty minutes. You want to see the dolphins?"

We swing by a snack hut to pick up sandwiches and sodas, then head to the arena where a trio of dolphins live. They're swimming lazy circles in the pool, which is smaller than I expected. We sit, and Piper tells me she eats lunch here most days, then explains about the series of pools behind the arena, which give Luke, Leia, and Han a lot more room.

"They're rescues," she says, picking a slice of tomato from her sandwich. "So while it probably seems like they'd be happier in the open ocean, they wouldn't make it."

"How'd they end up here?"

"Han was rescued when he was a baby. His mother stranded on a mudflat because she was sick. He followed her, and they both ended up with serious sunburns. She didn't recover, but he did. Because he was so young, though, he hadn't learned the skills he needed to survive in the wild. Leia's story is pretty much the same, and when she came to the park, she and Han bonded. Now they're a happy couple."

"What about Luke?"

"He's an old man compared to Han and Leia. He's partially deaf and mostly blind, so he can't hunt. But he's the smartest of the trio. At least I think so."

She's watching the dolphins, pensive and peaceful. It's obvious why. What I've seen of the Marine Conservation Park so far is awesome. Palms sway in the breeze, the air smells like sea salt and eucalyptus, and out beyond the dolphins' pool, the gulf sparkles.

211

I nudge her. "You really love it here, huh?"

She turns a grin on me. "Don't you?"

"Yeah. I think I do."

"My mom and dad helped open it."

I blink, this new layer of context dovetailing with all the things I already know about her. She's got a lifelong history with this place, with marine life. A passion for it has permeated her bones, infiltrated her DNA. Makes perfect sense that she'd want to follow in her parents' footsteps. "I didn't know that," I say, watching Luke chase Leia through the clear water of their pool. "Explains a lot."

"Right? My parents used to say that after Tati and me, the Marine Conservation Park was their greatest achievement. Turtle, my boss, mentored them, then partnered with them to get the park off the ground; I've known him forever. The animals too. I grew up here, like Han and Leia. A lot of times, I feel more understood inside these gates than I do anywhere else in Sugar Bay."

"Your home away from home," I say, my chest tightening with empathy. I've felt isolated before too, but it must be so hard for Piper, shuffling through the world feeling overlooked. Underappreciated. I'm glad she has the Marine Conservation Park, these animals she adores, and this cool connection to her parents, but it's bullshit that her sister and her supposed best friend have contributed to her loneliness.

She turns her face up to the sun. "I'm glad you get to experience it," she tells me.

"Yeah," I say, threading my fingers through hers. "So am I."

Piper

I COME HOME FROM WORK in the best mood.

Henry and I hung out for my whole lunch break, and then he explored the park on his own while I finished my tasks. We stopped on our way out to take a photo in front of the fountain, which came out like one of those dreamy #CoupleGoals images on Instagram. There's a spray of mist behind us, and our faces are lit by a sun flare. Henry's got an arm looped around my shoulders, and he's gazing at me, not paying any attention to the camera. He looks utterly smitten. I'm glowing and starry-eyed, grinning.

As we walked back to the Towers, he told me about his favorite exhibits. First, the manta rays because they look like soaring birds, then the gators because they're badass, and then the sea turtles, he said with a smile, because they remind him of the night we met.

It's been a good day—a good summer—but every time I start to feel fortunate, I remember that summer will end, and Henry will return to Spokane, and I'll be on my own all over again. The inevitability of it is messing with my head. How weird that I, a girl who has never wanted a lasting romance, now thinks about forever with a boy who can't stay.

Sometimes I catch him staring at me, his expression full of wonder. Sometimes he kisses me like he's trying to memorize the sensation. Sometimes he uses words like *later* and *someday*, even though we haven't talked about what'll happen after August.

Maybe I'll get accepted to Stony Brook University. Maybe Tati will let me go. Maybe Henry and I will reunite like we did in June. Maybe he'll visit me on his breaks from West Point.

That's a whole lot of maybes.

Ours is a summer romance; I knew what I was getting into when I signed on. Though I'll be lonely when he leaves, though I'll miss his hugs, his humor, and his easy presence, though so many of Sugar Bay's landmarks and all of my favorite spots will remind me of him, I'll be okay.

I'll have to be.

In the apartment, I toss my bag on the kitchen table, then rummage through the fridge for a snack. It's midafternoon, and I'm thinking about going down to the pool for a while. Henry and I are hanging out tonight—destination undetermined, though I'm tempted to get him somewhere we can dance again; he's better than he thinks—so I'll have to shower and shave my legs and deal with my curls eventually. But I'm nearing the end of *Siren's Secret*, and nothing sounds better than stretching out under the sun with a book.

I'm pulling a bag of baby carrots and the reduced-fat ranch my sister buys from the fridge when she scares the piss out of me by bursting into the kitchen.

"Are you going to share?" she asks, like it's perfectly normal for her to be in the apartment before dinnertime.

I slap a hand over my racing heart. "Why aren't you at work?"

"I'm telecommuting."

"Is that a thing if your workplace is an elevator ride away?"

She shrugs, smooth hair brushing her shoulders. She may be telecommuting, but that didn't stop her from wielding her flat iron and painting her lips red. "I'm taking care of business. That's what matters."

Okay, pod person.

I scatter carrots onto a plate, add ranch, and wave Tati over to the table. She comes with a spring in her step, wearing the most mom-ish coordinating leisure set I've ever seen.

"Cool threads," I say.

She sits, looking down at her outfit. "You think? Davis picked this out."

I lift a brow. Choosing outfits for each other? That's personal. A question occurs to me, one I probably should've thought to ask before now. "That morning I met him in the kitchen—was that the first time you guys...you know?"

She inspects her cuticles. "No. Not the first."

"The second?"

215

She drops her hands to the table and smiles brightly. "He and I went to the mall last night. That was fun!"

"Tati. How many times had he been over before I bumped into him?"

She sighs. "Several."

"Since when?"

She grimaces. "Christmastime."

"Christmastime?!"

"It's not a big deal, Piper. They were casual, those occasions when we…spent time together. And they were sporadic."

"Christmastime," I repeat. "Wow. But you were dating Officer Lopez in May. And Mr. Baseball in February and March."

"Mr. Baseball? Kevin worked in marketing for the Wahoos."

The Blue Wahoos are the minor league baseball team out of Pensacola. Tati doesn't like baseball, but she likes men with status, and this guy—*Kevin*—is high in the organization.

I roll my eyes. "Pardon me. So you were secretly hooking up with Davis while you were with Officer Lopez and Mr. Marketing?"

"Not *while* I was with them. Between. And don't even think about giving me a hard time. Davis knew what was going on, and he was an eager partner."

I snort. "I bet he was."

She shakes her head. "I know he comes off like a goofball, but he's different than you think. He's a good man. A good father."

"And an eager partner—don't forget about that."

She laughs, and my chest warms through. It's not often that

216

she and I talk this way. Like sisters. Like *friends*. I don't hate it.

"He got me through those breakups, if you want to know the truth," she says. "Helped exterminate those relationships from my system. He was the brandy you sip between the courses of a long meal. A *Trou Normand*," she says in an overblown French accent.

My stick-in-the-mud sister's been entertaining a casual bed buddy for more than half a year. My mind is officially blown. "Is he still a *Trou Normand*?"

She smiles. "No. Now he's…something different."

"Yeah. A personal shopper," I tease, hoping to keep her engaged.

I've missed girl talk.

I've missed *her*.

She smooths a wrinkle from her top. "He swore this would look good. I'm not so sure."

"It looks great," I say with sincerity. She reminds me of *me* during the pre-outing heart-to-hearts I have—*had*—with Gabi. I always spent ages in front of the mirror, fishing for reassurance. Gabi, who looks like she stepped off a runway after spending all of fifteen minutes getting ready, dished out compliments as readily as I trawled for them. The flattery went a long way toward calming my insecurities.

How interesting, this idea that my sister doesn't always feel as perfect as she seems.

Maybe we're more alike than I thought.

She crunches a carrot with intense focus, then dips another

and gobbles it up too. She zeros in on me, more solemn now. "How's work?"

"Good. It's fun." And hopefully only the first of many marine life–focused jobs on my resume.

"You're sure?"

"Yeah. I like it. Don't worry, I've been depositing half of every paycheck."

"I'm not concerned about your savings, Piper."

I sit back in my chair, crossing my arms. "But you *are* concerned?"

"Roger called."

Roger. No one calls Turtle by his given name. Even my parents used his nickname.

"About what?"

"He said something happened with a guest last week. He said you haven't been the same since."

Quills of worry pierce my skin. "He doesn't think I'm doing a good job?"

"He complimented your work ethic, actually." She says this with a surprised smile, like she didn't believe I was capable of putting my nose to the grindstone. "He's worried, though. He said you've been subdued."

I assumed no one had noticed. It's not like I've ever been a contender for the park's Miss Congeniality title. But I've been avoiding my coworkers. I've maintained distance from Turtle too, because I was hoping that if I kept my head down and busted my butt, he might forget that he had to reprimand me.

I force a laugh. "Have you ever known me to be subdued?"

"No, Piper. That's what bothers me."

"I'm fine," I say with conviction. "Promise."

"Who was the guest?"

"Doesn't matter."

"Roger said it was a boy—someone you knew. Someone from school?'

I groan. "I really don't want to talk about it."

"You dumped soda on someone. I want to know who it was and why you did it. Otherwise, you can stay in tonight."

I straighten in my chair. "You're going to ground me? For something that wasn't my fault? That's bullshit, Tati."

"I left work early to check on you," she says, keeping her cool, unlike me.

"I thought you were telecommuting."

She leans forward, her expression pleading. "Please, Piper. Tell me what happened."

I don't want to talk about Damon. I don't want to think about him. I sure as shit don't want to spend my work shifts looking out for him, hiding every time I see a scuzzy baseball hat, methodically counting shallow breaths until they've evened out enough that I'm sure I'm not going to hyperventilate. It's been forever since Gabi's party, but I'm as messed up today as I was the night Damon put his hands on me.

I want to cry.

"It was sweet tea," I say quietly.

"What?"

"It was sweet tea, not soda."

Tati gives me a wry smile. "Sorry."

"Mitchel Damon came to the park. Gabi's—"

"I know who he is."

"He reported me to management. I promised Turtle it wouldn't happen again.

"But why did it happen at all?"

Incredibly, she doesn't sound mad. She sounds worried. Sympathetic. Almost motherly. And that makes it just a little bit easier to say, "He was...bothering me."

My sister closes her eyes, probably recalling the picture Gabi painted for her at Publix. She presses her lips into a grim line. "Bothering you about what happened at Gabi's?"

"Yes," I say, my voice small.

"So..." she says, like she's genuinely trying to understand, "he's angry with you because Gabi is?"

For the bazillionth time, I consider telling her the whole story. Every humiliating detail. But it's hard to think the words, let alone give them voice.

"Something like that," I tell her.

She sighs. "I thought this would blow over by now. I understand why Gabi was upset, but you two have so much history. She knows how you are."

I flinch, taken aback. "How *I* am?"

"Spontaneous. Thoughtless, sometimes."

"God, Tati. That's really what you think of me?"

"I just wish you'd learn to control your impulses," she says, and god, I thought we were getting somewhere. Oblivious, she goes on, "I mean, you practically assaulted someone at your job. You've got to do better."

Beneath the tabletop, I ball my hands into fists, feeling like a kettle left on a flame too long. I want out—I want out *now*. "I told you what happened. Can I please go out with Henry later?"

"Of course."

She loves Henry, Mr. Good Influence. He'd never get himself into trouble at work. He doesn't have a thoughtless bone in his body. He's always in control of his impulses.

But that's just not me.

There was a time, long ago, when Tati applauded my spontaneity. Encouraged it, even. Like when I was in second grade and I used Sharpies to draw an undersea mural on the wall of my bedroom while my parents fixed dinner in the kitchen. They were less than pleased when they discovered what I'd done, but when Tati found out, she complimented my creativity and convinced my parents to put away the touch-up paint.

That mural lived on my bedroom wall until just before Tati put the house on the market. That's when she intruded on my space and my life, brandishing a can of boring white paint and a list of sky-high expectations.

I abandon my carrots and my sister and retreat to my room, where I climb into bed and bury myself beneath the covers.

I don't feel like going to the pool anymore.

Henry

"WANT TO DO SOMETHING WILD?" Piper asks.

We've just left Going Coconuts, a diner Piper suggested, where we ended up with a spread of desserts: apple pie à la mode, bread pudding, an enormous chocolate brownie with pecans, and two spoons. Our order was Piper's idea, which I went along with because she was in a crappy mood—something to do with Tati, though she was unwilling to elaborate.

I wasn't in a great mood either. When I got home from the park, I found a few texts from Silas and Ricky, telling me they'd run into Whitney downtown.

SILAS

Thought you two were over.

RICKY

Wouldn't've known it by the way she was talking.

SILAS

She was the same when we went for coffee a few weeks back. If you guys are done, she never got the memo.

And then there was a string of texts from Whitney. Nothing urgent—nothing new, even. Requests to call, appeals to talk, wishes sent out in little blue bubbles. Let's try again. It'll work this time. Please, Henry. These are roads we've walked, roads I can't keep walking. She has her parents and her friends, people better equipped to give her emotional support than I am.

Jesus—I need emotional support too.

Instead, I ended up nailed to the wall by guilt.

"What do you mean, wild?" I ask Piper.

"You know, out of your comfort zone."

I take her hand as we navigate the sidewalk, busy with the after-dinner crowd. "But I like my comfort zone. It's…comfortable."

"You don't ever feel like being spontaneous?"

"I'm sorry, have we met?"

"Henry. Please?"

I scrutinize her expression: earnest, eager, a little madcap. We walk on.

"What do you have in mind?" I finally ask.

She turns to smile up at me. "Let's go to the park."

"What, like a playground?"

"No! Jeez, are you eight? The Marine Conservation Park."

"But it's closed."

"I know."

I tug her to a stop, confused. "I was there earlier. You worked a six-hour shift. Why go back now, in the dark?"

"Because, like you said, it's my home away from home."

"I don't know, Piper." I reach up to rub the back of my neck. Like a loser, I ask, "What if we get in trouble?"

"We won't."

"How do you know?"

"Because I've been sneaking in for years."

I balk at the nonchalant way she admits to trespassing. "We could end up in deep shit, though."

"Henry, you worry too much."

"Well, yeah. Someone's got to."

She squints, like she's seeing the real me for the first time. She frowns, unimpressed, apparently.

"Okay," she says. "Then I'll go by myself."

She starts walking—not toward the Towers, where we were headed before, but in the opposite direction. Toward the Marine Conservation Park.

My choices are simple. I can let her go alone, ensuring that the possibility of misfortune stays far from me. Or I can tag along, make sure she's safe, and live a little. Like Whitney used to say. Like my dad still says.

I keep thinking about how it felt to dance with Piper on the pier.

224

How freeing it was to let go.

What's the worst that could happen?

You could get caught, my conscience whispers. *And if you do, you're fucked.*

But Piper's been going after-hours for years—she just said so. I don't know what happened with her sister earlier, but she obviously needs to reclaim her center. While I recalibrate by going on a run, she goes to the Marine Conservation Park, where her parents' memory lingers on clean paths, in cool pools, and through the protection and preservation of ocean life.

Who am I to judge?

I watch her retreat in her frayed denim shorts and loose white tank. Her ponytail swings, and her hips sway. Her Reefs slap the pavement as she marches down the sidewalk.

Instead of trying to get to the bottom of her mood, instead of trying to help her, I'm letting her walk away, this gorgeous girl who has decided to let me into her world.

What an idiot I can be.

Piper wouldn't risk her job or her good standing with her boss. It's not as if she sneaks into the park to cause trouble. The reverence she has for the product of her parents' hard work is the same as what someone else might feel for a monument or a church.

As far as she's concerned, the Marine Conservation Park is hallowed ground.

She's halfway down the block, and I'm vacillating like a moron.

I take off after her.

Piper

I'M SURPRISED HE'S FOLLOWING ME. He's so good, so principled.

And I'm inconsiderate. Untrustworthy. A pain in the ass.

Just ask my sister.

I want confirmation of Henry's commitment. I want him to want me, even when I'm challenging. Tati would say I'm testing him. She'd tell me this is wrong, both sneaking into the park and making Henry prove himself.

Though, look. He's game.

I link my arm through his. We walk until we reach the Marine Conservation Park. The ticket queues are eerily quiet. The tall gate is closed to block the entrance. A chain is wrapped around it, secured with a padlock. Henry and I stop just short of the glow of a lamppost.

"Are we climbing?" he whispers.

"No. We'll go around the back." Taking his hand, I say, "Come on."

We travel the park's perimeter, moonlight and dim solar-powered bulbs illuminating our path. There's a privacy fence lined with spiky shrubs. Orange signs that say KEEP OUT! PRIVATE PROPERTY! are posted on all the gates along the way. I catch Henry eyeing one apprehensively. Out on the sand, though, the warning signs disappear. There are breaks in the fence to make way for king palms nearly fifty feet tall. Those gaps are patched by rickety dune fencing that's easy to breach.

I stop at my usual entry point and pull back the fence, making a space big enough for Henry to slip through. He hesitates, peering down the sand that runs adjacent to the park. "You're sure this is a good idea?"

"Well. I never said it was."

He gives me a dubious look. "Security cameras?"

"Not where we're going."

"Night patrol? Trainers? Vets who check in on the animals?"

"The patrolman—a physically unimpressive rent-a-cop—does his first walk-through at ten; now that he's done, he won't be back for hours. No vets or trainers until morning. After dark, the animals just sleep or swim." I jiggle the fencing. "You're not chickening out on me, are you?"

He expels a breath and steps through the gap and onto Sugar Bay Marine Conservation Park property. I follow close behind.

We walk along a little-used path, one that circles the park's

227

border and is well out of range of the security cameras. Eventually, we'll end up at the manta ray exhibit, but first...

I stop and point at the ground, at a square of concrete different from its neighbors.

My parents' medallion.

"Whoa," Henry says softly, stooping down for a closer look. He runs his fingers over my dad's name, STEPHEN NIXON, and then my mom's, CONSTANCE NIXON. He gazes up at me. "I didn't notice this when I was here earlier."

"Most people just walk right over it."

"Does that bother you?"

"No, actually. It's here for me and my sister and Turtle and everyone else who loved my mom and dad. We appreciate it. That's what matters."

"Now I appreciate it too," he says, his voice steeped in fondness for two people he never got to meet. He rises, resting his hands on either side of my neck. He whispers, "I'm glad you showed me. Makes me feel like I know you better. Why you are who you are. Why you love what you love."

"I've been exploring my options," I tell him. "Like we talked about. Thinking about marine-focused majors. Considering schools."

Smiling, he asks, "Which schools?"

"There are a few in California, and I like the College of Charleston in South Carolina. SUNY Stony Brook is my top choice, though." I pull in a breath and meet his eyes. "It's in New York. On Long Island. Not so far from my grandparents," I add, because I don't want him to think I'm trying to chase him.

He cradles my face, the rough pads of his fingers brushing my jaw. "Not so far from West Point." Touching his lips to my hair, he murmurs, "I wouldn't hate being close to you next year."

I smile up at him.

I wouldn't hate that either.

———

We head for the manta ray exhibit. There are a few benches near the glass-walled pool, but we sit on the ground, stretching our legs out on the pavement. The rays glide through the water, stirring up the sandy bottom when they dip low. I could fall asleep watching them.

"It's kind of mesmerizing," Henry says.

"Totally. God, I wish I could join them."

He grins, more relaxed now that we're seated and still. "I bet you watched *The Little Mermaid* a lot when you were a kid."

"I did! I used to waste birthday candles wishing I could live under the sea with Ariel."

"Not to mention Delphina."

"That's right. My first true love."

He laughs, but I'm serious. My parents introduced me to *Delphina and the Starlit Sea.* They took turns reading a few chapters aloud each night. We finished about six months before they left for their getaway in Tampa. I read the subsequent books independently, repeatedly, and then I met Gabi, a girl as Delphina obsessed as I am.

229

My parents didn't know Gabi long, but they adored her. They were buddies with Maggie and Byron too. During those months when Mom and Dad and Gabi overlapped, our parents went out for drinks, and we had a couple of joint family barbecues. My mom often got on the phone with Gabi's mom to discuss us girls and this reality TV show about rich housewives that they both loved.

After the accident, it was hard to be at home but impossible to be anywhere else. Memories of my parents floated around me like bubbles in the sea. They were everywhere, but fragile, impossible to touch. Tati might as well have been a cyborg. She never once cried in front of me. She completed tasks from morning until night, handling the wake and the burial, keeping the house, managing the money, and dealing with my grandparents, who had been weepy and cross since they'd arrived in Florida.

I realize now that my sister was too busy and too stressed to cope with her own grief, much less walk me through mine, but at the time, I felt utterly abandoned.

After the accident, Gabi slept over for weeks, hugging me while I cried into the night.

Maggie checked in often, bringing meal after meal.

Byron helped with repairs and heavy lifting.

After the accident, I slept with *Delphina of the Starlit Sea* under my pillow, imagining Mom's voice lifting indignantly as she read Delphina's parts, Dad's tenor speaking Uncle Kye's lines like he knew the merman personally.

When Tati was prepping for us to move out of the

four-bedroom split-level we grew up in and into our two-bedroom apartment at the Towers, she packed up my room while I was at school and found the paperback in my rumpled sheets. When I got home, she confronted me, making me feel foolish, like sentimentality was for little kids who didn't know better.

"Keep your books on the shelves," she snapped, then left me to cry alone in my boxed-up bedroom.

Even at ten, I knew I should try to cut her some slack. She hadn't had a good night's sleep since our parents' passing; dark hollows had appeared beneath her eyes. She had paper cuts all over her hands thanks to the hours upon hours she spent wrapping valuables in packing paper. There was a shit ton of tension between her and our grandparents. She missed Mom and Dad and her life back in Boston.

But she was *so* snippy with me.

When Gabi came over later that day, I told her about my confrontation with Tati. She labeled my sister a wicked sea witch and tucked *Delphina* into the box with my folded linens.

"Why do you think mermaids are so often romanticized?" Henry asks now.

"Good question. Aside from the mermaids in the *Harry Potter* books, who are terrifying, they're usually portrayed as attractive. Irresistible. Once Delphina finds her way into the sea, mermen fall over their tails trying to get her attention. She only has eyes for Hurley, though."

Henry shakes his head, amused. "Hurley?"

"He's the love interest," I say, like *obviously.* It blows my mind

231

that there are people of my generation who aren't entrenched in the Delphinaverse. It's as weird as people Tati's age who've never read *Twilight*.

"He and Delphina are fated to be together," I explain, sighing at the ardor of it all. "It's beautiful and super intense. By the end of the final book, they can't keep their hands off each other."

His eyebrows furrow. "But that sort of attraction's pretty unbelievable. Living underwater, their skin would be all shriveled, and the salt would do a number on their hair. Also, how do merfolk procreate? Are they mammals who have live babies, or do they lay eggs like fish? And do mermaids nurse their merbabies, or do they leave them to fend for themselves like newly hatched sea turtles?"

I stare at him, wonderstruck by the way his mind works. But I'm also growing accustomed to his contemplation, to the charming way he puzzles over bizarre things.

"What?" he asks. "Am I being gross?"

"You're being adorable."

He makes a face. "Liar."

"Seriously. If I wasn't wild about you before, you'd have sealed the deal with these latest musings."

He grins. "Look, if I'm going to ditch my comfort zone to break and enter, you're gonna have to leave yours behind so we can discuss merpeople getting it on."

I laugh as he tucks me under his arm, pulling me close.

"Thanks for coming with me," I whisper, watching the rays.

"Thanks for inviting me. You know—"

A beam of light cuts through our corner of the park.

Henry goes absolutely still.

"Who's there?" a voice shouts.

My heart catapults into my throat.

"Who the fuck is that?" Henry whispers.

It's got to be the night patrolman.

He's late.

Or early.

Shit.

"Security guard?" Henry demands in an undertone.

In all the years I've been sneaking into the park, I've never encountered a soul. But tonight...tonight of *all* nights.

"Maybe?" I say, my voice trembling. "Probably."

"Jesus, Piper!"

I was casual and cool when I suggested coming to the park tonight. Not once did I seriously consider the possibility of being found out.

Of getting in trouble.

Of getting *Henry* in trouble.

The flashlight beam bounces through the manta rays' enclosure, skimming the top of their pool, the tops of our heads, illuminating Henry's panicked face.

The park is nearly a hundred acres, but the patrolman seems to have zeroed in on us.

"Come out!" he bellows. "You're trespassing on private property!"

All I can think of as I sit frozen on the pavement, dangerously close to cardiac arrest, is Henry. He follows rules, focuses on the future. He has goals. He has dreams.

West Point.

He could lose it because of me.

I scramble into a crouch, keeping my chin tucked, my head down.

He gives me a questioning look, mouth tight.

I grab his hand and whisper, "Follow me."

Henry

SHE DRAGS ME OUT OF manta ray territory and onto the footpath, hugging the row of hedges that lines it. We stay low, shuffling quickly but silently, keeping to the shadows. I'm focused—on not stumbling, not making a sound, not throwing up the two thousand calories of dessert I ate an hour ago. I'm scared as shit.

Behind us, the patrolman hollers for us to come out of hiding.

Would it be better to surrender now?

Will they go easier on us if we come clean before we're caught?

My mom's going to be so disappointed.

Piper ducks behind the partitioned wall of a bathroom entrance, yanking me in with her, raising a finger to her lips. Like I need a reminder to keep my mouth shut.

Footsteps echo down the path.

Piper presses a hand over her mouth, trying to muffle her

gasping breaths. I'm not huffing and puffing the way she is, but I'm pretty sure people all the way back in Spokane can hear my heart pummeling my ribs.

I tense as the footfalls draw closer. It sounds like there's only one person, and that gives me hope. We might outmaneuver a single patrolman. But if there's another close by, or a whole team, we're fucked.

He tromps past us, his shadow visible under the partition, flashlight beam like a meteor streaking across the sky. Piper's hand trembles in mine as the light swings back again, shining over the top of our hiding place.

He calls out another order for us to show ourselves, but he's winded, losing steam. I let my shoulders drop away from my ears as he moves on.

Piper's gaze meets mine. She points to the left, a different route than we took to get to the manta rays, but one that must lead toward escape.

I nod.

We're gonna run for it.

She slips off her Reefs. I tighten the laces of my Pumas. And then we launch ourselves onto the dimly lit path, silent and swift, two missiles firing through the night.

Thank *god*, the ramshackle fence comes into view quickly, the ocean just beyond it. We leave the same way we entered, then keep running down the beach toward home. I don't realize how far we've sprinted until Piper's hand becomes heavy in mine. I look back to see her dragging ass, practically wheezing. I slow to a stop, dropping my hands to my knees to catch my breath. I run distance, not dashes. When the stitch in my side loosens, I straighten to see the Towers about half a mile down the shore, lit up like twin Christmas trees.

Piper falls flat on her back in the sand, laughing in that noiseless, hysterical way that almost always ends in hiccups.

I glare down at her. "He could catch up, you know. We could still get busted."

She calms down long enough to say, "Henry, we're in the clear."

She tries to sit up, catches another fit of giggles, and falls back again. I peer down the moonlit beach, checking to make sure we're not being followed.

There's no one around but us.

I collapse beside her, then empty my shoes of sand. I focus on the waves, inhaling and exhaling in time with their crests, trying to get a handle on myself. If Piper deals with stressful situations by laughing uncontrollably, I bulge at the seams with anger.

Seems like a century ago that we were joking about mermaid sex.

Finally, she sits up. She scoots toward me, matching my posture, touching her toes to mine. I'm so frustrated by how this night has panned out, I kind of want to put distance between us. But that seems mean-spirited.

"It's okay," Piper says, more solemn now.

"Is it? What if he saw us?"

"I don't think he did."

"He knew we were on the property, so *someone* obviously saw us. Someone called security. What if your boss figures out the trespasser was you? What're you gonna do then?"

"That won't happen."

But she doesn't sound so confident anymore.

"It could. I shouldn't have let you—" I break off. I'm not going to slap her with all the blame. It's not like she dragged me through that fence.

"You shouldn't have let me what?" she prods.

"Nothing."

I move my feet away from hers.

Her face falls.

I don't know why I'm being so shitty to her. It's *myself* I'm angry with. I could've said no. Could've refused to trespass, but instead I let a girl sway me because I like her. Because I want her to like me.

I know right from wrong, but I still fucking folded.

"I'm sorry," she says, soft and rueful. "You're right. I shouldn't have asked you to come. I just—I thought it would be fine. It *has* been fine every other time I've done it." Her gaze drops to the sand. "Henry, if we'd gotten caught… God. I've been in trouble before—I can deal. But if I'd caused problems for you, I never would've forgiven myself."

She looks wrecked.

She looks like she might cry.

"Hey." I reach over to touch her knee. Her eyes find mine, and yeah, they're bright with tears. Shit—when we left the Towers a few hours ago, I never would've guessed we'd end up having what feels too much like fight. "It wasn't all bad," I tell her. "I liked watching the rays with you. I liked seeing your parents' memorial. I want to learn more about them."

"What, *now*?"

Laughter zaps what's left of the tension from my system. "Maybe not right now," I say, leaning back on my hands, stretching out my legs. "Like, tomorrow, or the day after that."

"You want to see me again after what I just put you through?"

She sounds exceptionally anxious, like the suspense might do her in. It's a lot like how I felt behind that bathroom partition, like another second of uncertainty would liquefy my bones. I shrug, letting her sweat it out for a second. And then: "Yeah, I want to see you again. I'm kind of into you. I thought you knew."

She lets a breath disappear into the breeze. "I'm kind of into you too."

The distance between us makes me feel like a buoy bobbing alone in the gulf.

I don't like it.

"Piper," I say with longing that's hit suddenly and insistently. "Come here."

She rises to her knees and edges toward me, gaze locked on mine until—Jesus, *finally*—she's hovering over my shins, my knees, my thighs. As much as I want to put my hands on her, this weirdly masochistic part of me likes the challenge of waiting to see what she'll do without influence. She leans close, pressing her chest to mine, setting her cool palms against my hot neck.

She kisses me once, softly, barely, leaving traces of vanilla on my mouth.

I exhale, feeling like a grenade without a pin.

Her face catches the moonlight. She's pleased with herself, with the power she must've just now realized she has.

I grapple for composure, but anticipation's coursing through me, a second surge of adrenaline. I focus on her, dragging my hands over her ankles, her calves, her thighs, trapping grains of sand between her soft skin and mine, until I find the tattered hems of her cutoffs. I rub the denim between my fingers, wondering how far she wants this to go.

She's breathing erratically, watching me, waiting to see what I'll do next.

My hands blaze trails over her hips, her waist, her spine. I kiss her, a kiss that feels powerful in a way I've never experienced. I've moved from fiery devotion to absolute frustration to horniness that borders on embarrassing in the span of minutes.

It's brain-melting.

I slow down, struggling to find even the most tenuous self-control because I want to enjoy kissing her, not barrel through it. She must understand, or want the same thing, because her body relaxes. She eases back, returns to me, eases back, swoops in again, teasing with lips and tongue and hands.

We dissolve into the sand.

When our fire fizzles out, I sit up.

I'm in over my head.

No, Piper's not careless. She cares about her job, her sister,

240

and her future. She cares about whatever happened with her best friend. She cares about minor stuff like mermaid books and acai bowls.

She cares deeply, maybe to her detriment.

And now she cares about me.

I need to get a handle on what's happening between us, because August is closing in. I need to be certain I'm not going to tear a rift through her by leaving in a few weeks. But if she's feeling anything close to what I'm feeling, I'm not sure that's possible.

I fold her into a hug for my benefit as much as hers. Her scent washes over me: her rose-garden hair, her vanilla gloss, salt stirred up by the gulf air and our sprint.

I hold her close, breathing her in, changed in this colossal but indefinable way.

"Henry," she whispers, her breath tickling my neck. "What are we going to do when it's time for you to go back to Spokane?"

I bury my face in her curls.

I have no idea.

All I know is that I don't want to go anywhere.

Piper

TATI'S IN MY WAY.

She's standing at the counter with her I NEED MY SPACE! mug, separating me from my cereal. The mug is filled with coffee, and she's spent about a century drizzling almond milk into it. She slowly swirls a spoon through the liquid, adds another drop of milk—a *literal* drop—and stirs again.

Yeah, she needs her space, but she's also *lost* in space.

"Scoot." I hip check her.

She replaces the milk's cap.

"I need that," I tell her, gesturing toward my dry cereal.

"Oh, sorry." She turns and puts the carton back into the fridge as I stand there, dumbfounded, empty hand suspended in the air.

"Jeez, Tati. What's up with you?" I ask, claiming the milk.

"I'm tired." She sips her coffee. "I was up late waiting for you."

Usually, steam spews from her ears when I come in after

curfew. Last night, Henry and I stayed on the beach until way after. But when he dropped me off at our apartment and waved to my sister from the front door, she came over wrapped in Mom's afghan and made a couple of minutes of affable small talk. Not a word about the late hour.

"Sorry I missed curfew," I tell her now.

She sits at the table. She's showered, wearing her bathrobe, her hair twisted up in towel. Even without her smooth bob and flawless makeup, she looks better than I do on my best day.

"Text next time," she says. "It's not difficult."

No. I guess it's not.

"I know you think I'm a hard-ass," she goes on. "And maybe I am. But only because I worry about you."

"I get it," I say, bringing my cereal to the table.

"I don't think you do. How would I get by if something happened to you, Piper?"

This is getting real deep, real fast. "Nothing's going to happen to me."

She gives me a look that says, *You can't know that for sure.*

She's got a point. Who could've imagined that our parents would be taken so suddenly?

"I feel better," she says, "knowing you're out with Henry."

"Because he's such a hunk?" I'm joking, trying to lighten the mood, but I'm also remembering the way the muscles in his back contracted under my hands on the beach last night.

"Because as far as I know, he doesn't make bad decisions," she replies.

With the exception of yesterday, anyway. Acid rises in my throat as I recall his fear while we were hiding. He never would've snuck onto private property if I hadn't pressured him. Tati thinks he's a positive influence, and he is.

I'm a *terrible* influence.

That feels...really awful.

"He's a good egg," I say, flipping my curls like I haven't a care in the world. "Thank god for Henry Walker."

Tati, who's reanimating thanks to her coffee, grins. "Let's send up thanks for Davis Walker while we're at it."

I gag like the thought of my sister happy with a man disgusts me, but truly, I couldn't be more grateful. I appreciate her better moods and her more relaxed expectations. It's nice not having to tiptoe around the apartment, worried about some task I didn't complete or some choice that was less than responsible.

I like having my big sister back.

Henry

GULF COAST LINKS IS A bitch.

There's no way I could suck more at whacking a small ball into a small hole.

My dad tosses out pointers. "Focus on your knees when you swing—that'll give you more power. You're too tense, buddy. You're getting tied up in the mechanics. *Feel* the swing."

A couple of weeks ago, his tips would've irritated me. The sun would've broiled the life out of me. I would've been desperate to get back to the Towers and into a cool shower.

Today, not so much. I mean, I'm sweating my balls off and playing like shit, but I'm having an okay time. My dad's trying to help, yeah, but he's not smothering me with bro-hood. Being with him is like it used to be when I was a kid, before he left Spokane, when we'd hit the snow and he'd help me with short turns and carving.

I'm pretty sure the change has to do with Tati.

When I suggested setting them up, I was hoping for something casual to help him burn off energy. But he sees her every day now, and when he talks about her, his face becomes a high-watt bulb. It seems like they're getting serious.

We're finishing up the fourteenth hole, a gauntlet with a couple of sand traps and a water feature that's home to a legit alligator. Somehow I've gotten my ball onto the green without a lot of trouble. Grumbling, Dad has to chip his out of the sand. Still, he putts easily into the hole, earning a fifth stroke. I choke and spend three strokes on the green while he suggests I relax my stance and drop my hands.

We take a break after that, pulling off to the side, letting the golfers behind us pass while we cool off on a shaded bench. A refreshment cart cruises by, and Dad flags it down. He buys a couple of sodas, which are so cold the bottles immediately start sweating. I pop mine open and guzzle almost half. Dad roots through his golf bag until he unearths a flask. He opens his soda, downs about a third, then tops it off with whatever he brought along. He doesn't offer me any, to his credit, but come on. I get that recreational golf and drinking often go hand in hand, and I guess it's nice to have something to take the edge off, especially if you're out on the course with your buddies. But it's midmorning, and I'm his kid.

I almost say something, but then I hear Piper telling me to go wild, and Whitney telling me to live a little, and Mom telling me to give Dad a chance.

He doesn't need me to lecture him about day drinking.

"You're getting better," he tells me, tucking the flask back into his bag.

"If that's true, it's thanks to your coaching."

He chuckles. "Were you not paying attention back there when I was kicking up sand?"

"Oh, I was paying attention." I pull our scorecard out of my pocket and toss it on the bench between us. "According to this, though, you're the superior golfer."

"You run six-minute miles."

"You own your own business. A pretty successful business, at that."

"A *very* successful business," he says, bumping me with an elbow. "I'd say you could run it with me someday, but you've got different plans, huh?"

"West Point."

"West Point," he repeats with a nod. "Like your pop."

I wonder if it bothers him that my aspirations were inspired by my maternal grandfather. I hope not. Dad has plenty of qualities I'd like to emulate, like his confidence and his people skills. His drive. His mellow temper. But I don't want to live in a beach town, serving beers and fried cod. That's the right path for him, but mine veers in a different direction.

"You'll come visit me in New York next year, right?"

"Whenever I can get away. I want to run something else by you, though." He props an ankle on his knee, then gives me a solemn look. It's like he's nervous or something. "You don't have to give me an answer today. But it's something to think about, okay?"

Shit—this ought to be good.

"Yeah. Okay."

"What if you stayed in Sugar Bay for your senior year?"

I shift on the bench, trying to make sense of his question. "Like, live here full time?"

"Why not?"

"Because I can't just pick up and move."

"Sure you can. The high school here is real good. Their cross-country team's exceptional." He laughs, thumping a hand against my shoulder, knocking what's got to be a dumbstruck expression off my face. "I looked into it. I'll do what it takes to keep you around."

"But Mom—"

"Your mom and I talked about it. She doesn't think it'd be so bad for you to take a longer break from Spokane. She's okay with whatever you want to do."

"Wow. Really?"

Mom and I are tight. All my life, she's been present and protective. It's surprising to hear that she's not itching to have me back home.

"Yeah, really," Dad says. "She misses you—of course she does—but it upset her, what happened this past spring. She doesn't want to see you hurt all over again. Neither do I."

I pull my hat off and run a hand through my hair, looking out over the golf course. It's a big ask: moving across the country, changing schools, getting settled in a new town, all for only a year. I'd have to give up living with Mom, and I'd have to give up my role as captain of the cross-country team, a spot I busted my ass for. Hell, I'd have to start all over with a new cross-country program. On the flip side, staying in Sugar Bay would mean three thousand miles from Whitney and the space I need to finish healing.

Better than that, I'd get to spend the year with Dad.

And Piper.

If Dad had made this suggestion at the beginning of the summer, I would've laughed in his face. It would've been an immediate no.

But now...

"I don't know." I peel the label of my soda. "It's something to consider."

He looks at me from beneath the bill of his hat, hopeful. "You don't hate the idea?"

"I mean, it'd be a huge pain in the neck, but also...not so bad."

He grins.

I say, "Just...don't give me shit about it, okay? There's some stuff I've got to figure out. I've got to reach out to my guidance counselor and my Field Force rep. After I talk to them, I'll let you know what I decide. Cool?"

He downs the last swig of his spiked soda. "Yeah, buddy. Totally cool."

Piper

ON FRIDAY, THIRTY-SIX HOURS AFTER Henry and I snuck into the Marine Conservation Park, Turtle catches up with me during my lunch break. Somberly, he asks me to come to his office for a conversation.

The blood rushes out of my face like the *whoosh* of a toilet after its flusher is pressed, leaving me light-headed, unsteady on my feet.

I have to command my head to nod.

I follow Turtle into the admin building, my feet iron-heavy, and down the corridor to his office. He gestures to one of the empty chairs across from his desk, his expression as stern as I've ever seen it.

My heart *thud-thud-thuds*.

I have an idea why I'm here, but it's still a nightmarishly out-of-body experience, sitting across from my stone-faced boss, my dead parents' mentor, a man who treats me like family: with kindness, without judgment.

He hasn't spoken yet, but my throat's already clogged with sadness.

"Two nights ago, there was a break-in here at the park."

I keep my face neutral but chafe my palms against my shorts. It's killing me, but I maintain eye contact.

"Do you know anything about it?" he asks.

"No," I say, aiming for innocence, for ignorance. Bile inches up my throat, riding the lie's wake. I might be better off coming clean, begging for forgiveness, but there's the tiniest, *tiniest* chance Turtle's bluffing. Maybe he's talking to all the employees. Maybe he's collecting intelligence, attempting to discern who knows what. If I can sit out this interrogation with as few words as possible, I might be okay.

Or maybe that's the grandest of delusions.

Turtle watches me, spine curved, shoulders by his ears.

He looks *so* disappointed.

"The park is equipped with security cameras, Piper. Surely you know that."

I remember coming with my dad after they were installed. In his office, he pulled the system up on his computer and showed me how the different zones were captured in grainy black and white. The other night, as always, I was careful to keep out of the cameras' range, right up until Henry and I were nearly caught. That sprint from the bathroom to the exit—that path was in a covered area.

251

Turtle isn't collecting intelligence. He's calling me out.

"Yes," I say. "I know."

"Did you forget about them while you and your friend were running from security?"

My gaze falls to my lap as I try to manufacture an excuse. What reason, what story would make him pardon the unpardonable?

But I can't lie. Not this time.

"Turtle, I'm so sorry."

He expels a breath. "I'm glad to hear it. Unfortunately, that doesn't excuse the fact that you betrayed my trust. How could you do such a thing, Piper?"

I was having a rough night. A rough week. A rough summer. I'm a bird flying alone, searching for a place to roost. I do stupid things because sometimes—a lot of the time—my wings get so tired, and there's no place to land. Somehow, the buzz of mischief lifts me.

But none of that justifies sneaking into the park, and it wouldn't make sense to Turtle, a man rooted in his principles.

I'm not going to insult him with a tale of woe.

"We didn't mean any harm," I say, looking down at my hands. An irrelevant truth at this point. "We didn't come to cause trouble. We sat with the rays and talked. That's it."

He hums, a sound of contemplation. A sound of bewilderment. "You couldn't have had a conversation elsewhere? On the beach? At a restaurant? At home?"

I lift my gaze to his. God, he looks as gutted as I feel. "Yes, of course. But the park is special to me—you know that. I love it here. I'm happiest here. I see now, though, that I made a huge mistake. I'm sorry, Turtle. I'll *never* do it again. You have my word."

He regards me for a long moment. A bead of sweat cascades down my spine as I consider his possible responses. Finally, gently, he says, "I'm going to be very honest with you, Piper. Your word doesn't hold weight with me anymore. You're a hard worker and a lovely girl, and I was proud to give you an opportunity here. But I can't disregard this breach. What you did was foolish and dangerous. It speaks to a deficit in maturity. It pains me to say this, but you are no longer part of the Marine Conservation Park's staff."

"But Turtle—"

"I'm sorry. You're welcome during operating hours—you always will be—but as far as your employment goes, my decision is final."

Losing the source of my income, the letter of recommendation I've been hoping for, and Turtle's trust in me all at once...it's too much. Mom and Dad would be *crushed*.

"I understand," I say quietly, and I do. Regret feels like two strong hands wrapped tightly around my throat. This is nobody's fault but my own. "Will you give me a chance to tell Tati? She should hear it from me."

He nods, and I leave his office after a final apology, one that's meant sincerely but sounds hollow.

I walk the corridor with my chin up, my shoulders back, trying—poorly, I'm sure—to project false confidence. I manage to avoid crying as I enter to the locker room to gather my things,

253

then make a quick detour to my parents' memorial. I'm still battling tears as I bend to touch their names, gleaming in the sun.

They'd be so sad to know what I've done.

I don't fall apart until I'm through the park gate, on the sidewalk, dragging my feet toward home.

Henry

FRIDAY MORNING, I EMAIL MY guidance counselor and my Field Force rep to ask how a transfer would impact my post-graduation plan. Then I run six miles down the beach and six miles back, pondering the idea of staying in Sugar Bay through senior year.

Aside from the question she whispered the other night at the beach, Piper and I've sidestepped what I've been assuming was inevitable: saying goodbye at the end of this summer. It never occurred to me that I could stay. That maybe I *should* stay. I'm pretty sure Piper hasn't thought of me in Sugar Bay beyond August either. Now, I'm freaked about spooking her with the prospect of my looming presence.

When I get home, the apartment's empty; Dad mentioned last night that he wanted to get to the restaurant before the lunch rush today. I shower and down a sandwich, glad for the quiet, paging through an SAT study guide while standing at the kitchen counter. I'm rinsing my plate when I hear a gritty cough, then a throaty groan coming from down the hall.

I nearly piss myself.

I turn off the water and move slowly, silently, out of the kitchen. I pass my bathroom and my bedroom—both empty—before approaching Dad's room at the end of the hall. His door's barely ajar. I consider finding a golf club or some other makeshift weapon, but I'm six two and can crank out seventy-five push-ups in two minutes. If there's an intruder in the apartment, I'll hold my own or end up with a bullet in me.

I strain to listen...breathing, ragged and irregular.

"Hello?" I call.

Another groan.

Someone's in my dad's room.

I close the distance to his door and shove it open.

Dad's on his stomach on top of the bedding, arms at awkward angles like he plummeted from a high window and landed just that way. He's wearing what he left in last night to meet Tati. His breathing is open-mouthed and noisy, a circle of drool visible on the comforter. His hair's all over the place.

What a fucking mess.

His shoes, on the other hand, sit neatly on the floor near the foot of the bed, laces looped up and over. There's a glass of water on the nightstand. The small bathroom trash can is positioned on the floor near his head. I highly doubt he had the forethought to put it there.

"Dad!" I say sharply.

He snorts awake, rolling over with effort, dragging a hand over his pallid face. "What time is it?"

"Like, noon."

"Oh. Shit."

"Tell me you're sick."

He squints like the sunlight streaming through the blinds burns his retinas. "I'm sick."

"Bullshit."

"I think I'm supposed to be at the restaurant."

"Yeah, that's what you said last night. You don't look like you're in any shape to get yourself there, though."

He manages to sit up. He looks like a Weeble, these teetering egg-shaped toys my mom played with when she was little and saved to share with me.

He groans again. "I'll be all right. Just need a shower. And some hair of the dog."

I lean against the doorjamb. I have no idea what he means by *hair of the dog*. His eyes fall closed as he seesaws on the mattress, using his hands to brace himself on either side.

"Are you going to throw up?"

He hauls his eyes open, swallowing thickly, considering the trash can. "I think I'm good."

He gets up like a man who hasn't been on his feet in months, then hobbles into the bathroom. The door shuts, the shower powers on, and I leave him to it.

I don't understand people who forfeit control this way. It used to drive me crazy when Whitney would call late at night, drunk with her friends. She'd go on about how much she loved me, her words sluggish, too syrupy to be sincere. All I ever wanted was to get off the phone because that girl—loose-tongued and sappy—wasn't who I'd signed on for.

Dad overdoing it is even worse. He's too old to be getting so sloshed he's gonna feel like shit the next day.

In the kitchen, I text Piper:

My dad's nursing a wicked hangover. Tati too?

She responds after a few minutes.

No idea.

It has to have been Tati who brought Dad home. She must've gotten him into bed. She took off his shoes and made sure he had something to heave into. For all the crap Piper talks about her sister, she's not so bad. Drunk Davis isn't for the weak of heart. Tati stepped up.

I shoot Piper another text, telling her I'll come by tonight, then set my phone on the countertop as Dad comes lumbering in. He looks human, more or less. He opens the fridge, plucks a Corona off the shelf, and pops the top with his trusty bottle opener.

I watch, my jaw unhinged. "Hair of the dog?"

"Yeah," he says, followed by a weak laugh. "Quickest way to cure a hangover." He pulls peanut butter out of the pantry, grabs a spoon, and scoops out a huge dollop. He devours it. "Second-quickest way to cure a hangover," he says, his mouth sticking and smacking. "Greasy bacon works too."

"Gross."

"You'll thank me one day."

I shake my head—I can't believe these are the life lessons he's imparting to me.

"I'm going to Piper's later," I tell him. "You going in to work?"

He checks the time. "In a while."

"What about Tati? Are you seeing her tonight?"

He blinks, brows knitting together.

"Dad, what?"

"Last night..." He wades out of his haze. "I think I pissed her off."

"How?" I ask with trepidation.

"Hard to say, buddy. Hasn't all come back to me yet." He laughs this off, like getting so tanked that you have little recollection of the night before is hysterical.

"You might want to give her a call," I suggest, thinking of Piper's message. There's not a lot of nuance in texts, but she didn't seem amused by my *wicked hangover* observation.

"I'll do that." Dad double-dips himself another scoop of peanut butter, then parks himself on a stool. He's still got bags under his eyes, and despite his shower, I swear to god I can smell booze leaching from his pores.

"I'm gonna go out for a while," I tell him, heading out of the kitchen.

I've got nowhere to be, but if I have to look at him slurping peanut butter off a spoon like an anteater for another second, I'll lose my shit. I feel like telling him how uncool it was, walking into his room midday and seeing him bedraggled and incoherent. He'll say I have a stick up my ass and everything's fine. He'll toss back his Corona and go on about how he knows what he's doing, he's got a handle on it.

He's Davis Walker, for fuck's sake.

I could call my mom. Maybe I *should* call my mom. But she'll buy me a one-way ticket back to Spokane, scheduled to depart tonight, using her emergency credit card because this is not a purchase she's budgeted for. As far as she's concerned, Davis is a decent man and a good dad, but she won't let me stay with him if she thinks his drinking's out of control.

I'm not ready to leave Sugar Bay.

I spend the afternoon cruising the pier, edgy and overwhelmed.

Piper

BY THE TIME I GET back to the Towers, I've dried my tears and formulated a plan. I'll have to tell Tati about losing my job eventually, but that's a worry for Future Piper. For now, I'll come and go as if I'm still employed, if only to put off a blowout. During the hours I should be at work, I'll hunt for a new job. Any job. When I secure one, I'll come clean about what happened at the park.

At home, I change out of my Marine Conservation Park T-shirt for the last time and nearly fall apart all over again. I steel myself, throw on a white tank, and wash my face. Then I give myself a pep talk. *Forget about upsetting Turtle. Forget about how heartbroken Mom and Dad would be. Forget about Tati and the shitstorm she'd stir up if she knew. You've survived worse. You've got this.*

I make a pot of rice on the stove, drop in a generous pat of butter, and sprinkle on salt and pepper. Standing in the kitchen, I eat every last grain.

I'm feeling infinitesimally better when my phone buzzes with a text.

TATI
Are you home?

God—did Turtle call her after all?

TATI
I need you to come to my office.

The last thing I feel like doing is visiting my sister in her office, a windowless cavern where goodwill goes to die. She only ever asks me to come down there when she's got something dire to complain about or when I've done something above and beyond what usually aggravates her. Like when I've been fired and my boss—my *former* boss, a friend of the freaking family—notifies her before I do.

Piper. Please, she texts.

Okay, this feels different. Not like Tati knows I did something wrong, but like something's wrong with Tati.

I slip on the Adidas I ditched at the door when I came in and head for the elevator.

Tati's assistant, Brigitte, is a middle-aged woman who tried to mother me when she started at the Towers a few years ago. She

262

knocked it off only when I growled that *no*, I didn't need help with my math homework, and *yes*, I was eating enough vegetables. Brigitte is usually eager to chitchat, but today—thank god—she waves me toward my sister's office without any inane questions.

Tati's behind her desk, signing off on a document. "Close the door," she mumbles.

I do, catching Brigitte's curious look just before it clicks shut.

I take a seat in one of the two armchairs meant for new applicants or tenants who've come to bitch. This feels a little too similar to being in Turtle's office an hour ago, and I have to breathe through a swell of anxiety before I say, very casually, "What's up?"

She lifts her chin. Her eyes are bloodshot, with dark shadows beneath them. She's not wearing lipstick—unheard of outside the walls of our apartment—and her hair looks lusterless, like she resorted to dry shampoo instead of her usual morning wash.

I pull in a breath. Something's definitely wrong.

The day our parents were killed, Tati and I were together. She'd come from Boston to stay with me while Mom and Dad were in Tampa, and she made what she called a *staycation* of our time together. We ate acai bowls daily, saw late-night movies, and spent long afternoons on the beach. She showed me how to put a heart-shaped sticker on my stomach so that later, when I left the sun's warmth, I'd have a sort of inverse tattoo.

When the call came, we were back at the house, getting ready to pick up Gabi and go to dinner. My sister pressed her phone to her ear, listening raptly as the caller spoke, and then she

263

collapsed onto the couch as if her muscles had turned to goo. She didn't ask questions, and she didn't cry. Her eyes became terrifyingly vacant.

They're the same now: unseeing, unfeeling.

"Tati, god. What happened?"

"Davis...I think we're over."

My stomach bottoms out.

But I should've expected this. The men Tati dates don't stick around. Being with her is arduous, and she's practically got a kid. She's stunning, so dudes always try to make it work, at least for a while. But it turns out very few men are game to sign up for forever with a taxing woman and a bonus teenager.

Davis, though...he's got a teenager of his own, and he's so easygoing, a counterbalance to Tati's rigidity. She's been happier in the weeks they've been dating than I've seen her in our seven years of cohabitation.

"You *think* you're over?"

"Last night...he drank a lot," she explains. "And he wasn't a fun, *let's go sing karaoke until two a.m.* drunk. He was completely obnoxious. I had to pay for dinner because he couldn't slide a credit card out of his wallet. I had to help him out of the restaurant. I had to drive him home. And, Piper, he was kind of a dick."

"To you?" I'm unable to keep the alarm from my voice.

"He was short with me. That hasn't happened before. And he was just *rude* to everyone we encountered. Our server. A group of people coming in as we were on our way out. There was a tourist driving through the parking lot—rental car, you

264

know—and he must've been looking at the GPS on his phone because he almost rolled into us. I thought Davis was going to drag the guy out of the car and hand him his ass."

I sit back in my chair, mind whirling. I recall Henry's earlier text: My dad's nursing a wicked hangover. Yeah, I'd assume so. I've seen Davis throw back a beer or two in the confines of his home, and he was indulging the night Henry and I arranged for him and Tati to cross paths at Blitz Brews. But he's always seemed in control.

I think back to the nights I've had a drink (or three) too many. A lot of times, my actions were spurred by an impetuous need to throw caution to the wind—to chase fun. But sometimes, something set me off: a fight with Tati, a less-than-stellar grade, a dream about Mom and Dad so vivid, so haunting, that I'd wake up thinking I was in my old bed in our old house, fixed firmly in my former wonderful life.

Or, like today, getting fired.

Two months ago, I would've called Gabi, then gotten too drunk to see straight.

"What if Davis was having a bad day?" I ask Tati. "What if he argued with Henry, or Henry's mom, or some random person who made him feel like crap?"

"Doesn't matter," she says, more exasperated than sad now. "I have bad days all the time. I argue with you all the time. Have you ever seen me so drunk I slur my words? Have I ever vomited in the kitchen sink? Have I ever once passed out before I could tell the person I'm dating *thanks for a nice evening*?"

265

Oh god.

"That's how it ended? He puked, went to bed, and you left?"

"That's how it ended," she confirms, rooting around in a desk drawer. She pulls out a compact, opens it, and glares into its mirror. "I put a glass of water and a trash can near his bed, then rolled him onto his side. I felt like I was back in college taking care of some idiot roommate, not saying good night to a grown man who knows better."

"Have you talked to him today?"

She presses powder onto the bridge of her nose. "I don't have anything to say."

"Maybe you should see if there's anything he wants to say to you," I suggest gently, wary of setting her off again, yet compelled to give Davis the benefit of the doubt.

It just doesn't seem right that he could be so Jekyll and Hyde. I hate to see Tati throw away a good thing; she's a lighter, brighter version of herself when she's with him.

Her gaze narrows. "Why are you on his team?"

"His *team*? I'm not on anyone's team. It sounds like he was a disaster. But he's also human. He's not perfect."

"I don't expect him to be perfect. I expect him to act his age."

"Tati, it was one night."

She snaps her compact closed, turning to glower at me. "I asked you to come down here because I wanted to vent. I should've known you'd defend him. You two are cut from the same cloth. Of course you can't see his faults."

I don't even know how to respond. She's spent the last five

266

minutes disparaging this man, only to turn around and remind me that he and I are alike. She's infuriating, and kind of a jerk. It's no wonder Davis overdid it. He had to tie one on to put up with her shit.

"You know what, Tati? You're so high and mighty, you can't see a good thing when it's standing right in front of you. Davis cares about you, and I know you're into him. But you're going to nitpick him to death, the way you do every guy you date. It's no wonder none of them stick around. You're *exhausting*."

She stares at me, neck flushed, eyes swampy.

"Go home," she says.

For the second time today, I'm awash in shame. It's not that I didn't mean what I said, but I could've framed it better. I could have been more sensitive. More sisterly. "Tati—"

"I don't want to hear it," she says, shuffling through a stack of papers.

"But I didn't—"

"Piper!" she yells, slamming her hand down on the desk.

I startle.

Her head whips toward the closed door. Brigitte has to have heard.

Tati takes a breath. Then, in a terrifyingly calm voice, she says, "Get. Out."

She turns her chair to face the wall behind her desk.

For seconds that feel like eternities, my mouth gapes soundlessly while I scrabble for a way to make this right. But I know she won't hear me out. I pushed too hard—I get that—but Tati, as usual, refuses to entertain the idea that maybe, every once in a while, she's wrong.

I slink out of my sister's office, meeting Brigitte's shocked gaze for a fleeting moment.

I leave the Towers through the lobby doors, stepping into the warm sunshine.

What a glaring contradiction to the day I've had.

———

I walk to a gelato shop tucked into a strip mall a mile from home. I eat a scoop of hazelnut, sitting on the curb, breathing in exhaust and defeat.

I think about calling Henry.

I think about changing my hair again.

I think about texting Gabi. She's good at working through conflict—at least, she used to be. The report card I brought home after the first anniversary of my parents' accident was littered with D's, and Tati went through the roof. I couldn't understand why she wouldn't cut me some slack. My parents were *dead*. I called Gabi to complain, and after spending a few minutes commiserating, she pointed out that maybe it wasn't the grades, exactly, that'd made Tati mad. Maybe it was the fact that I wasn't doing my best.

"You're super smart, Piper," she'd said. "I know that, and so does your sister. But you've still got to work hard. I think that's what your parents would want, and it's obviously what Tati wants."

And yeah, in hindsight, she was right.

After I finish my gelato, I wander the length of the strip mall, my shoes scuffing the sidewalk with each forlorn step. I don't enjoy fighting with Tati, but we've had such a combative dynamic for so long, I don't know how to shift it. I'm not going to apologize for an argument that was equally her fault. I'm not going to stop being myself.

And my job...I'm still breathless with the loss. I practically spat in the face of the good man who could've helped me make my dream a reality. I let a hailstorm of emotion drive my decision-making without bothering to consider the ramifications of my actions, just like Tati's always saying. I sullied my sanctuary, my happiest place.

A storefront with a colorful sign catches my eye: Ink Isle. A tattoo parlor I've never paid attention to because my sister hates body modifications and has threatened me with boarding school should I ever come home with a speck of ink.

WE PIERCE TOO! announces a sign in the window.

I push open the door, ramifications be damned.

Henry

I BELIEVE WHAT DAD SAID about having had a conversation with my mom regarding me staying in Sugar Bay, but I'm not convinced she was as enthusiastic as he made it seem. When she calls late in the afternoon on Friday, she surprises me.

"Henry! Of course I'm okay with it," she tells me while I sit in one of Blitz Brew's booths, wolfing down the Reuben I earned walking the pier. Davis rolled in half an hour ago. I haven't spoken to him since he gargled with peanut butter. "I'll miss you with everything I've got," Mom goes on. "I already do. But I've been lucky to have you with me for almost eighteen years. It's only fair that your dad get some time too."

"You're sure?" I think about all the stuff I take care of around the house—stuff my pop did for Mom and me before he passed, like mowing the lawn, cleaning the gutters, hauling bins of holiday decorations in and out of the garage. It's not like Mom's helpless;

she's been pushing the mower all summer. But she shouldn't have to, not on top of work and school and everything else.

"I'm very sure. Don't worry about me."

"Whitney's gonna lose her mind if I'm not back in Spokane in a few weeks."

"Whitney's not your responsibility."

She's right; I know this, rationally. So why do I feel like I've got to do everything I can to avoid hurting her feelings? Is it guilt? Shared suffering? Habit?

Davis comes out of his office, spots me, and flashes me a peace sign.

I roll my eyes.

"Your dad said you've been spending time with one of his neighbors," Mom says.

Jesus H—is nothing sacred? Piper's no secret, but I would've liked to tell my mom about her in my own time, in my own way.

"Yeah. Her name's Piper."

"Is she a factor in whether you enroll at Sugar Bay High?"

"I mean, it wouldn't suck, spending the next year with her."

"If you like her, I do too. Just…please be careful."

My face goes hot. Her appeal's as subtle as a sledgehammer. But she's a mom and a nurse, and I have a history. She's obligated to say this shit to me.

"Don't worry," I reply, which probably only makes her worry more. I could tell her Dad has made sure I have a reserve of condoms at my disposal, but that just seems mean. Instead, I try to reassure her. "I've learned my lesson."

271

"I'm glad to hear that. You let me know what you decide about your living situation. If you want to talk it out, call me."

"I will."

"And, Henry, don't think about me when you're making your choice. Don't think about Whitney, don't think about your dad, and don't think about Piper. Do what's right for you."

She tells me, like always, that I'm her whole heart. We hang up, and I finish my sandwich, pretending to read while I watch Dad do his thing with guests and staff.

He's good at his job. He handles his business. Everyone adores him.

It's stupid of me to get bent out of shape about one wild night.

I'm pulling cash for a tip out of my wallet when a trio of guys walks past my table. My hackles go up. It's the sack of shit who harassed Piper here and at the marine park, plus a kid who I bet is his younger brother and a man who's got to be their father.

They're rambunctious, and they're drawing a lot of attention. The scumbag—Damon, Piper called him—is whaling on his brother, taking cheap shots at the back of his head as they follow Cassie, the hostess who's stuck dealing with them. The little one snakes a hand out to pinch the back of his brother's arm. Damon retaliates with a slug to the gut, sending his brother hurtling into the chair of a middle-aged man trying to eat a burger. Their dad brings up the rear, distracted by his phone while his offspring act like wild animals.

The restaurant's din lowers, like the newcomers are sucking the spirit out of the place.

When they reach their table, their father finally takes notice. He pockets his phone, grabs Damon's arm, and yanks him aside. He hisses a warning, nostrils flaring. He clenches his kid so tight, I bet there'll be marks tomorrow. Beneath the bill of his filthy hat, the lowlife scowls. He twists out of his father's grip, rubbing his arm and muttering under his breath.

He gives his brother the finger as soon as he's sure their dad's not looking.

Cassie drops their menus on the table, then hurries back to the host station.

I realize I'm staring when the three of them finally settle into their seats. I'm not the only one; everybody in our section seems to let out a simultaneous breath of relief.

My dad's watching too.

His fists are planted on his hips, and his mouth is set in an uncharacteristic glower. He doesn't like when the chill vibe of his sports bar is disrupted, or when his staff isn't treated kindly, but more than that, he's got zero love for parents who get physical with their kids.

Our eyes meet. He cringes, lifting his shoulders in a rueful shrug that says, *I'd die before I'd treat you like that.*

Shit—he and I have had our ups and downs, but I've got it good.

I'm pretty sure Dad would boot this guy and his kids if doing so wouldn't cause an even bigger commotion. For now, he

273

lingers near the bar, keeping an eye on their table, making sure I'm safe, as are the rest of his patrons, his employees, and the punk kids who seem to be growing into mirror images of their asshole father.

Piper

WHEN TATI GETS HOME, SHE takes one look at me, then turns and walks back out of the apartment.

By the time Henry swings by at nearly eight, she still hasn't returned.

He stoops down to peer at the tiny sparkling stud in my nose.

"I like it," he declares.

"My sister hates it."

"Who cares?" He kisses me, smiling against my mouth. "It's hot. Did it hurt?"

I've decided to keep the news about losing my job from him as well. I'll tell him as soon as I secure something new, same as Tati. I'll pretend it's no big thing—story of my life.

"Nope," I say with a sunny smile. "Not even a little."

We order a pizza, then joke and laugh while we wait for it to arrive. Henry, who can't sit still to save his life, clears the kitchen counter of an empty seltzer can and the bowl I ate grapes from earlier.

"You don't have to do that," I say, watching from a barstool.

"I know. Sorry, it's become habit. My dad never puts anything away."

"How'd he get by before you showed up?"

"He has a housekeeper who comes once a week. It's not that he's lazy. I just don't think he notices clutter. He's too busy looking for the next exciting adventure."

You two are cut from the same cloth. Of course you can't see his faults.

It bothers me that Tati's not wrong.

"You want to hang out in my room?" I ask.

Henry's expression is a mixture of intrigue and wariness. He's been over plenty of times, but we've always stayed in the common areas.

"Your sister won't care?"

"My sister's not here."

"What about the pizza?"

"Oh, Henry," I say, comforted by how totally and completely dependable he is. "We'll hear the buzzer."

His mouth curves into a smile. "Okay. Yeah. Let's hang out in your room."

———

"This is so *you*," he says of my space.

276

I think so too. The far wall, where my bed sits, is painted in horizontal black and white stripes. My headboard is a saturated teal, almost identical to the color of the ocean outside the window. My linens are white, and there's a graphic black-and-white rug covering most of the hardwood floor. Gabi helped me decorate two summers ago, after convincing my sister that the pink explosion she'd chosen when we'd moved to the Towers was too juvenile. With a tight, Tati-approved budget, Gabi and I ordered the bed and the rug online, then went to Pensacola with Maggie to shop for everything else. We painted the stripes ourselves after watching how-to videos on YouTube.

Sorrow knocks me off-balance. I've thought about Gabi a lot this afternoon—too much. Being fired wouldn't hurt so badly if I could process it with her. If she was still around to act as my champion, Tati's beastliness might stop deadening pieces of my soul. She'd love my little nose piercing. Before, she would've had her belly button done in solidarity.

God, I miss my best friend.

Henry steps over mountains of clothes and beach towels scattered across the floor. I spend a second worrying about whether the disorder bothers him before convincing myself that it doesn't matter. He likes me, flaws and all.

He checks out my bookshelf, which is stuffed with a bunch of fantasy series, plus Nora Roberts and Curtis Sittenfeld novels I lifted from my sister. My Delphina books are there too. I have three complete sets of the trilogy: the dog-eared paperbacks my parents originally bought me (the copies I continuously

277

reread), plus the movie tie-in paperbacks and a pristine set of signed hardcovers. The author appeared at a book festival in Tallahassee a few years ago, and Gabi's parents drove us all the way there so we could hear her speak, then spend hours standing in her signing line—totally worth it.

Henry draws his finger across the hardcover spines, which in combination form the image of a shimmering mermaid tail. "Whoa," he whispers.

"Different from your bookshelf, I bet."

"A little." He tosses a grin over his shoulder. "But now I know who to come to when I'm ready to dive under the sea."

He heads for my unmade bed. He spends a minute standing over it, looking at the rumpled burrow of cotton I sleep in. His back's to me so I can't see his face, but I'm dying to know what he's thinking.

He turns around to tell me: "Not gonna lie, I've imagined myself here a few times."

I smile. "Same."

I go to him. I pull him down onto the soft sheets. I kiss him, and the disaster that was this afternoon dissipates. We stop only when the pizza arrives. We hear the buzzer, as I told him we would.

We return to my room with dinner on paper plates and glasses of water garnished with lemon wedges, spreading out picnic-style on the floor, which I clear with a few hasty swipes of my foot. I let Henry get through a slice of pizza before I raise the topic we've been avoiding.

"So, what went on with your dad earlier?"

He frowns, wiping his hands on a napkin. "Well, he slept until noon. I didn't even know he was in the apartment until he started snoring louder than a trash compactor. After he dragged himself out of bed, he ate some peanut butter off a spoon and—get this—downed a beer. Not his best showing."

There are a couple of things I could delve into. First, alcohol does cure a hangover. Damon taught Gabi, and Gabi taught me, and I've kept the lesson in my back pocket for the direst of mornings. That said, it's pretty gross having to pop a top to kickstart functionality. Second, I've had a couple of mornings that sound similar to Davis's, and that doesn't make me proud. But the first knot that needs unraveling is, "Does he remember fighting with Tati?"

Henry winces. "He didn't really go into it."

I put my plate with its half-eaten slice of pizza next to his. "I only got Tati's side, but it didn't sound good. The way she tells it...your dad was kind of terrible."

I'm not trying to make Henry feel bad, but I'm not going to let Davis off the hook—not again. The more time passes, the more I wish I'd been supportive of Tati this afternoon.

You're exhausting, I told her.

I'd take it back if I could.

"How pissed is your sister?" Henry asks.

I sigh. "She's been through a hundred breakups and she's always low afterward, but this feels different. She seemed more heartbroken than angry."

"She brought him upstairs," Henry says, red-faced, like he's embarrassed on Davis's behalf. "She took off his shoes and set him up with a trash can."

"I'm not surprised. Even when she's mad enough to breathe fire, she's good at taking care of people."

He lifts a brow. "I think that's the first nice thing I've heard you say about her."

"It's the truth. She wades through shit to make sure the people she cares about are okay. She doesn't always do it with compassion, but she does it."

He ponders that for a minute. "I'm sorry my dad made her sad."

"I know, Henry, but that's not your apology to make." His empathetic nature is one of the things I've come to like most about him, but it's got to be awful, shouldering the hardships of others. I reach for his hand and ask the question that's been on my mind since Tati and I talked in her office. "How often does your dad drink like he did last night?"

Henry's posture wilts. He's obviously considered this before, and that worries me.

"I don't know. He drinks socially. He owns a sports bar. It's part of the job."

"Is it, though?" I ask.

He lets go of my hand to tear a hunk of crust from a second slice of pizza. He shovels it into his mouth like that'll keep him from having to respond.

After too many quiet seconds, I whisper his name. I have no

idea what I'm going to follow up with, but the solemnness of his expression pierces holes through my heart. I need him to look at me.

He does, his eyes swirling with emotion. "I don't know what you want me to say, Piper. Does my dad overdo it sometimes? Maybe. Do I wish he wouldn't? Fuck yes. Is his drinking the reason he and your sister fought? I have no idea, and I don't think it's fair to automatically slap him with all the blame. You know Tati's not easy to get along with. And to tell you the truth, it's not really our place to psychoanalyze what's going on between them. They argued. They'll work it out or they won't. It has nothing to do with us."

I'm starting to feel a little prickly. "That's easy for you to say. You weren't called down to Tati's office. You didn't have to see her looking all dejected. You didn't say the wrong thing, as usual, and end up catching her wrath." I pick up speed. "How nice to be you. Your dad got wasted and acted like an asshole, and you're okay with pretending that's fine."

He stares me down.

Once again, I've spewed the wrong words in the wrong way.

Once again, I've left careful consideration in the dust.

Once again, I've hurt someone I care about.

My breath catches as I realize that Henry could walk out before we've resolved this.

He could walk out for good.

Henry

I CAN'T BELIEVE SHE'S PAINTING Tati as superior. I can't believe she's dragging my dad through the mud, hauling the fears I've worked my ass off to bury into the glaring light.

Quietly, she says, "Henry, don't leave."

An ache fills the space behind my ribs. "I'm not going anywhere."

"You're looking at me like you hate me."

She's so far off the mark.

I loosen my jaw and roll my shoulders. "I don't."

"This is too hard," she says, staring down at her lap.

The ache becomes sharp. "Too hard, like you don't want to see me anymore?"

Her head snaps up. "No! I don't want to stop seeing you—not that. I just can't understand why you'd defend your dad when not five minutes ago, you seemed pretty freaking irritated with him."

"I'm not defending him, but I'm also not going to dump all over him because he did a stupid thing. You of all people should understand that."

She flinches. "What's that supposed to mean?"

"Nothing," I say reflexively.

"No, tell me."

"All I'm saying is that you're acting holier-than-thou when in reality, you've got some experience with making choices you regret later."

Her mouth becomes a circle of shock. "I apologized for that night at the Marine—"

She falters, swallowing hard.

Shit—I've hurt her. I want to recant because none of this even matters, but my foot's crammed so far down my throat, there's not a chance in hell I'll be able to yank it out in time to salvage this conversation. "Piper—"

"Yeah, okay, sometimes I do things I *might* reevaluate later," she says, her voice growing stronger, "but that doesn't mean you get to throw them in my face."

"I'm not—"

"You are. You say I'm acting holier-than-thou as you sit there judging me. You're not perfect, Henry. You're sheltered, set in your ways. You think misfortune is a dad who's excited to take you golfing. You know that's not an actual problem, right?"

I've got nothing.

She was onto something weeks ago, when she worried that getting Tati and Davis together might mess things up between her and me. That's what's happening. We're arguing, firing low blows, and neither of us is hearing the other.

All thanks to my dad and her sister.

She watches while I stack my paper plate on top of hers. She watches while I collect our napkins. She watches while I get up off the floor.

"I'm gonna go," I tell her, even though what I'd like to do is forget the last ten minutes and climb back into bed with her.

"You said you wouldn't," she whispers with doleful eyes.

"That was before." I reach out to smooth her hair. "This isn't how I thought tonight would go. I don't want to fight. I'm not even mad, really. But we're not getting anywhere, and I don't want to say something that makes things worse. Let's talk tomorrow, okay?"

She nods, but her face is shadowed with doubt.

How many people have promised her tomorrow, then walked out of her life?

I head for the door, but before I step out into the hallway, I turn back and say, "Piper, I promise I won't disappear."

Piper

TATI AND DAVIS SPEND ALL weekend apart.

Her phone doesn't move from its charging port on the kitchen counter. I peek at its screen every time I walk by. Davis has called a few times. He's sent a lot of texts too, but I can only see one, stacked on top of the rest: Can we please talk?

As far as I know, Tati doesn't respond.

Henry and I keep our distance too, though there are scattered texts, and a couple of choppy phone calls..

With the exception of eating and peeing, I spend all of Saturday and most Sunday in my room. I get sad every time I think about how Friday fell apart, and Tati's as frigid as ever, but what's really bothering me is knowing how much better I'd feel if I could talk to Gabi. She's the best buffer when it comes to my sister and me, and she's a master at putting boy troubles into perspective. If Damon hadn't screwed everything up, I'd text her now. She'd be at the door in half an hour with magazines, face masks, and a pint of Peanut Butter Fudge.

I worry about her. She thinks she's found a prince in Damon. She thinks her parents and I judge him unfairly because he's rough around the edges. She won't—can't?—see who he really is, and that terrifies me. Friends or not, I love her. I never want her to experience her boyfriend's cruelty.

Late on Sunday afternoon, I draft a message in my Notes app, not the text thread Gabi and I used to blow up at all hours. God forbid I accidentally hit send—I'm not ready for that. But I am ready to put words to the truth.

Damon wants you to believe I started what you saw. I didn't. I didn't want him to touch me. I didn't want him to kiss me. I told him no, but he wouldn't listen. I don't know how far he would've pushed if you hadn't walked in. He's not good for you, Gabi. He's dangerous.

I close the app and toss my phone onto the bed.

Maybe now my wounded heart will scab over.

Restless, I go to the kitchen. Tati's there, sifting through papers at the table, half a mug of coffee to her right. She's dressed and made up, but it's a front. Her ragged cuticles and bouncing knee betray her agitation.

I pull a seltzer from the fridge, then say mildly, "You should call him."

286

She taps the edges of the papers on the tabletop, aligning them, avoiding my gaze. "You should mind your own business."

"Come on, Tati. You can fix this if you want to."

"I shouldn't have to fix it."

"He's trying. He's called. He's texted. You're not giving him a chance."

"Piper, I swear...I don't want to talk about Davis."

"But you care about him. I know you do."

She flings the papers. They go sailing across the table, then flutter to the floor. They're lease applications, I see now, and they're everywhere. She shoves her chair back so hard it rams into the wall, leaving a scuff, then pushes to her feet, snapping, "Sometimes caring isn't enough. Sometimes caring leads to more trouble. More hurt."

I blink, taken aback by the way she just voiced the position I maintained right up until I reconnected with Henry.

She adds, "You only want me to call Davis so you can make peace with Henry."

"How do you know he and I aren't at peace?"

"Because he hasn't been over here all weekend, and you haven't left the apartment. You miss him, hence your opportunistic suggestion that I call his father. Everything you do—everything you say—is self-serving."

Something heavy materializes in my stomach. Why does she *always* put me down? "That's not true. I've been watching you mope since Friday. Is it such a stretch that I want you to be happy?"

287

"Yes," she says, taking an antagonistic step into my space. Her gaze flicks to the stud in my nose before she meets my eyes. "You go out of your way to push my buttons, to wear down my patience, to make me worry, all because I'm not—"

She's standing so close I can smell her jasmine perfume. She overlined her lips, faking a fuller mouth, before she layered on her Ruby Woo. God, she pisses me off.

"You're not what, Tati?"

"Nothing." She sets her mouth in a hard line, breathing heavily for no good reason.

"Say what you were going to say. I'm sure it's nasty, and that's what you want, isn't it? To hurt me?"

"Yes, Piper, that's always my goal," she says, rolling her eyes. "What I was *going* to say is that you make me feel like shit all the time because I'm not Mom and Dad. Because I *can't be* Mom and Dad."

"You're right about that. Mom and Dad loved me. They gave me chances, and taught me things, and wanted me to grow. To thrive. All you want is for me to turn out like you."

She shakes her head in disgust. "I want you to be an independent, productive member of society. Not a drunk. Not a criminal. Not a leech."

I got wasted at Gabi's party.

I broke into the Marine Conservation Park.

I lost my first and only paying job, and I'm too cowardly, too embarrassed, to tell anyone.

Tati's accusations might be malicious, but they're not untrue.

288

"I'm not mean for the joy of it," she goes on. "It's not easy, putting in forty hours a week at a job I dislike, taking care of a teenager who hates me, living in a town I spent my adolescence desperate to leave. I'm lonely. I'm stressed. And I'm tired."

I feel bad for her—a part of me has for years—but my pity is overshadowed by animosity.

"I'm *so sorry* Mom and Dad left you to do the dirty work," I say, my volume rising. "At least you had a normal childhood. At least you got to grow up with them!"

"Yeah, lucky me," she replies with so much disdain I lose my breath.

How dare she disparage our parents?

Can't she see that I'm hurting? Doesn't she care?

"They shouldn't have chosen you to be my guardian," I tell her. "They should've known you'd treat me like a burden. They should've known you wouldn't want this life."

She stares at me, her eyes sparking with an emotion I can't name: *fury* is inadequate, *devastation* too weak.

"You have *no idea* what you're talking about," she says.

Crying hot tears now, I sink down, squatting on the kitchen floor with my chin to my chest. She stands over me, offering no comfort, patronizing as usual.

"Piper," she says finally, and because I'm desperate to be looked after, I raise my gaze. But her tone is vicious. "You always do this. You say something ugly or do something stupid, and then you make this big production of falling apart. But you don't want to be comforted. You want to go on feeling sorry for yourself. You like believing the world is against you, so you push people until they break. You do it with me, and you probably did it with Henry. You sure as shit did it with Gabi. "

I straighten. I'm done letting Damon's actions make me look selfish and slutty. "I didn't push Gabi, and I didn't break her. I didn't kiss her boyfriend, either. If you'd asked me what actually happened, I would've told you: Damon kissed me."

Tati huffs.

I barrel on. "He trapped me in Gabi's room and got in my face. He touched me. I'd been drinking, yeah, but I told him to stop. I told him I didn't want to be with him, that it'd crush Gabi, and that—" I trip over a sob, but I'm in too deep to stop now. "I told him he was hurting me. I told him *no*. If Gabi hadn't interrupted when she did…"

Tati gapes at me, her face horrifically pale. I'm humiliated under her stare, scarred by the memory I just unearthed from its dark hole so I could throw it in her face.

Hands shaking, chest heaving, I attempt to rebury it with shovels full of dirt and denial.

I wasn't sure Tati would believe me.

I wasn't sure anyone would believe me.

I think my sister believes me.

"Piper—"

"Don't. You assumed the worst of me, same as Gabi."

I shove past, ramming her shoulder with mine.

I hear her call after me, but I don't turn back.

I go to my room, retrieve my phone from my bed, and open

the Notes app. I copy the words I wrote for Gabi, then paste them into our text thread, the one that's been unused for weeks. I stare at the blinking cursor for a long moment, and then, because I *am* reckless and impulsive, because maybe I *do* want to be miserable, I fire off the message.

Delivered, my phone assures me.

Later, when I'm sure Tati has left the kitchen for her room, I sneak down to the pool, hoping Henry will show. Hoping he'll sense my need the way he has in the past.

He doesn't.

For hours, I sit in the dark, alone.

Henry

I STARTED READING *DELPHINA AND the Starlit Sea* the night Piper and I ate pizza in her room.

When I got back to Dad's apartment, he wasn't home. Good thing, because I was riled up. I poured a soda, purposefully ignoring the clanking beer bottles stored along the shelves of the refrigerator door, then went to my room and pulled out the Kindle I rarely use.

Delphina's an orphan, I learned that night.

Also, *Starlit Sea* is one hell of a story.

I read until I finished. It was close to dawn when I downloaded the two sequels and dove into *Delphina and the Siren's Secret*, pushing on until I couldn't keep my eyes open.

Saturday and Sunday were a blur of sleeping and reading. I barely spoke to my dad, but not for his lack of trying. I called Piper, though maybe I shouldn't have. My questions felt forced, and her answers sounded clipped. I was sure that if I could see her, we could work things out. But she didn't ask to meet up, so I didn't push.

Sunday night, I feel a sudden compulsion to go down to the pool, like the water's shouting up at me. But that's silly, because I don't feel like swimming, and if Piper was going down, she would've let me know.

I stay on the couch with *Delphina and the Coral Crown*, hoping Dad will burn the midnight oil at Blitz Brews.

He barrels into the apartment just before ten.

"What's up?" he asks, shoving my legs over so he can flop down on the couch.

I don't answer; I'm in the middle of a book.

"Whatcha reading?" he pushes, jostling my foot.

I glance up, annoyed. "The third book in the Delphina trilogy."

I don't expect him to have heard of it, but he says, "I've seen the movies. Good stuff."

I swear to god, every time I think I've got him nailed down, he surprises me.

I power off my Kindle. "Piper loves the books. That's why I started reading them."

"You didn't read them when you were younger?" He chuckles. "They're everywhere. You must've actively avoided them."

Maybe. But was it because I was disinterested or because I thought I was better than the masses who're obsessed with it?

"Did you talk to Tati today?" I ask.

"Nope. Did she come by?" He casually combs his fingers

through his hair, like my reply doesn't matter to him one way or another, but the hope in his voice is hard to miss.

"No. Do you think you ought to reach out to her?"

"I have. She's gone dark."

"So that's it? You're giving up?"

"I tried, Henry. She doesn't want to talk." He shrugs. "I don't like knowing someone's angry with me, but what happened the other night wasn't that big of a deal. She might not be able to get over it, but I already have."

I don't get him. He's a people pleaser—always has been. But his relationship with Tati is more important than catering to customers at Blitz Brews or making friends with strangers on a fishing excursion. He's got real feelings for her, but instead of doing the work to make things right, he's tossing in the towel.

"Dad, Tati told Piper you were out of control."

He laughs. "By Tati's standards, maybe."

"She had to drive you home and put you to bed."

"Nah. I was good, buddy. No regrets."

I stare at him, disbelieving. His eyes are clear. He's enunciating his words and sitting up straight. He's not smashed…but I can smell beer on him. What I'm starting to realize is that Davis's baseline is three drinks in.

The apprehensive feeling in my gut tells me it'll get worse: four drinks, then five, then six. It's going to start impacting every facet of his life, from work to home to finances.

To me.

I know this with alarming certainty. I also know that if I point

294

out what I'm finally starting to understand is a problem, I'll come off as sanctimonious. Like I'm trying to parent him. Like I'm taking Tati's side.

Davis is gonna do what Davis wants to do.

I'm not sure I want to stick around and become a casualty of his choices.

Piper

MONDAY MORNING, I LEAVE THE apartment like I'm going to the Marine Conservation Park. In my bag, I've packed a floral halter bikini and *The Coral Crown*, plus snacks, sunglasses, sunscreen, and a towel. I walk all the way to a public beach denounced by locals for its tourist crowds and stake out a spot. It's warm, but not as humid as it's been over the last few weeks.

I spend a solid four hours lying out on the sand.

Even considering that I'm not talking to Tati and barely talking to Henry, I leave the beach feeling better than I did all weekend, thanks to the sunshine, the sea, and the solace of a favorite book.

I'll start looking for a new job tomorrow.

I'm lost in thought all the way home, cataloging reasons Gabi might've opted not to respond to the text I sent last night. *She was already asleep. She realizes she was wrong and can't figure out how to apologize. She hates me more than ever...* I'm so tied up in my thoughts, I'm nearly on top of her before I notice her sitting by the fountain outside the Towers.

She's wearing a white maxi dress, and her hair, which she usually wears in natural coils, has been woven into micro braids falling long down her back. She's shielding her eyes from the sun and looking right at me.

When she stands, adrenaline floods my system, instinct demanding that I veer away because our last few interactions have been miserable, and what if Damon's here someplace too?

I swerve toward the building's entrance, picking up my pace.

"Piper, wait," she calls, hurrying toward me.

I don't turn around.

Why did she come here?

Why not return my message instead?

"Piper, please!"

She makes a grab for me, her pianist's fingers wrapping around my wrist.

Heart racing, I look skittishly around, over her shoulder and then mine, sure Damon's lurking nearby.

I don't see him.

I don't see any familiar faces, besides Gabi's.

"I read your text," she says. "I've read it a lot, actually."

My mouth is dry, my brain muddled as I stare into her umber eyes.

Her shoulders droop, her expression more diffident than I've

297

ever seen it. "I wish you'd told me the truth about that night," she says quietly. "I wish you'd told me what Damon did."

I push a question into the space between us. "Would it have mattered?"

She considers, reaching up to brush a braid away from her face. "I don't know."

Her candor surprises me. She could've said yes, portrayed herself in a favorable light, especially considering what I pulled during spring break. She could absolve herself of accountability and point at my past behavior. Instead, she says something truthful, unflattering but *real*, and god, I love her.

"I broke up with him last night. What he did…I'm sick over it, Piper. I'm so sorry. That's what I came here to say. I can't imagine what this summer's been like for you. Just awful, probably." Her eyes are bright with tears, but she holds my gaze. "I'm sorry about how I treated you at Clementine's, and about telling Tati what I *thought* happened that day at Publix. And I'm so, so sorry for what happened at my house… I should've asked for your side of the story. I should've seen him for who he is. I should've made sure you were okay. I should've known, Piper. I should've known you'd never betray me that way."

I slip my sunglasses from my face and push them onto hers, because she's crying for real now. I can't believe she's here, admitting she was wrong, apologizing. It's everything I've hoped for all summer long.

"I'm glad you came," I tell her. "And I'm glad you're done with Damon. I can't stand the thought of him hurting you too."

298

"He won't," she says, shaking her head. "I blocked his number, blocked him on socials. My parents know he's not welcome at our house anymore. I'll never speak to him again."

We stand there, Gabi and me.

I'm not sure where to go from here.

She must not be either, because she says, "So...what now?"

"I don't know."

"I miss you, Piper."

I hesitate, not sure if I'm ready to dive into the open waters of honesty yet. But I can't put up a front—not with Gabi. "I miss you too."

Her face is shadowed with worry. "Why do I feel like you're going to tack a *but* onto the end of that statement?"

I smile, happy to be known. "I *do* miss you, but it's hard for me to forget what happened. You're right: In a lot of ways, this summer has truly sucked."

She's still wearing my sunglasses. A tear falls from beneath them. "I'll leave you alone if that's what you want. I'll give you space if that's what you need. If it's up to me, though, I'd like to earn back your friendship."

Since fourth grade, Gabi's been like a sister to me. More so, a lot of times, than my actual sister. Our history supersedes arguments and mistakes—even massive, foundation-shattering mistakes. We've argued, we've forgiven, and we're stronger for it.

"Can we start with breakfast tomorrow morning?" I ask.

She smiles, reaching out to squeeze my hand. "Definitely."

Henry

NEARLY A WEEK HAS PASSED since Piper and I last hung out. Walking to her place has been a serious temptation since I finished *Coral Crown*, but there's a wall between us, one I can't figure out how to breach.

It seems like the longer I spend away from her, the weaker the draw should be.

In reality, the distance makes me want her more.

Late Thursday afternoon I'm hungry, and there's nothing to eat in the apartment. Dad's at Blitz Brews, so I head over to take advantage of the free food. I snag my usual spot at the bar because Mateo's working and it's been a while since we last caught up. He's got a crowd to deal with, but he keeps the sodas coming and makes sure I have plenty of tartar sauce for the huge plate of fries Dad brought out when I showed up.

Mateo pulled him an IPA. The now-empty glass sits behind the bar.

When things slow down, Mateo tells me he's taken April, one of the hostesses, out a few times. "It's a whole new world," he says, retying his apron. "Being with Lana was a shit show. April's so chill. A lot of fun." He swipes a cloth across the bar. "What've you got going on in the romance department? I've seen you in here with a cute brunette a few times."

"That's Piper," I say.

"She your girl?"

"I guess." I'd feel weird calling her *mine* under the best circumstances because my mother raised me to respect women and their autonomy, but if that's the explanation that makes sense to Mateo, I'll roll with it.

"Where's she now?"

"Home, I think. We're in a weird place. You know how it goes."

"Do I ever," he says, offering me a fist bump of commiseration. "Work it out, bro, if you want to be with her."

I do—about that, I'm sure. What I can't get straight is whether I *should* be with her. I keep asking myself: Will things be different with Piper? Or will it end in disaster, like Whit and me?

"You're thinking too hard," Mateo says, sliding another soda in front of me.

"Yeah, overanalyzing is kind of my thing."

"There are worse ways to be." He glances across the restaurant to where my dad's laughing raucously with a bunch of customers. They've got a half dozen pitchers of beer spread across their

301

table, and Dad's topping off glasses, offering loud commentary on the Marlins game most of the TVs are broadcasting.

Thanks to a recent Google search, I now know what a functioning alcoholic is.

Pretty sure I'm living with one.

Dad's acquired a fresh glass. He fills it with beer, foam sloshing over the brim and onto his patrons' table. They don't notice or don't care. He joins their toast, shouting "Cheers!" so loudly that his voice rises above everyone else's. He throws back the beer—not quite a chug, but not the civilized sip of a proprietor, either.

"He's somethin'," Mateo says, looking dubiously at Dad. "He can really sock 'em back, especially lately."

"Yeah. I've noticed."

He goes back to work, shaking his head. I pick up my phone, ready to text Piper. Ready to apologize for my part in our argument. Ready to beg for guidance on what the fuck I should do about my dad.

I really want to hear her voice.

A text comes through.

WHITNEY 5:26 P.M.

I need to talk.

HENRY 5:27 P.M.

Busy. Later?

WHITNEY 5:28 P.M.

It's important.

5:30 P.M.

Henry. I'll call your mom if you don't call me.

This is a new low.

I call her, even though it's loud in the restaurant.

She answers with a hiccupping sob. I can't help it—I grimace. She's used tears to manipulate me in the past, both before and after our breakup.

It was stupid to take a flying leap the second she told me to jump.

She launches into a rundown of every emotion she's experienced since March. Guilt about the decision. Relief. Guilt about the relief. Justification. It's all one garbled run-on sentence, but I'm softening. It's hard to maintain distance from this girl when we've been treading in the same shitty sea.

I give her a version of the platitude my mom's given me: "You did the right thing. It'll get better. *You'll* get better."

"But you got over it so fast," she wails.

I picture her in her room, on her bed, surrounded by crumpled tissues. It's not a hard image to conjure. I've seen her exactly this way more than once since spring break.

"I haven't gotten over it, Whit," I say, competing with the noise of the dinner crowd. "I'm surviving it. Same as you."

"You took the easy way out."

"That's not fair," I say, waving to Mateo. I slide off my stool

303

and head for the door. My face is going hot, my forehead prickling with sweat. On the off chance Dad decides to pay attention, I don't want him to know how worked up this call's getting me.

It's not much cooler outside, but it's definitely quieter. I park on a bench and listen to Whitney cry like she's in physical pain.

Maybe she is.

"It wasn't fair of you to leave," she slurs through a series of hiccups.

"Jesus, have you been drinking?"

"Does it matter?"

"Fuck yes, it matters. If you need to talk, I'll talk to you, but don't drunk text me."

"I'm not drunk. I'm *sad*."

"Yeah. Me too," I say quietly.

She's silent for a second. And then: "I can't wait for you to come home. I want us to work through this together."

I know without a doubt that I can't work through my emotions alongside Whitney.

I owe her understanding. Patience. An apology, maybe.

I don't owe her my future.

"We'll make a new beginning," she says. "You'll remember how good we can be."

Even if Piper wasn't a factor, even if I wasn't considering staying in Florida for senior year, even if I'd never heard of West Point, I wouldn't get back together with Whitney. I wish her all the good in the world, but I don't want to be part of her life.

"I've got to go, Whit."

I've got my finger ready to end the call when she says, "Henry! Please!" I press my phone back to my ear. "Tell me you'll think about trying again. Just *think* about it."

"Fine," I say, desperate to be done. "I'll think about it."

"Okay." And then, triumphantly, "We'll talk soon."

I end the call with the lie I just told turning my stomach sour.

I don't feel good about bullshitting her, but she has a tough time accepting no as an answer, and I don't have it in me to try and reason with her tonight. Still, I can see the whole forest. All she can focus on is the tree right in front of her.

I walk along the beach back to the Towers. The sun is warm, moving westward. When I get to Dad's, I hustle through a shower, then throw on shorts and a clean T-shirt. I head for the door, where my shoes are waiting.

Work it out if you want to be with her, Mateo said.

Conviction is the one good thing that came of my conversation with Whitney. I want to be with Piper.

I've got to make things right.

Piper

AS PLANNED, GABI AND I met up for breakfast Tuesday morning. It was *so* good to spend time with her. What a treat to indulge in iced coffees, croissants, and girl talk.

She updated me on her parents (busy, happy, all up in her business), her little brother ("He's a punk, but he's *my* punk"), and piano (still has her sights set sky-high on Juilliard). I filled her in on everything I'd learned about Stony Brook University, then explained how I'd lost my summer job and how my recently formed post–high school plan might be on hold indefinitely.

"Oh, Piper," she said, "I'm sorry. I can help you look for other options, if you want."

Because talk of jobs and higher education was bumming me out, I switched to gushing about Henry, whom she immediately recalled from the stories I'd told her three summers ago. She suggested I bring him to this Friday night's house party, hosted by Hudson, whose parents are taking his sister to Orlando for a long weekend.

"It'll be small," she said. "I already confirmed that Damon won't be there. Cole's travel baseball team has a three-day tournament in Montgomery, and according to Hudson, their dad's making Damon go. Bring Henry—I'm dying to meet him!"

I waffled, unsure whether I wanted to subject Henry to my past life.

A few days later, after a morning spent dropping my resume off at boutiques, cafes, and souvenir shops, I called Gabi, still waffling about Hudson's party.

"I just don't know..." I had her on speaker so my hands would be free and I could put some effort into cleaning my room. I wasn't above taking such steps to patch the gigantic hole Sunday night's explosion with Tati had created. "Last time I went to a party, it didn't end well," I said, slipping a sundress onto a hanger.

I didn't mean to make her feel bad, but the line went quiet.

"Sorry. That wasn't—"

"No," she cut in. "You say what you need to say. I'll deal. If you don't want to come, it's totally fine. I just need you to know that you're invited, and I'd love to see you. You *and* Henry."

I told her I'd let her know, then got back to cleaning.

———

Thursday evening, I ride the elevator to the eighth floor of the east tower.

Working things out with Gabi has gotten me thinking: Henry and I have allegiances to our respective family members, and that's how it should be, but fighting with him about my sister and his dad isn't worth it. Instead of enjoying the time we have left together, I've put a week's worth of energy into proving a point.

I knock, hoping he's home and Davis isn't.

Henry pulls open the door, and when he sees me, he grins.

My heart lifts.

He looks like he very recently stepped out of the shower. His chestnut hair's damp, and there are spots of water across his gray T-shirt, like he threw it on without bothering to towel off completely. He's wearing chino shorts, and his feet are bare, revealing flip-flop tan lines, an attribute that's so very Florida. I smile, thinking of my own perpetually striped feet.

"I was just heading over to see you," he says, waving me inside. "I wasn't sure you were ever gonna come this way again."

"Oh, Henry. Like you could get rid of me so easily."

He shuts the door, then snags my hand. "You're assuming I want to be rid of you," he says softly. "And that's where you're wrong."

He kisses me, a gentle press of his mouth that feels like *I'm really glad you're here*. It's a shame when he draws back—such a shame that I loop my arms around his neck and hug him close, breathing in his soapy scent, finding comfort in his height and his solidity. He holds me like there's nothing else in the world he'd rather be doing.

Tears of relief well in my eyes.

I should've come sooner.

"Do you want to do the apology thing?" he whispers, his breath moving the hairs at the back of my neck, making me shiver. "Or should we just agree that the last week's been shit and arguing isn't worth our time?"

I smile. "Let's go with the second one."

He reaches up to unwind my arms, then takes my hand and walks me to the couch. I curl up beside him, feeling better than I have in a long time. I might not have found a new job yet, and I can't look my sister in the eye without a rush of resentment, but Gabi and I are okay. Henry and I are okay.

Life is okay.

Henry

SHE TELLS ME ABOUT MAKING up with Gabi, which she hasn't mentioned in any of our sporadic surface-level texts over the last few days. I'm frustrated with myself, knowing that this huge thing happened in her life and I was too stubborn to be around for it.

She traces her fingertips over my palm, sensing my aggravation. I relax as she tells me about the slow mending of her most important friendship. She doesn't delve into what fractured it in the first place, but I'm so happy to see her happy, I resist the urge to pry. When she asks if I want to go to Hudson's—one of the lesser dicks, she reminds me—tomorrow night, I tell her I'm in.

Then she asks what I've been up to. I give her the rundown: running, studying, keeping track of my dad. "Oh, and I read *Delphina*," I say, like I'm only just remembering.

She pops upright. "Shut up."

"What?" I shrug. "I did."

Her gaze narrows. "The first book?"

"Yeah. And then the rest of the trilogy."

She looks genuinely shocked.

I laugh. "You've gone on about how good the story is. What'd you expect?"

"Uh, *not* that you'd read them," she sputters. She swats at my chest. "So? What'd you think?"

"Unputdownable," I say honestly.

"Ha!" she chirps, grinning. "I *knew* you'd be into them!"

I'm into you, I think.

Six months ago, I was sure I was in love. Maybe I was; maybe love comes in many forms and varying degrees. What Whitney and I had was intense and exciting, scary in a way I don't need to experience again. It's different with Piper. Our relationship is also intense and exciting and a little scary, but a lot less taxing. Arguing with her sucks, but making up doesn't feel like surrendering.

I can't go back to Spokane.

The realization hits me like a jolt of electricity.

It's so right, staying in Florida. I can't believe Dad had to lob the idea my way.

This week, I heard back from both my guidance counselor and my Field Force rep. While neither of them seemed enthusiastic about the idea of me transferring, neither could give a compelling reason as to why I shouldn't. It's an inconvenience, application-wise, for everyone involved—me especially—but it's not an impossibility.

311

Yeah, I'm gonna miss my mom, but staying in Florida will give me the space I need to heal. Staying in Florida means more time with Piper. And staying in Florida will allow me to continue cultivating my relationship with Dad—not to mention keeping tabs on him.

He needs me here.

I'm taking stock of everything I'm gonna have to do make a move happen—have my records transferred, register at Sugar Bay High, research their cross-country program, figure out how to get important shit I left in Washington to Florida—when Piper reaches up to smooth my furrowed brow. "What are you thinking about?"

I go right for it: "Staying. In Florida. For senior year."

Her mouth drops open, and a hand flies up to cover her heart. "But...could you even?"

"Sure. My parents are okay with it—it was my dad's idea. I think it'd be cool, hanging out in Sugar Bay for longer than this summer. But I don't want to impose on your territory."

A smile cracks her face wide-open. "You wouldn't be imposing."

"You're sure?"

"I'm *totally* sure."

I sweep a curl off her face. "I thought you'd need a few minutes—or, like, a few days—to think about it."

"As if the idea of you staying in Florida for the next year hasn't crossed my mind? I've thought about it. I've thought about it a lot. I just never imagined it'd be something you'd want."

"I didn't either, until I went too long without seeing you. Piper, I don't want to say goodbye anytime soon."

She takes my face in her hands. "Then don't. Stay in Florida. Stay with me."

Piper

ON FRIDAY, I SPEND THE time I should be at work—or looking for work—shopping for something to wear to Hudson's party. I end up blowing way more money than Tati would approve of on a breezy dress with a deep sweetheart neckline and a hem that whispers well above my knees. The retail therapy turns out to be just what I need.

After a quiet dinner with my sister, I slip into my new dress, pausing to admire my reflection in the mirror, then twist my hair into a topknot, brush a second coat of mascara onto my lashes, and swipe vanilla gloss over my lips.

Henry and I walk to Hudson's. He lives about a mile from the Towers in a rambler that's part of a planned community. Jayden's and Gabi's cars are in the driveway, plus Hudson's dad's Subaru. The family minivan is likely parked outside one of the Disney resorts.

"Did you go to a lot of parties in Spokane?" I ask Henry as we head up the drive.

"Is my neon LOSER sign not burning brightly enough for you?"

"You're not a loser." I link my arm through his. "And even if you were, I wouldn't care because you'd be *my* loser."

He laughs. "You really know how to stroke a guy's ego."

Hudson lets us into the house with a raucous hello. He thumps Henry on the shoulder like they're old friends, then moves in to hug me, welcoming me back into the fold.

Gabi's in the kitchen with about a dozen people from our class, including Jayden. Anna and Michaela are there too, and apparently wormed their way into Gabi's good graces while I was on involuntary hiatus. As soon as Gabi sees me, though, she skips over, grinning.

"I'm so glad you came!" She glances over her shoulder at Anna and Michaela, then mock whispers, "You're so much more fun than they are."

I introduce her to Henry, hoping the two of them will hit it off. They're my most valuable people, after all. Henry's polite and gracious as usual. Gabi looks floored by the majesty that is this gorgeous boy who gently fixes the slipping strap of my dress before draping his arm around my shoulders.

We hang around the kitchen for a few minutes. Gabi's got a hard cider, and there are bottles of strawberry vodka, Captain Morgan, and Jäger on the countertop, along with a few two-liter bottles of soda and a lot of spills. I don't know if it would bother Henry if I

315

decided to drink, but it seems insensitive, considering our recent conversation about his dad. And anyway, I'm not in the mood.

Hudson works on arranging Solo cups on the dining room table, then breaks volunteers into teams for Flip Cup. His mom would die a thousand deaths if she could see the way he's slopping cheap beer all over her beloved reclaimed wood.

"Let's go out back," I say to Henry.

Hudson's parents put in a really nice patio a couple of summers ago. There's a stone fire pit, a built-in grill, and a big table with six chairs under a pergola. Henry and I head for a group of loungers away from the house. He chooses one, dropping his wallet and phone onto the adjacent table. I nestle between his knees, letting my back melt into his chest, tipping my head to rest on his shoulder. He presses his cheek to the crown of my head, inhales, then releases a contented breath. He's in this as deep as I am, I realize, which makes me the very best kind of happy.

I lift my chin and meet him in a kiss.

His phone chimes once, interrupting us, then twice more in quick succession. I pull away, trying to sneak a subtle peek at who's texting him, but it's screen down on the table.

Another chime.

He tenses.

"Your dad?" I ask.

"No."

He dips his head, ready to kiss me again.

"Don't you want to see who it is?"

316

He sighs. "I know who it is."

"Okay…?"

"It's Whitney. Only Whitney texts compulsively until she gets a reply."

"Who's Whitney?"

His frown is deeply miserable. "The girl I broke up with back in March."

Henry

"OH," SHE SAYS TONELESSLY.

"It's not a big deal."

She inspects her nail polish, which is black and glittery. She disagrees—that's obvious. And who can blame her? My whole demeanor has changed.

It's a big fucking deal.

She turns in our chair to face me, crisscrossing her legs. "So, what happens if she doesn't get a reply?"

I rake a hand through my hair. "She keeps texting. Or she calls my mom, who's close with her mother. As many times as I've asked my mom to stay out of it, she's got loyalty where Whit's concerned. And a whole lot of sympathy."

"*Whit,*" Piper repeats, making the name sound like an expletive. "Why'd you guys break up?"

"There were a lot of reasons."

"Okay. Give me a few."

When I'm quiet, she stretches a hand toward me, pressing her palm to my cheek. The gesture helps me understand her motivation. She's not asking to be invasive. She's concerned. I guess that makes me a sinking ship, visible from shore.

I drop my elbows to my knees, dragging my hands down my face. Our pasts were bound to catch up to us eventually. I've encountered Damon and met Gabi. Piper's gonna learn about my breakup. We can't go on pretending we didn't have lives before this summer.

Still, I hate talking about Whitney.

Leaning into the chair's cushioned back, I gesture for Piper to come with me. She does, taking my hand, twining her fingers through mine in a show of support that, mortifyingly, raises a lump in my throat.

I swallow. "Whitney and I are very different people. It was all good at first, but eventually she wanted me to become someone I'm not. It...it wasn't working. Still, I was too chickenshit to end it. She was the first girl I'd been serious with, you know? I kept putting it off, hoping things between us would get better. And then she ended up pregnant." I pause, then revise. "*We* ended up pregnant—it's not like she managed it on her own."

Piper goes very still. "Oh. God."

I push out a breath, trying not to rouse the anguish I've spent months wrestling into submission. "We were always careful. *I*

319

was always careful, even though she's been on birth control since she was fifteen, for cramps or whatever. But one night I didn't have anything, and she promised it'd be fine."

Chill, Henry, she said. *It'll be okay.*

I figured she would know, since she was the one who was using the pill, and knew her cycle, and always said she was in tune with her body.

I shouldn't have taken the risk. I should've insisted we find a condom or put things on hold for the night. I should've been smart. Responsible. *Safe.*

I was none of those things, and as a result, I nearly lost West Point. I nearly became another link in the too-young-to-parent chain Mom and Dad started. And Whitney…baby or no baby, she paid severely.

Jesus—my heart is *pounding.*

Piper opens our joined hands, then studies my wrist, my palm, my fingertips, squinting through the darkness. She's quiet for so long, I start to wonder if her mind has been properly blown, if she's decided that she's heard enough.

But I'm not sure I want her to let me off the hook. I can't be perpetually shackled to this anchor of regret, dragging it through every moment she and I share.

She links our hands again, looking up at me.

So I continue. "Whit and I had a huge fight after she showed me the positive tests. She couldn't stop talking about how she'd have to quit dance and give up college and how we should've used a condom after all. Like, no shit. I couldn't shut up about West

320

Point, how you can't apply if you're married or if you have a legal obligation to child support. There was yelling. A lot of crying. I was scared shitless. I can't even imagine what she was going through."

"Henry, I'm so sorry."

"You shouldn't be, though, because here's the worst part: When she told me she thought we should end the pregnancy, the first thing I felt was relief. Not worry or sorrow, but *relief*. What an asshole, right?"

"You're not an asshole. It was a shocking, stressful situation. I'm sure you handled it the best you could."

I shake my head. "You're giving me too much credit."

"No," Piper says softly, reaching up to touch my face. "I don't think so."

Whitney and I were over, but I didn't feel right about bailing on her, so I asked if I could go with her to the clinic. She made an appointment for spring break, when her parents would be at work. Afterward, I drove her home with the prescription, some magazines, and a bag of her favorite snacks. She read over the doctor's directions, took the medication, and sent me on my way. By then, we weren't fighting anymore. We were hardly speaking.

"Whit's mom called the morning after her appointment," I tell Piper. "My mom had just gotten home from a twelve-hour shift, and then her friend's on the phone, losing her mind about how her daughter's been admitted. My mom woke me up and drove me back to the hospital she'd just left. In the car, I came clean about the clinic and the pills, about going to sleep that

321

night even though Whit hadn't answered the texts I'd sent to check in on her. I was furious with myself and freaking out about how sick she'd become."

"But she's okay," Piper says, her voice wobbly. "Whitney's okay, right?"

"Physically, yeah. Now, anyway. Medical abortions are statistically safer than childbirth. I've done a ton of reading on this stuff since it went down. She was just really unlucky. She hemorrhaged, and then there was an infection." I look at my hands, wrapped around Piper's. "She might've died if her mom hadn't found her when she did. And what was I doing? Fucking sleeping."

"Henry, there's no way you could've predicted what would happen. Even if you'd been awake. Even if you'd been with her."

"Maybe not. But still…the what-ifs are brutal."

I made it a point to be around for Whitney in those weeks after she was discharged. Like being compassionate and accommodating after the fact could make up for everything that had gone wrong between us, not to mention the health complications she experienced. Every time I looked at her, guilt ate me up.

"I wish it had been different," I say. "Not that Whit and I had stayed together. Not that she'd stayed pregnant. I just wish the end had been cleaner. It's a shitty feeling, knowing that she's dealing with the full burden of what happened while I walked away unscathed."

"I don't think you're unscathed," Piper says gently.

322

"I am compared to her."

"It's a loss for both of you, though. You can't measure yours against hers."

"Sure I can. It all happened to her—she was pregnant, she was sick, she was left behind. I'm a witness—a witness and a runaway. But...I'm still messed up."

"You have a huge heart, Henry. It'd be weird if you *weren't* messed up. You can't force yourself to get over something like this. Healing takes time. A lot of time."

I squeeze her hand. "I get the feeling you're speaking from experience."

She shrugs. "After my parents' accident, I spent ages trying to sort through what happened. I was sure I'd done something to anger the universe. There had to be a reason Mom and Dad had been taken from me. I spent hours with the counselor at school and months with a therapist Tati found for me, but nothing they said stuck. I felt I was somehow at fault—that was the only way I could make sense of something so senseless."

I'm blown away by how similar her past mindset is to my current mind fuck. I hate what she's been through, but I'm feeling a hell of a lot less alone.

It's wild how powerful empathy can be.

"That line of thinking," I say. "How'd you get past it?"

"Gabi. She convinced me that what had happened to my parents wasn't cosmic punishment. *Sometimes life is just really unfair,* she said one night after I'd spent hours crying. Somehow, her simple logic rose above months of irrational self-blame."

"She sounds smart."

"She totally is. So, Henry, I'm going to tell you what she told me: Sometimes life is just really unfair."

I smile. She's chipping away at the wall self-appointed culpability has spent two seasons building. "I just wish there were something I could do to turn things around for myself, and especially for Whit. She's still really struggling."

Piper's expression is serious, introspective. "I wonder if she keeps reaching out to you because she wants to reclaim the person she was before all of this. Or maybe she's looking for permission to move on from the loss. Or maybe she's waiting to be shown that she's still worthy of the life she wants, even after suffering through this terrible thing."

My mom has expressed similar theories and doled out comparable advice. For whatever reason, though, her words have never sunk in the way Piper's are now.

"If I could go back in time," I say, "I'd do a million things differently."

Softly, she says, "Me too."

Piper

HENRY'S HISTORY WITH WHITNEY—*WHIT*—isn't the stuff of average high school romances.

They could've had a *baby* together.

I can't help but wish he'd told me this story before now. It's heavy—the hurt he's endured, the connection he shares with her, regardless of whether they're together or apart. Trauma has so obviously marked him, leaving a scar on his soul.

This layer, this *secret*…I almost feel like I'm meeting him for the first time.

Though who am I to toss stones? I live within the cold confines of a glass house.

I should've told him the truth about what happened with Damon weeks ago.

"Hey," he says. "You okay?"

I nod, but emotionally, I'm wrung out.

"You want something to drink? I can run inside."

"Yeah, thank you. Water? Or soda?"

My voice sounds froggy, like I've spent the night screaming through a concert.

He watches me for a minute, worry pinching his features, then leaves me on our chair and jogs toward the house. The windows are alight, vibrating with a bass beat. I catch sight of Gabi inside with Anna and Michaela. She laughs, tossing her braids over her shoulder. I haven't seen her so carefree since before she and Damon got together.

I'm so glad she's rid of him.

Henry's been gone only a minute when his phone chimes again.

I regard it like it's a scorpion, tail raised, ready to strike.

Don't do it, I tell myself, but holy balls. How am I supposed to *not* look?

I glance back at the house. I can see Henry in the kitchen. He's getting a drink. For me. Like a gentleman.

And here I am, seriously considering invading his privacy.

Another chime; another text.

I nudge his wallet out of the way so I can slip his phone off the table. His background is the picture we took together at the marine park, in front of the fountain, which…how adorable. It's almost enough to make me put down his phone, respect his boundaries, trust that he's handling things with his ex in the best possible way. But our faces are partially obscured by text messages, stacked atop each other. I can only see one, and it is in fact from Whitney.

WHITNEY

Thank you for saying you'll try again. See you soon.

There are heart emojis, a whole slew of them.

Yesterday, he said wanted to stay in Sugar Bay. He said it'd be cool to spend senior year together. He said he liked me a lot. And he just poured his heart out to me, holding tight to my hands, checking to make sure *I* was okay when he was done recounting one of the hardest experiences of his life.

I read the text again. This can't be right.

Whitney must be confused.

But...she doesn't sound confused.

Henry told her he'd try again? Try *them* again? And she'll see him soon?

It's right here in a text bubble.

I put his phone back on the table, screen down, the way he left it. And then I get up from the chair and cross the yard toward the house.

Is Henry playing me?

It's a preposterous idea—utterly incomprehensible—and yet I'm suddenly nauseated.

I sneak inside, slipping past his turned back. He's caught up in a conversation with Jayden, two bottles of water tucked under his arm, oblivious to the fact that I just caught him in...in what can only be a massive lie.

In the empty hallway, I stop to lean against the wall, intent on getting my blood pressure under control. Bending, I brace my

327

hands against my knees. I focus on breathing, on counting the tiles that lead to the front door. There are goose bumps on my arms, and the music is so loud my head's starting to pound.

I need to go back outside, where it's warm and quiet and dark.

The front door opens, getting caught on the woven doormat, wrinkling it before detaching and swinging clear. I raise my gaze to see who's rolling in so late.

My heart claws its way into my throat as Damon walks into the house.

Henry

BY THE TIME I SHAKE off Jayden—who seems like an okay guy, actually—I find that Piper has ditched our chair. I grab my stuff off the table, giving Whitney's latest message a cursory glance: Thank you for saying you'll try again. See you soon.

Jesus H.

It's gonna be a nightmare dealing with the fallout of my stupid deception.

Gabi comes through the back door as I'm about to open it, cider in hand. She's close to my height, with long legs, long hair, and long lashes. She's like gallery art: striking and intimidating.

"Where's our girl?" she asks.

"Not sure. I figured she'd gone inside."

"I haven't seen her. Bathroom, maybe." She twists the top off her cider, then takes a sip. She's hard to read, but if she's Piper's best friend, she's got to be all right. "Don't like to drink?" she asks, gesturing to the waters I snagged from the fridge.

"Nope."

"You've rubbed off on Piper. She passed up Hudson's bar."

I shrug. "She does what she wants."

"Isn't that the truth. God, I've missed her." She swallows a sip of cider, then says, "I can't believe I let Damon come between us. What he did to her...I could castrate him."

Damon's given Piper shit more than once this summer, which is enough to make me want to jump him in a dark alley. But what Gabi just said makes me think there's more to the story than obnoxious jokes and pervy gestures.

I meet her gaze. "She doesn't ever talk about him. I don't like to push, but sometimes I worry about her." It's a knife to the heart, remembering the times her eyes clouded over, her muscles went rigid, her hands trembled. "She can be so evasive, you know? I don't want to cross any lines, so tell me to go to hell if I'm overstepping, but could you fill me in on the Damon story?"

Gabi takes another pull of cider, considering. And then: "He and I started going out in January. Piper thought I could do better. So did my parents. But there was something between us. A spark to outshine the haters. At least, that's what I thought. I had people over the night after school let out, and things got kind of wild. Piper went really hard. It was after midnight when I walked in on her and Damon. They were kissing—at least, that's what I thought was going on. But I should've known Piper

330

wasn't into it," she says, her voice unsteady now. "She was hardly coherent, barely able to stand on her own. Still, Damon made it sound like she'd been all over him. It wasn't until a few days ago when Piper told me that she'd said no. That she'd tried to push him away. That he wouldn't let her go."

Spots of crimson flash in my vision as I think of Damon, his brother, and his dad at the restaurant. He's an asshole and a bully—I've seen that firsthand—and now, after this glimpse into the true darkness of his nature, I don't give a flying fuck about the hardships that made him who he is. I'd like to smash something unyielding into his face.

"And you believed him? Piper would never do that to you—to anyone."

"I know," Gabi says miserably. "It was easier to take Damon at his word than to accept that I'd spent five months with someone who'd cheat on me. Worse, someone who'd take advantage of my best friend."

I tighten my hands into fists, for the first time truly understanding the expression *seeing red*. I'm seconds from projecting my pent-up frustration on Gabi, a girl I've only just met. I know that's so, so shitty, but at the moment, I don't care.

"Take advantage?" I repeat, my voice low and tight. "He *assaulted* her. Let's not sugarcoat it. Piper sure as shit doesn't have that luxury."

I leave her on the patio, her eyes brimming with tears.

I almost wish Damon were here tonight.

I'm a can of gasoline waiting for a spark.

Piper

DAMON SEES ME.

I'm all he sees.

He must've found a way to skip the Montgomery trip. He must've come looking for Gabi. He's probably hoping to coerce her into getting back together with him. Or maybe he's here to find a new victim. Someone isolated and vulnerable.

Like I am right now.

He strides toward me, all swagger and heavy footfalls.

I want to turn away. I want to run.

My feet have grown roots.

"Piper." His voice is deep and confident. He's used to getting what he wants, either by asking or taking.

Henry's probably back outside, looking for me. Gabi's gossiping in the kitchen with Anna and Michaela. Hudson and Jayden and the rest of the guys are preoccupied with Flip Cup, clueless that their buddy has arrived, ignorant about who he truly is.

"Leave me alone," I say, managing a half turn and a clumsy step before he catches my wrist and yanks me back.

He doesn't let go.

"It's over between Gabi and me," he says. "Because of you."

"No. Because of *you*."

"She hates me, thanks to your lies."

"They *aren't* lies." There's grit behind my words. Telling Tati and Gabi about those horrific moments back in May banished the uncertainties that tormented me in the weeks that followed. I know I didn't do anything wrong.

"You overpowered me. I said no. You refused to hear me."

I try to pull away, but his grip tightens.

"Let go of me, Damon."

He forces me backward, until my spine presses into the wall. "You're going to fix this." He pulls my wrist up and traps my hand between us. His forearm comes to rest on the wall by my head, and I know that if someone were to walk by, this would look reciprocal.

"If you don't let me go, I'll scream."

He laughs, quietly maniacal—a paralyzing sound. "Go ahead," he says, eyes traveling down, down, down.

I look where he's looking: my suntanned chest, sprinkled with freckles; the rapid rise and fall of my ribs; the swell of cleavage accentuated by my dress's neckline; my shoulder strap, slipping down my arm again.

"No one will believe you," he says. "The way you look, the

way you drink, the way you act…they'll jump to the same conclusion they did last time."

It's terrifying that he could be right.

He touches my hair. His face is so close to mine, it's hard to focus on any one of his features. But I catch his smile as he says, "Now that it's over between Gabi and me, you and I ought to give things a shot."

"I'd rather *die*," I say, trying and failing to twist my arm free.

Somewhere, a door slams. Footsteps close in, audible even above the music and the laughter and the whirring in my ears.

A flash of movement catches Damon's attention. He shifts back enough that I can pull in a full breath. He doesn't let me go, but his expression changes from cocksure to ruffled. I follow his gaze. Henry's standing in the hallway.

His eyes cloud over.

Does he think I'm complicit in what's happening?

My heart shrivels.

Gabi comes around the corner, nearly bumping into Henry. She stops short. "Damon! Let go of her!"

He acts as if she hasn't spoken, but Henry doesn't. He zeros in on the way Damon's gripping my wrist. He sets his jaw, his expression contorting into one of ruthlessness.

"Get away from her," he says, ice cold.

Damon's a pig, but he's not an idiot.

He frees me, taking a step backward. He puts his hands in the air like he's innocent. Like he's been misunderstood. He's almost convincing, but his bluster returns too quickly.

334

He snickers.

One second Henry's across the hall, and the next he's in Damon's face, bunching the front of his shirt in his fist, slamming him against the wall.

"I fail to see the humor," he seethes. "She doesn't want you to touch her. She doesn't want you anywhere near her. Got it?"

"Yeah, bro," Damon says, his words sounding choked. "Got it."

"I'm not your *bro*," Henry spits out, releasing his shirt. "If you put your hands on her again—or on any other girl who's not enthusiastically encouraging your attention—you and I are gonna talk. Don't misunderstand: It won't end well for you."

"Yeah, got it." Damon's cheeks, his neck, and the tips of his ears are an angry red. "Now get the fuck away from me."

Henry takes a step back, swinging an arm toward the kitchen in the most disingenuous welcome gesture I've ever seen. But Hudson and Jayden, along with Anna and Michaela, have come to check out the commotion.

Hudson steps toward Damon. "You need to go, dude."

Damon's jaw drops. He hooks a thumb toward Henry. "You're taking his side?"

"I'm taking Piper's side," Hudson says. "Gabi's too. They don't want you around, and now I've got an idea why. I'm not cool with you being here if the girls are uncomfortable."

Damon huffs. But Hudson's glaring, and Jayden looks like he's got homicide in his heart. Despite my trembling hands and imminent tears, their support shines a warm glow through me.

"Damon," Hudson says. "Go."

Damon turns for the front door, meekly at first. As he moves past, though, he drills me with a glare and mutters, "Bitch."

Henry lurches forward, grabs the neck of his shirt, and whirls him around. He cocks his arm back, then crushes his fist into Damon's face.

I'm *stunned*.

Damon staggers, hands flying up to cover his nose, which is spurting blood all over his shirt and his shoes and the floor. He stands there, dazed, while the rest of us hold a collective breath, waiting to see if he'll retaliate.

He doesn't, which is a surprise, even to my hazy mind. He's a wrestler. He's aggressive. He's arrogant as hell. But Henry just proved that he's a badass, and I'm pretty sure he can count on Hudson and Jayden for backup. Damon must realize the same; he gives his head a disgusted shake and walks out the front door, leaving a trail of blood in his wake.

Gabi rushes to my side, linking her arm through mine. "God, Piper. Are you okay?"

"I'm fine," I whisper.

The biggest lie.

Henry's breathing hard, shaking out his hand, avoiding my gaze.

I should go to him. That's what everybody's expecting.

He defended me, but *after* he lied about his ex-girlfriend.

I shiver, fingertips to toes.

Gabi brushes loose curls from my clammy forehead. "You sure you're all right?"

336

I nod, rubbing my wrist, trying to erase the ghost of Damon's grip.

Anna and Michaela go back into the kitchen, talking shit about Damon. Jayden inspects Henry's hand; his knuckles are already puffy. Hudson passes him a tea towel packed with ice. He leans against the wall, holding the ice to his hand, looking dead on his feet. Jayden and Hudson each pull on a pair of yellow kitchen gloves and scrub Damon's blood from the floor.

As I watch, frenzied laughter fizzes up my throat. I don't know why. I'm scared and sad and not even a little bit amused. Choking the cackles back, I make a sound like a sob.

They all look at me: Gabi, Hudson, Jayden, Henry, their concern encircling me like a fog.

I turn to Gabi, clasping my hands to hide their shaking. "Walk me home?"

"Piper," Henry says.

I leave the house with Gabi.

I leave him behind.

Henry

I STAY AT HUDSON'S WITH a towel full of ice pressed to my throbbing hand.

He and Jayden are amped, rehashing what happened, tossing out compliments on my form and my force.

"Dude, you should box," Hudson says, throwing quick one-two punches into the air.

"Yeah, not really my thing." I don't mention that before tonight, I've never hit anything but a punching bag. I don't tell them that I feel like shit about clocking Damon—not because he didn't deserve it, but because I lost control. Acting brashly, going all hypermasculine...that's not me. At least, it didn't used to be.

It's hard to breathe in this house. All I can see is Damon and Piper. His hands caging her in. Her face contorted with fear. I keep remembering Damon—that *prick*—showered in blood.

I last another few minutes before I bail.

I walk home, wondering if this is it—the end of Piper and me. She's never looked at me like she did in that hallway.

Like I betrayed her.

Like she loathes me.

I can't figure out why.

I take the elevator to the eighth floor of the east tower, checking out my hand on the way. Gingerly, I make a fist. I stretch out my fingers and rotate my wrist. My knuckles are swollen, and my whole hand hurts like a bitch, but there doesn't seem to be any serious damage. It was infinitely stupid, though, hitting that guy. The confrontation could have escalated into a full-on fight. I could have fucked up my hand permanently.

But god, it felt good.

When I walk into the apartment, something's off.

The kitchen counter looks a lot like the one at Hudson's, littered with bottles. Except the mostly drained liquors here look like they're top-shelf. There are three—two rums and a tequila—along with an unopened two-liter bottle of Sprite and most of a jug of orange juice.

Dad started mixing drinks, then settled on booze neat?

My Pumas stick to the floor as I move into the kitchen. The fridge is wide-open. I bump the door closed. There are a few glasses in the sink and a half-eaten pepperoni pizza on the table. A slice with one bite taken from its crust is sitting on the tabletop.

Jesus H.

Where the hell is Davis?

I trudge to the back of the apartment. At my bedroom, I

339

pause to toss my phone onto the bed, which looks pretty freaking appealing right now. Then, aggravated—why can't Dad be an adult tonight of all nights?—I head for his room.

The air stinks of sweat and vomit. His bed's disheveled but empty.

My pulse vibrates through my body.

Where is he?

My heart crash-lands when I spot him. First his feet, then his legs, supine on the floor, sticking out of the bathroom doorway.

I bolt toward him.

He's breathing, but he's out cold, white as the porcelain tub. There's puke in the toilet bowl, running down its side, splattered on the floor. And shit, there's blood. Enough to make me lightheaded and positive I can't handle this on my own.

Dad's phone sits on the countertop. I grab it and punch in the code he shared with me weeks ago—the month and day of my birthday—to unlock the screen.

Instinct says to call 911, but I force myself to take a breath, to take stock of the situation. Because what if I'm overreacting? There's puke, but drunk people throw up sometimes. It's probably good that he's getting the alcohol out of his system. There's blood, but not so much that he's going to bleed to death, and I still can't see any cuts or scrapes. Do I really need a parade of paramedics traipsing through the apartment?

He gives a jolt that looks painful, then rolls onto his side and spits up foamy liquid. The back of his head is busted, the skin split and oozing. His hair's matted with blood.

340

My stomach turns over.

I call the only person I can think of who will definitely know what to do.

I'm surprised when Tati answers. As far as I know, she hasn't spoken to Dad since their fallout. But it's late, and she's practically a parent. She must have a sixth sense when it comes to things going wrong in the dead of night. I barrel into a hoarse description of what I see.

"I'll be right there," she tells me.

She knocks on the door not three minutes later, hair in a ponytail, wearing leggings and a Blue Wahoos T-shirt. She hurries to Dad's room. I stand in the bathroom doorway while she hovers over him. She's all business, evaluating the gash on the back of his head, pressing two fingers to his neck to feel his pulse.

"How much did he drink?" she asks when she's done counting.

"I don't know—I wasn't here. But the kitchen…a lot, I think."

She bites her lip, studying Dad's pallid face. "Do you know how long he's been out?"

"No idea. Jesus, Tati. Is he going to be okay?"

"I'm not sure. I'm not so worried about the cut. It doesn't look deep. What concerns me are the unknowns: the amount of alcohol in his system and how hard he hit his head. He could have a concussion."

I drag a hand over my face. "What should I do?"

She looks at me, her expression drenched in sympathy. "We need to call for help."

The way she says *we* makes my chest tight.

I turn away.

I dial 911.

Piper

I'M IN THE KITCHEN THE next morning, scavenging for breakfast, when Tati walks through the front door.

I hadn't realized she wasn't in the apartment. She was home when Gabi and I came in last night, on the couch watching *The Notebook* with Mom's knitted blanket and a box of tissues her only company. Gabi sat down to talk to her while I went into the bathroom to wash my face. I ended up on the floor, crying into a bath towel until my throat ached, leaving splotches of mascara on the white terry cloth.

Tati will be pissed.

Her outfit is uncharacteristically sloppy: a Wahoos T-shirt she must've inherited from Mr. Marketing and leggings that are usually reserved for lounging at home. Loose wisps of hair hang in her face. She looks exhausted.

"Are you okay?" I ask, forgetting all about the recent silence between us.

"Not really." She pulls her I NEED MY SPACE! mug from the cabinet and fills it with cold coffee left over from yesterday. "Davis was admitted to the hospital last night."

"Oh. God. I didn't know. Henry and I—"

I'm not sure how to explain what happened at Hudson's. My heart hurts every time I think about what I saw on Henry's phone, and how he let me walk out without even trying to salvage what we've spent the summer building.

Tati waves me off. "He found his dad unconscious. You need to get in touch with him."

"I don't think he'd want—"

"Piper, don't be petty." She sets her coffee down and crosses her arms. "If you care about him at all, be there for him. He's struggling. Trust me, I'm not the person he wants sitting beside him in a hospital waiting room."

There it is again, her assumption that *I'm* the problem.

When Gabi found me crying in the bathroom last night, she sank down beside me and grasped my hand. She whispered reassuring words. She rubbed my back and wiped my tears and put toothpaste on my toothbrush. She stood by while I scrubbed my teeth and washed my face for real, then tucked me into bed.

"I'll stay until you fall asleep," she promised.

Where was Tati?

"He could call me," I tell her.

I wait for her to ask why he didn't.

344

I'm begging her to invest in me. To love me.

She says, "Why are you always so selfish?"

She picks up her coffee and walks out of the kitchen.

Henry

LAST NIGHT, TATI INSISTED ON following the ambulance in her car, then stuck around at the hospital even after the ER doctor shared her diagnosis—alcohol poisoning, head laceration, minor concussion—and her plan for treatment: oxygen therapy and a steady drip of fluids, vitamins, and glucose.

"We used a few staples to close the wound on his head," Dr. Bowen told Tati and me with zero inflection. "He's going to be sore when he wakes up, but he's lucky. Drinking as much as he did can be life-threatening."

After she left, I let my head fall into my hands and blew out a heavy breath.

I stayed that way a long time.

Tati sat beside me, silent, for the duration.

"You should go home," I told her sometime around two in the morning. "You've done more than enough."

She looked at me like I'd insulted her. "I'm not going anywhere."

A long time passed before she spoke again, quietly and with a lot less poise. "I'm afraid this is my fault."

I gaped at her. "How do you figure?"

"Your dad came by last night. He wanted to talk things out." She lowered her voice, leaning in a little. "He'd been drinking. Too much. I can't enable that kind of behavior. I can't subject my little sister to it, especially considering what happened to our parents. Also, I don't have the emotional energy to act as someone else's mother. So I told him to go home. Two hours later, you called. I knew in my gut that something bad had happened."

"God, Tati." Her parents—Piper's parents—were killed by a drunk driver. It's no wonder she has no tolerance for Davis's bullshit. I swallowed around the stone that had been lodged in my throat since I'd walked in on Damon cornering Piper. "I'm sorry he bothered you. I'm sorry he—"

Lost control, is what I was going to say, but is that even it?

Is Davis capable of controlling his drinking?

"No need to apologize," Tati told me. "You're not to blame for your father's actions."

"Yeah, well, he's not up for making things right at the moment. I hope you know that tonight, and whatever happened between you guys last week...that's not my dad. I mean, it is, these days. But he's better than that. Or he used to be."

The truth is, I hardly knew Davis before this summer. The

347

last six weeks, he hasn't been authentic. He puts on this cool-guy facade that's so overblown it'd be comical if it weren't so tragic. But he's not a jerk at his core. He's lonely and possibly a little sad, and he needs help. I knew, sitting there in the waiting room, that he probably needed more help than this tiny hospital was gonna be able to offer him.

"I've known your dad a while now," Tati said.

"Since Christmas. Piper told me."

She smiled, sheepish. "He's compassionate, driven, and funny. But it seems like he's losing that version of himself."

I nodded somberly. She'd put my worries into words. It felt like permission to be scared. To be pissed. To ask for help. Permission to demand that *Dad* ask for help.

She patted my arm. "He and I need some time apart, but you're welcome to call me anytime. I'm always around if you need someone."

"Thanks," I said, hoping she understood how much I meant it.

I miss my mom, but last night, Tati was a pretty okay substitute. *Piper's lucky.*

Like she was listening in on my thoughts, Tati said, "Have you talked to my sister?"

I shook my head. "I don't want to bother her with this."

She gave me a mystified look. "She wouldn't feel bothered. She'd want to be here with us. With *you*." She sighed, closing her eyes a minute. When she opened them, she looked bone-tired. "She came home from Hudson's with Gabi. Why, when she went there with you?"

348

Because a lot of crazy shit went down, I thought.

But I had no idea how much Piper had shared with Tati, and I wasn't about to tell her story without her approval. I went with, "I figured out some stuff about why she and Gabi spent most of the summer not talking."

"Ah," Tati said. "The Damon story."

So she did know.

"That guy's a—" *Fucking jackass,* I wanted to say. But talking to Tati felt too much like talking to a parent, so I finished a lot less colorfully, "Troublemaker."

She laughed without humor. "He should be confined to a cage with a dead bolt and no key."

"Agreed." I held out my hand, knuckles starting to turn purple. "He ran into my fist."

This time, she laughed genuinely. "To think that your dad's always going on about how wholesome you are."

I gave a self-deprecating shrug. "Nobody's perfect."

"Chivalrous is better than perfect. That little shit needed to be put in his place."

"That's how I saw it too." This thing with my dad has been terrible, but learning what happened to Piper, then witnessing a near sequel has been unbearable.

"Not gonna lie," I said to Tati, "watching Piper leave with Gabi sucked."

She gave me a sympathetic smile. "I've watched her leave a lot of times. Running from hurtful situations is how she copes. I'm not making excuses for her—she can be insufferable—but she's

349

a lot like those sea turtles she loves so much. Protective shell, soft and vulnerable underneath."

We fell quiet. Tati moved to the other side of the room and lay down across two chairs, curled up with her arm crooked under her head, eyes falling closed. I was running on adrenaline and dealing with major sensory overload. The hospital lived and breathed, doctors and nurses hustling by, people filtering through the waiting room, beeps and alarms and intercom pages echoing through the corridor. It was busy, considering the hour.

Through the high windows, I watched the sky slowly lighten.

Tati startled awake when Dr. Bowen arrived with an update.

"Mr. Walker is doing well," she announced. "Rehydrated. Breathing stably. Still resting. You'll be able to see him soon."

"Thank you," Tati said.

While I was relieved, a new sort of dread eddied around me. What was I gonna say to my dad, this man who was supposed to shelter me but had scared the ever-loving shit out of me instead?

After the doctor walked out, Tati turned to me. "I'm going to head home. I need to check in with Piper. But I can come back if you need me. I'm a phone call away."

She squeezed my shoulder, and then she was gone.

Piper

TATI SPENDS THE BETTER PART of the morning locked in her bedroom, and I loiter restlessly in the kitchen, worrying about Davis and Henry. I hear the echo of my sister's earlier question: *Why are you always so selfish?*

I text Gabi: Am I selfish?

Her response is immediate. No. Don't let Tati mess with your head. She sends a series of kissy-face emojis, followed by, Gotta run. Piano lesson. Talk later.

I pocket my phone, thinking about how good it is of her to jump straight to reassuring me. But is she full of best friend shit?

I take a mental step back and try to analyze myself objectively. I'm curious. Devoted. Naive, maybe. Spontaneous. I'm defensive, which I want to be better about. Tati has said I'm a dreamer, an idealist, a romantic, which is flattering. I've got a complex when it comes to being left behind, that's for sure.

I wonder how Henry would describe me.

I'm not sure it matters anymore. After last night, I have no idea where we stand. That text from Whitney has been bouncing around in my head all morning, and I've yet to make sense of it. Now that my initial fury has lessened, rationality has elbowed its way in. It's possible I misconstrued Whitney's words. It's possible she misconstrued Henry's.

Or maybe Henry is phenomenally shady. Maybe he's spent the summer stringing me along—using me. Whitney *and* me.

I just can't make that theory stick.

I *know* him.

He and I...what we have is special.

Still, maybe it'd be best if he went back to Spokane in a couple weeks. His mom is there. Whitney and their tangled history are there. Maybe they *should* get back together. Maybe they owe each other the time and effort. Maybe they're meant to be, soul mates. I want to accept that as a possibility. I want to be gracious. I want to put Henry's well-being ahead of my own.

But the thought of him *not here* makes me feel like I'm descending into darkness.

I drag myself outside for a walk.

I'm spiraling. I don't have the bandwidth to argue with Tati, and my bedroom reminds me too much of Henry now to serve as a sanctuary. I miss the Marine Conservation Park; I wish I could take refuge there for a few hours.

Instead, I shuffle down the sidewalk, dazed and disassociated, like I'm hovering overhead, watching a raven-haired girl wander without purpose.

She looks sad and tired.

She looks like she needs a hug.

She looks so very lost.

Henry

MY PHONE'S NEARLY DEAD, BUT now that Tati has left and I've got an update on Dad, I've got to call my mom.

She answers, sounding as worn out as I feel. She just got home from a shift, she tells me before I give her the condensed version of the last several hours. I wrap up with the doctor's latest report, making sure my tone's as confident as hers was.

"He's sleeping now," I finish. "He's good."

Through my account, Mom's kept quiet. Now she erupts.

"He is *not* good, Henry. Nothing about what you just told me is *good*. My god, will he ever grow up?" She's obviously not expecting an answer and follows up immediately with another question. "Has this happened before?"

"No. Well…not really. I mean, he has a drink now and then."

"Henry. Don't you dare cover for him. How often?"

I tip my head back to rest against the wall. "Every day."

"How many drinks?"

Jesus—why do I feel like I'm tattling? "I don't know. It varies. Several, usually."

"But nothing like last night?"

"There was one other time…it wasn't as bad, but he passed out."

She groans. "I could kill him for putting you through this. You can't stay the year with him. You have to come home. Now."

"Come on, Mom. It's not that serious." Even as the words leave my mouth, I know they're bullshit. My dad drank himself into a stupor and let his kid find him unconscious and bleeding in a puddle of puke.

It's pretty fucking serious.

"What kind of parent would I be if I let you continue living with him?"

"This isn't about what kind of parent you are. This is about Dad. I'm his kid—his *only* kid. If I leave him alone, he's gonna get worse. I won't abandon him when he needs me."

"Henry—"

"Mom. You were cool with me staying in Florida last time we talked. You said it was my decision. I want to stay. And anyway, my birthday's in two months. If you make me come home now, I'll just fly back when I turn eighteen."

She goes quiet. I picture her at the kitchen table, still in her scrubs, with a mug of tea. It's rare that she and I disagree, even rarer that I'm downright defiant. But she's not heartless. I know I'm getting through to her.

She says, "Your dad's got a problem."

"I get it. But I want to give him a chance to work on it."

"Two weeks. If there aren't changes between now and then—changes I'll discuss with him privately—you're coming home. I'm going to trust you to be honest with me. If he backslides, if anything even close to what you went through last night happens again, I need you to tell me."

"I hear you. I'll keep you posted."

Dr. Bowen pokes her head in. She sees me on the phone and lifts a brow.

"I've got to go," I tell Mom. "His doctor just came in. I'll call you later."

When I've hung up, Dr. Bowen says, "He's awake. Do you want to see him?"

Piper

LATE IN THE AFTERNOON, I wake up on the couch, disoriented.

The sun's hanging low in the sky. My mouth is dry and my forehead is clammy. I've been covered in the cherished ocean-blue knit blanket. I sit up, folding it back. My sister's in the nearest armchair, holding her trusty mug in both hands.

"I want to talk to you," she says.

"Give me a sec." I go into the kitchen, guzzle a full glass of water, then take a can of Red Bull from the fridge. I grab an apple too, because I skipped lunch in favor of walking to nowhere. If Tati and I are going to throw down again, I need sustenance. I fall into a corner of the couch, snack at the ready. "How's Davis?"

"Improving. Henry's sure been through a lot."

"I haven't talked to him," I admit. "Because I'm scared, *not* because I'm selfish."

I brace for judgment. Instead, Tati leans forward and says, "I know you're not selfish. I shouldn't have said that. You're a teenager, and you've had a rough go of it. You're doing pretty well, considering."

I pick my jaw up off my lap, then give her a hesitant smile.

"Piper," she says, looking remarkably serious for someone who just paid her little sister a compliment. "I need to tell you something."

I pop the top of my Red Bull, then change my mind and set the can on the table. "Okay...?"

"You think I feel burdened. You think I'm stuck with you. You think Mom and Dad heaped this responsibility on me against my will and that I'm unhappy as a result. Is that right?"

It sounds extra rotten when she says it all aloud that way, but not untrue. "I mean, that's the general impression I've gotten over the years, yeah."

"Then I'm very sorry. Rarely does my unhappiness have anything to do with you. But I get frustrated and take it out on you. I'm not proud of that."

In seven years, Tati has never once apologized to me. For a moment, the world feels askew, like I woke up in a parallel universe. But no. My sister's sipping coffee, and I'm wearing my favorite denim cutoffs, and the eucalyptus-scented candle that's lived a thousand lives on our coffee table flickers merrily. I'm where I'm supposed to be. Except that for the first time, Tati and I are on equal footing—two sisters engaged in a mature conversation.

358

"I read somewhere that you're your worst self with the people you love most," I tell her. "Because you trust that they'll forgive you. You know they'll be there for you regardless."

She smiles. "If that's true, then you and I must love each other *a lot*."

"I do love you, Tati. Even though I'm not always the best at showing it."

"I love you too. So much that I think it's time you know..." She purses her lips for a moment, then says, "Piper, Mom and Dad didn't choose me to be your guardian. I fought for the privilege."

I furrow my brow, then shake my head. "But...their will."

She leaves her chair to join me on the couch, turning so we're face-to-face. "I don't know where you got the idea that they had a will, but they didn't. I'm not sure why not. Probably because they never in a million years imagined that they'd die together, especially when you were still a minor. After they passed, Grandma and Grandpa assumed they'd take custody of you. That made sense on paper, I guess, because they'd raised a daughter. And they had the money to provide for you."

For several months after my parents passed, my grandparents loitered in Florida, staying in a hotel near our house. I'd always known Grandma and Grandpa to be warm and funny, but during that time, they were overwrought, short with me, and even shorter with my sister. I figured their behavior and the exceptionally long visit were due to grief and the stress of helping to manage my parents' affairs.

"If Grandma and Grandpa wanted to be my guardians, how come…"

"Custody doesn't automatically go to grandparents in situations where there's no will," Tati says. "It was up to the court to decide guardianship based on your best interests. Grandma and Grandpa filed a petition. I did too."

She lets her declaration hang in the air while I gape at her, hugging my middle like the wind's been knocked out of me.

"They were furious with me," she goes on. "There was a lot of arguing, mostly while you were at school. On that, we agreed: we wouldn't bring our dispute into your world."

"But if you wanted to take care of me, why wouldn't they let you?"

"There were a lot of reasons. I was twenty-five. I had no idea how to parent, and I was just getting on my feet financially. They wanted to keep you close—you're a piece of Mom. But nothing they said dissuaded me."

"But…*why*? Why were you so determined?"

"Because you're my sister. I love you more than anyone in the world. And Grandma and Grandpa wanted to take you back to Albany. They would have moved you away from Gabi and the beach, enrolled you in a new school. I thought it was cruel to rip you away from everything you knew, especially after you'd already lost so much. Mom and Dad's memory is here. If they couldn't bring you up in Sugar Bay, I wanted to do it." She shrugs. "The judge saw it my way."

I'm still staring at her, trying to keep my breath steady as my perception of the past is reshuffled like a deck of playing cards.

"After the custody hearing, Grandma and Grandpa left. I know they've kept in touch with you and I'm glad about that, but they've hardly spoken to me. I don't think they'll ever forgive me."

I reassess the hand I've been dealt. My grandparents' rushed departure. Their refusal to return to Florida. The Christmas and birthday cards they send, generous checks enclosed, made out solely to me.

"Do you regret it?" I ask quietly.

"Piper, god. Of course not. I miss them and I wish things could be different, but I'd choose my life with you no matter the consequences."

"That's kind of funny, because I've always felt like I ruined your life."

"I have *never* said that."

"You don't have to. Our apartment, your job, your relationships, *me*—this isn't what you imagined for yourself."

"You're right, it's not. But that doesn't mean I have regrets. I don't like my job, but a lot of people would say the same. And you have nothing to do with my relationships, or lack thereof. Do I wish you'd keep your room clean and stick to curfew? Obviously. But you're smart and determined and cool. I like to think I played a part in some of that. You bring me a lot of joy." She sets her mug on the table and wraps me in a hug. "Honestly, Piper. You're the part of my life I'm most proud of. I'm sorry for the times I've made you think otherwise."

361

I hug her hard and say, weepy, "I'll clean my room when we're done here."

She laughs, letting me go. "Maybe when you're finished, you can call Henry? He's upset about his dad, but he's *very* upset about whatever went on between the two of you."

I frown, raising my mental ramparts. What business is it of hers?

She gives me an encouraging smile. Her sincerity infiltrates my defenses, and I make a resolution: From now on, I'm going to be real with my sister.

I tell her about Henry and Whitney. The text I peeked at. The sorrow that swallowed me when he let me leave with Gabi, and never came after me.

"I can't forget his expression when he saw me with Damon," I say. "It was half a second, but it was like…he wondered, Tati. I've never felt less understood."

"I get why you're upset," she says. Not *don't be needy* or *quit being dramatic.* "But, like you said, it was half a second. He must've been surprised or hurt. He didn't have much information to go on. And he's a seventeen-year-old boy. He's kind and smart and principled, but he's not immune to messing up." She lifts her brows, a little smug. "And didn't he redeem himself by punching Damon's sleazy face?"

I give her a reticent smile. "He told you about that?"

"He showed me his busted hand. Generally, I think it's gross when dudes fight. But for him to step up and protect you that way…he's got it bad for you, Piper."

My cheeks warm because god, this is a weird conversation to have with my sister. Still, her good sense supersedes my hasty presumptions. Now that she's laid it out so rationally, it's hard to deny: Henry cares about me.

"What about the text?" I ask. "He told Whitney he was planning to go back to Spokane. He told me the opposite. You don't think he's playing me?"

"I don't think he has it in him to play you, but you won't know until you have a conversation with him." She reaches over to squeeze my hand. "I'm not going to bug you about it again. I know you'll do the right thing."

The right thing? *Me?*

I cringe, hanging on to her hand, hoping her benevolence lasts through what I've got to say next. "Yeah, speaking of doing the right thing…now's probably the time to tell you that I'm unemployed."

Henry

DAD LOOKS LIKE SHIT.

His hair's matted and greasy, and there are half-moon shadows beneath his eyes. There's a tube in his left arm connected to a bag of clear fluid. He's wearing the hospital's obligatory gown, and a starchy-looking blanket covers his lower half.

He gives me a hangdog smile, raising his arm, hand curled into a fist. I bump his knuckles with my good hand before dragging a chair toward the bed.

The TV's on a baseball game, which is set to mute. The Marlins are winning.

"I'm okay," Dad says, his voice raw. "I don't want you to freak out."

"Too late for that."

His red-rimmed eyes dart around the room. He's

uncomfortable—good. He scared the piss out of me last night. He ought to be very uncomfortable.

"Dad," I say. And then: *"Davis."*

Now he looks at me, contrite. "Let's go with Dad."

"You sure?"

He nods, then winces, gingerly touching the back of his head. "Henry, I'm not real sure what to say. All I know is that I've made a mess of things. I'm humiliated, if you want to know the truth."

"Does that mean it'll never happen again?"

His brows draw together. His typical good humor is nowhere to be found. "I don't want it to. But I haven't figured out how to make certain it doesn't."

Don't drink, I want to say.

But I know it's not as easy as that.

"I used to go to meetings," he tells me.

This is a surprise. You don't walk into an AA meeting unless you've acknowledged, at least on some level, that you've got a problem. "Why'd you stop?"

He lets out a dry chuckle. "Well, they weren't much fun."

"And getting so wasted that you bust your head open *is* fun?"

"I didn't say that. I don't drink because it's fun, usually. Having a few loosens me up. Gets me out of my head."

"I'm in my head all the time, Dad. There are other ways to deal."

"Yeah. Maybe I should take up running."

"Maybe."

"Or read those mermaid books."

365

I crack a smile. "Why not? Those stories are the shit."

He grows serious again. "I can't think of anything I want to talk about less than the last twenty-four hours, but I owe you an explanation. This thing with Tati's been rough. I'm furious with myself for driving her away, so I keep doing the thing that drove her away. It doesn't make sense, but a lot of times, I just can't make myself care until it's too late."

"I called her last night," I tell him. "She helped me—helped *you*."

"Oh, hell," he says, sinking into the pillows behind him. "I'm sure she was thrilled."

"Not exactly. I'm glad she was around, though. She's pretty great."

He gazes up at the ceiling, wistful. "Yeah, she is."

We let quiet fill the room, both of us focusing on the game. When it breaks for a commercial, Dad says, "I've never told your mom about the meetings."

"How come?"

"She already thinks I'm a screw-up. If she knew about AA, she'd be all over my ass."

"I don't know about that. Look at the trouble I found myself in last spring. If she was pissed, I never knew it. She was just there for me. She gives people a lot of grace, Dad."

"When it comes to failed attempts at sobriety, though? I don't know, buddy."

"I do—I talked to her earlier. She wants you to do what it takes to get healthy, and if a meeting is the first step, she's gonna support you. So will I."

"But isn't it weak, having to sit with a bunch of strangers and admit that you don't know your limits?"

"I think it's the opposite of weak. It takes balls to ask for help." I run a hand through my hair. Difficult as this conversation is, I've got to put it all out there. I've got to tell him how badly he scared me. "I don't want to see you unconscious and bleeding ever again. If talking things out with strangers a couple of times a week keeps you on your feet, then I think you should do it. And if you're not willing to try, I won't stick around."

"Henry—"

"No. It's that simple."

He sighs. "You sound like your mom."

"Is that supposed to be a dig?"

"Not even close." He rubs his eyes like someone kicked dust in them. When he looks at me again, his expression is less distressed than it was when I walked into the room. "If getting sober is what it takes to keep you in Florida, I'll do it. Meetings, sponsor, booze down the toilet—the whole thing. But don't go getting a big head. I'm gonna do it for myself more than anyone. I'm tired of not remembering what happened the night before. Of feeling like shit every morning. Of disappointing the people who care about me. I want to take back control."

"What about your job?"

"What about it?"

"You own a sports bar."

"I don't have to drink while I'm there—I haven't always. I'll do the work. You've got my word."

I let out a breath, rolling the kinks from my neck. I'm freaking drained, but I feel liberated too. Finally, the stress that's been weighing on me has lessened. Finally, resolution is in sight. Dad wants to recover. He wants to be around for me, and I want to be around for him. His conviction has seeped into me; if he can do hard things, I can too.

I need to clear the air with Whitney. Hurt feelings or not, I need to be honest with her. Piper too—I don't know where she and I stand after last night, but I want to try and fix what's broken between us. No more secrets. No more guilt. No more half-truths.

"I'm gonna stay in Sugar Bay through senior year," I tell my dad.

He grins. "Florida looks good on you. She's giving you a kickass tan."

I laugh. "Yeah, that weighed heavily in my choice to stick around."

Later, I go to the cafeteria in search of something to drink while my parents have it out on the phone. When I get back to Dad's room with a Gatorade for him and a soda for me, he's hung up with Mom.

"She's tough," he says, but he doesn't seem beaten down.

The opposite, actually.

"Only when she cares," I tell him.

I leave for the Towers. I'll head back to the hospital when Dad's discharged, but for now, I'm craving a hot shower, a nap, and a couple of Advil. The hospital's a few miles from home—it's weird to call Dad's apartment *home*—so I summon a rideshare. The app says I've got a few minutes to wait. I use the time to dial Whitney.

"Hey," she answers. "I was hoping you'd call. I thought—"

"Hang on." I sink onto a bench outside the hospital's entrance. "I've got to say something, and you're not gonna like it."

I put it all out there. I tell her that even though I was sad about ending the pregnancy, I was relieved too. I tell her how awful I feel about our fights leading up to the breakup, and after. I tell her how much I hate it that she got so sick. I tell her she was the first girl I ever fell in love with, and then I tell her I'm not coming back to Spokane next month. I tell her I'm sorry.

She listens.

And then she cries.

I feel like the world's biggest asshole, hurting her again.

"I'm sorry," I tell her, like echoed apologies are the Band-Aid she needs.

"God, Henry. Stop saying that."

"Okay." And then, because it's almost reflexive: "I'm sorry."

She laughs. It's a pitiful sniveling sound that makes her laugh harder, more believably. "You're the worst."

"Maybe. But, Whit, I don't want to be another reason you're sad."

Quietly, she says, "You met someone else, didn't you?"

369

I sigh. "Yeah. But she's not the reason you and I can't be together. We don't make sense, Whitney. We don't make each other happy—not like we used to."

"But you let me believe you were open to trying again. I've clung to that."

"Why, though?"

"Because I just...I want to go back to the way things were. Before. I want to feel happy and not wonder if I'm allowed. I want to start looking toward the future instead of asking *what if?* about the past. I want to feel lovable again."

A lot like what Piper said.

I've been stuck in a similar state of shame since March. It sucks, feeling empty and unworthy. But hearing those sentiments come out of Whitney's mouth gives me clarity I haven't had in months.

"Whit, you *are* lovable."

"But you don't love me anymore," she whispers. "And my parents won't look me in the eye. My friends...they're trying to help, but they treat me like I'm broken. I *feel* broken."

I sigh, wishing we'd had this conversation in person before I left for Florida. I want to meet her gaze as I say, "Not to undercut your emotions, because you feel what you feel, and I get what you're saying—I swear I do—but Whitney, you are *not* broken. It's okay to get excited about the future; you deserve that. And I'm personally giving you permission to feel happy again. Whenever you're ready."

My ride pulls up to the curb. I signal that I need a second, and the driver nods.

370

"Whit, tell me what you're thinking."

She exhales. "I'm thinking that you wouldn't bullshit me."

"I wouldn't. Especially not about this."

A few beats pass before she says, "When you come visit your mom, do you think we could get coffee or something?"

"Yeah. That'd be cool."

A few minutes later, when we say goodbye, I know in my gut that it's for real.

I get to my feet, and despite all that's happened in the last twenty-four hours, I feel lighter. Like I've cut an anchor free.

Piper

AS TATI AND I ARE getting ready to sit down to Chinese takeout, Henry texts my sister to let her know his dad's been discharged.

"You guys traded numbers?" I ask, scooping fried rice onto my plate.

"This morning. I told him to get in touch if he needs anything."

"That was nice of you."

"I'm hardly the wicked witch you've spent years making me out to be."

I pick up a wonton and snap my arm back like I'm going to throw it at her. She ducks behind the door of the fridge, laughing. "Don't you dare!"

"I won't, because that'd be a waste of a perfectly good wonton." I drop it onto my plate and head for the table. When Tati joins me with a plate of her own, I say, "I'm going to Henry's later. You were right—he and I need to have a conversation."

She nods, smiling down at her food.

It's not often that I admit she knows better than I do.

She didn't react to the news about me getting fired the way I thought she would. I mean, she was disappointed for sure, but she didn't yell, and she didn't make me feel worse. More than anything, she was bummed that I'd put Turtle in such a difficult position, which bothers me equally.

"I'm going to reach out to him," I told her this morning. "I want him to know how sorry I am and that I learned from my screw-up."

"I think he'd appreciate that," she said. "He may not want you to work for him anymore, but he'll always care about you. He knows we're more than our mistakes."

She's right. It's been a hard-won lesson, but this summer more than any other time in my life, I've realized the importance of forgiveness, of assuming good intentions, of compassion, and of conviction. I want to keep surrounding myself with people who embody those traits, and I want to strive to exemplify them myself.

My sister is the best example.

"You know, I can help you look for a new job, if you want," she tells me now.

I make a mopey face and say with a sigh, "Maybe. I was hoping for a letter of recommendation from Turtle, though. I'm gonna need some stellar endorsements for my college applications."

She reaches out to squeeze my shoulder. "It'll work out. You'll get letters of recommendation from your guidance counselor and a couple of teachers and your next boss, probably. Your GPA is strong. You'll get into a good school."

"I don't want just any good school. I want to go to Stony Brook University."

"In New York?"

"Yes, in New York. I want to study marine biology, Tati, like Mom and Dad. I've been doing tons of research, looking into lots of different schools, learning about programs all over the country. There are a few I'd like to apply to, but I've just got this feeling— Stony Brook University is it for me. I know you don't think I should leave Florida. I know it's super far away, and I know out-of-state tuition is bananas, but I'm going to apply for scholarships, and I can take out loans if I need to. Will you keep an open mind?"

She lets out a hefty sigh, and I sense it—the turning of tides.

"I'll make you a deal," she says slowly, like she's still working it out in her head. "I'll keep an open mind if you will too. Promise me you'll consider some Florida schools as well."

"Tati—"

"Look, I know it's selfish, but you're my baby sister. I don't want you to live far away."

"But think of it as an opportunity for you too. If I leave Sugar Bay, you've got nothing keeping you here. You could move anywhere. Back to Boston, or LA, or Europe. Get back into interior design, or something else entirely."

She considers this as if she's only now realizing that she's got a whole lot of life ahead of her. Then she reaches out to take my hand. "I'm going to miss you no matter where you go."

I smile. "I know. But look on the bright side: Your home will be *so clean* when I'm not living in it."

Poking me with her foot, she says, "I'll try to wrap my head around college out of state if you keep your nose clean. I mean that figuratively *and* literally. No more piercings."

"Okay—yes. No more piercings. Best behavior."

She grins, giving me a resolute nod. And then she launches into a story about how when she was home from college one summer, she was *not* on her best behavior and ended up getting fired from her job as a beach lifeguard.

"Apparently, you're not supposed to snag a key from your supervisor's office, use it to unlock one of the guard towers, and sneak in with a random summer hookup," she finishes with mock indignation.

I die laughing.

Maybe she and I aren't so different after all.

———

After dinner, I shower and tame my curls. I put on a sundress, even though it's nearly dark, and the espadrilles Gabi finally returned, because they make my legs look almost as good as hers. I use mascara and perfume and my favorite vanilla lip gloss.

Tati said she'd wait up, so I leave the apartment empty-handed—no phone or keys or gloss for touch-ups. I'm free; I feel like I'm moving in the right direction for the first time in a very long time.

During my trip down in the elevator, I list the things I need to say. *Last night hurt me. I want us to be honest with each other. Thank you for punching Damon's stupid face.* I also review the things I don't want to do: get defensive, back down, storm off.

As the elevator stops, butterflies lift off in my stomach. I hesitate when the doors open, like my cute shoes have glued themselves to the floor. I force myself to step into the lobby. I'm nervous, but Henry has earned my effort.

I make my way into the softly lit courtyard. The sun has set, but the sky still glows lavender. Palm fronds dance in the breeze. I approach the pool, which is deserted, looking up at the east tower as I move across the deck.

Maybe he's out grabbing dinner.

Maybe he's sleeping off the horribleness of the last twenty-four hours.

Maybe he's with his dad, enjoying a guys' night now that Davis has been sprung.

"Piper?"

My gaze drops from the eighth floor to the other side of the pool.

Henry.

I stop like I've come up against an invisible wall: abruptly and without grace.

"Where are you headed?" he calls.

To you.

But the words get caught in my throat, and my eyes are welling with tears. I shrug like a half-wit, then cover my face with my hands.

When he says my name again, this time with concern, he sounds much closer. I peek out from between my fingers, mortified by the way I've fallen apart at the mere sight of him, to find that he's hustled around the pool. He's wearing a white T-shirt and tan shorts and flip-flops. His chestnut hair is hidden beneath a backward baseball hat. He looks listless, like his spirit has been siphoned out of him.

"Tell me why you're upset," he says, and the way he phrases it, like my unhappiness is a burden he insists on sharing, breaks me apart.

He doesn't wait for an answer.

He opens his arms in the loveliest invitation.

My cheek nestles against his sternum. I clutch his shirt, and he wraps his arms around me, exhaling so deeply that I feel all his frustration, anger, and sadness retreat in that swell of air.

We stand there until the wind dies down, leaving the night warm and still. When I draw back, he smooths my curls, which have already gone frizzy. "Are you okay?"

"No, I'm a mess. Are you okay?"

He smiles down at me. "I'm getting there."

Henry

WE HEAD TOWARD THE POOL, the place we met three years ago. This is where I first noticed how pretty she is. Where I first decided I wanted to know her. I kick off my shoes and sit on the deck, sinking my feet into the cool water. She does the same, trying not to flash me as she maneuvers in her dress. I study the stars until she's settled, and then I focus on her.

"How's your dad?" she asks.

"Okay. He went to bed early. Been a long day."

"For you too, I bet."

"I watched him pour a half rack of beers and a dozen bottles of booze down the drain, so it hasn't been all bad."

She smiles.

I expect her to ask about Whitney, or my hand, which aches. Instead, she says, "Henry, I shouldn't have left you at Hudson's. That was awful of me. But when you went inside, I read this text on your phone, and then Damon... I just had to get out of there."

How is she so poised and steady-voiced after what she went through at Hudson's?

She says, "If you're mad, I understand. I betrayed your privacy by looking at your phone, and then I ditched you. If you don't want to see me anymore, I get it. I would hate that, though, and I was coming to tell you as much."

She lets me weave my fingers through hers.

"I was coming to tell you the same thing. Well, not the same thing, exactly. I was coming to tell you that last night sucked and I want to make it right. That text you saw...it was from Whitney?"

"Yes. I was confused. I *am* confused. I thought—"

"It was a miscommunication. A mistake on my part. I set it straight. I'm staying in Florida, Piper. As long as my dad's sober, I'm staying. Whitney's part of my past. That's all."

She looks at our joined hands. Gently, she runs a fingertip over my bruised knuckles.

"Do you believe me?" I ask.

She lifts her gaze, nodding. No more tears.

"Is there something else?"

She nods again.

I trail a hand up her arm, then down again. It comes to rest against her wrist, her pulse beating under my palm. "Piper, what?"

"When you saw me with Damon," she says, whisper-soft, "you knew I didn't want anything to do with him, right?"

379

"Yeah. Shit—of course I knew."

"Your face, though. When you came around the corner. It seemed like you weren't sure."

My cheeks catch fire. How—*how*—could I have put that idea in her head?

I wrestle for a comprehensible explanation. "I'd just talked to Gabi. She'd told me what Damon did to you. Seeing you with him, knowing the backstory, knowing what he put you through...I've never felt so out of control. This instinct kicked in, and Jesus, I wanted to choke the life out of him. It lasted a heartbeat before I remembered that you were a thousand times more important than retribution. Then all I wanted was to be sure you were okay."

"I *am* okay."

"I know. You're tougher than I'll ever be."

She raises her eyebrows. "I'm not the one who drilled my fist into someone's face."

I shrug. "You should've seen me at the hospital last night. I was half a second from weeping on your sister's shoulder."

She sits quietly, swirling her toes through the pool's illuminated water before she voices a question. "Henry, do you think we're defined by our mistakes?"

I ponder that for a minute. "Shaped, maybe, but not defined. At least, I'm trying not to let hard stuff from my past shit all over the good stuff in my present."

She smiles up at me. "I like that."

"Yeah, I can be pretty philosophical."

380

She laughs. There's forgiveness in her eyes, and her palm is warm against mine. She leans into my arm, her weight and her presence a grounding wire. As much as I've come to care about her this summer, I've fallen flat-on-my-back in love with her in the last five minutes.

I lift a hand to touch her cheek, and she presses back against my palm. I swear to god my heart blasts skyward.

"Can we kiss now?" she whispers. "Or do you have more deep things to say?"

"I'm definitely done talking."

She slips a hand around the back of my neck, drawing me closer. She kisses me, tentatively, like it's our first time all over again. I cradle her face, urging her vanilla lips open. She smiles against my mouth. We build from a warm-up jog to an all-out sprint to a leisurely cooldown that lasts until we've reclaimed the breaths we lost to each other.

"Want to go swimming?" she asks.

I arch an eyebrow. "I'm not wearing—"

She tips into the pool, water splashing up behind her.

When she surfaces, I'm laughing. "I'm having déjà vu."

She pushes her wet hair off her face. "That was intentional—not like last time."

"It was equally graceful, though."

She shoots a stream of water at me, soaking my shorts. "Now you have no excuse."

"Oh, I'm coming in." I lose my hat, pull my shirt over my head, leave my phone and key ring in the bundle. Then I hop into the pool, dipping to submerge my shoulders. I grab her hand and reel her in. She drapes her arms around my neck, hooking her ankles behind me. There's a glint of mischief in her eyes.

"I'm cool with swimming," I tell her, linking my hands at the small of her back. "But I wasn't done kissing you."

"Good," she says, leaning in.

Piper

A WEEK LATER, I MEET Henry at Clementine's for late-afternoon acai bowls. He's scored a spot by the window, and he's waiting with spoons and napkins and bottles of water.

He stands as I near the table. I rise onto my toes to kiss him.

"I ordered," he says. "I got you a Sunrise Bowl, but it's not too late to switch if you want something else."

"Nope, that's perfect."

"You're all dressed up," he says, taking in my outfit: black cigarette pants with Mary Janes and an emerald tie-front shirt on loan from Tati. He looks uncertainly at his frayed-hem shorts and faded T-shirt. "Should I have worn something nicer?"

I swat his arm. "You always look good."

"So do you," he says, tucking a curl behind my ear.

The guy behind the counter catches his attention; our bowls

are ready. I take a seat while Henry goes to the counter to get them. Then he slides into the booth beside me.

"What'd you do today?" I ask, mixing granola into my blended acai.

"Golfed with my dad." He grins. "I beat him."

"No way! Was he grumpy after?" I've never actually seen Davis grumpy, but I know he's competitive. Unsurprisingly, I can relate. Losing makes me super irritable.

"Nah. We had a good time. I know it's only been a week, but I swear I can see a change in him. It's like his skin fits him better."

I smile. "That's amazing."

"Yeah," Henry says, scooping up a banana slice. "He's excited to have you on at the restaurant."

"I can't wait to start."

Davis has hired me as a hostess. They had an opening, and after getting Tati's blessing, I ran the idea by him the other night while I was eating takeout with Henry at their place.

"We'd be lucky to have you," he said. "When can you start?"

I'm not sure if Davis and Tati will ever get back together, but I wouldn't mind if they did.

"You want to guess what I did before I came here?" Henry asks, twisting the top off a bottle of water.

"Hmm...went on a run? Read something enriching? Took an SAT practice test?"

"Wrong, wrong, wrong." He smiles broadly, drawing out the suspense. He clears his throat. "I registered for classes at Sugar Bay High."

384

I knew he was planning to, but senior year with Henry didn't feel real until this moment. He's going to live in Sugar Bay. He's going to start school with me in a few weeks. We get a whole year together. And after that, maybe more.

I drop my spoon, sandwich his face between my hands, and lay a kiss on him.

He laughs, then eclipses my kiss with one that's softer and sweeter, his warm hands coming up to take mine. "You're happy?"

"I'm *ecstatic*."

"Me too." He pulls me into a hug.

I press my lips to his neck, beyond grateful that we reconnected this summer.

I can hardly remember life before him.

He lets me go and hands me my spoon, nudging my snack closer. After a couple of bites, he asks, "What'd you do today?"

"I went to Gabi's this morning. Her dad made a big breakfast—biscuits and gravy, grits, and sweet milk waffles, and then I helped her pick a dress for the concert she's giving in Tallahassee next month. It took forever. She likes to look as perfect as she sounds. And she will, of course."

Henry grins. "I'm glad things are good between you two. Your face...your whole demeanor...you're an incandescent bulb. Or, like, a star. Polaris! Brightest star in Ursa Minor."

I bump his shoulder with mine, laughing. "You're such a nerd. But yeah, I had a good morning. At least until..." I wrinkle my nose, reluctant to talk about the appointment I sat through after

385

leaving Gabi's. But I'm working on being more open. Especially with Henry.

I draw in a breath and tell him, "Tati took me to consult with an attorney. She wanted advice on filing for a restraining order. She doesn't want Damon anywhere near me. One of the rare topics we agree on."

"Shit," Henry says, resting a comforting hand on my leg. "I'm right there with you guys. Are you gonna do it?"

"I think so. It'll be tricky because we go to the same school. No judge is going to deny him his right to education. But it's not impossible, so long as Sugar Bay High cooperates. He's been harassing me and causing me"—I throw up air quotes, because this is a phrase Tati has taken directly from Florida code—*"substantial emotional distress.* Basically, he makes me fear for my safety, and that's illegal. Also, it *really* sucks."

"Yeah. Understatement of the fucking century."

Fondness bubbles up within me. He was right—since Gabi and I made up, since my sister and I had our heart-to-heart, since he decided to stay in Florida, since I established a future to work toward, my outlook has been so much brighter. Lately, life feels too good to be true. A tiny part of me is afraid it's only a matter of time before my joy is snatched away.

Who am I to deserve such unbridled happiness?

When I mentioned my worries to Tati in the car earlier, she smiled and said, "Life is highs and lows, Piper. It's not always going to feel this perfect, so soak it up."

I'm doing my best.

I turn a grin on Henry. "Want to know what I love about you?"

His cheeks go pink at the word *love*, I think. He swallows and says, "I absolutely do."

"I love how you look all upstanding and respectable, how your vocabulary is, like, double mine, how you're so thoughtful and gentlemanly—standing when I walk into a room, ordering treats for me—and yet you drop the most perfectly placed f-bombs like it's nothing."

He bursts out laughing. "You really love that?"

"I really do."

His gaze catches mine and holds tight. "You know what I love about you?"

I shrug. "Probably everything."

He swoops down to kiss my cheek, then whispers in my ear, "That's exactly right."

Acknowledgments

Thank you, first and foremost, to the readers who have bought and borrowed my books, who have read and reviewed, who have posted on socials, and who have gifted copies to friends and family. Thanks to those who've reached out to tell me how my stories impacted you. Thank you to those who've annotated, dog-eared, and cried into the books I've written. This job is the best, and without you, I wouldn't get to do it. ♥

I'm so lucky to be a Sourcebooks author! Annette Pollert-Morgan, working with you continues to be a fulfilling and joyful experience. Your knowledge and enthusiasm are unmatched; you care about my stories as much as I do, and I am endlessly grateful. To everyone at Sourcebooks who had a role in getting this book into readers' hands, including Kay Birkner, Jenny Lopez, Lia Ferrone, Thea Voutiritsas, Sarah Brody, Stephanie Rocha, Gabbi Calabrese, Alison Cherry, Karen Masnica, Rebecca Atkinson, Delaney Heisterkamp, Tracy Nelson, Jess Elliott, Keri Haddrill, Sarah Brody, and especially Dominique Raccah, thank you so very much for your talent and time, your ingenuity and hard work.

I can't imagine navigating this industry without my incredible agent, Pam Gruber. Your advice and support are invaluable. A warm thank-you to the entire team at High Line Literary Collective, and additional appreciation to Heather Baror-Shapiro at Baror International for her foreign representation.

Elodie Nowodazkij and Alison Miller, I simply could not do this without you. All the hearts! Much gratitude as well to Temre Beltz, Jessica Patrick, and Christina June; I'm so fortunate to have a fantastic circle of writer besties.

Loads of appreciation, as always, to my family, including Mom and Dad, Bev and Phil, Mike and Jena, Zach and Michele, Danielle and Andy, Sam and Kacie, my wonderfully encouraging aunts, uncles, and cousins, and all my nieces and nephews.

My very favorite girlies, Claire and Lizzie, I write with you in mind. Thank you for being my biggest cheerleaders. Matt, I love that we get to do life together. Thank you for standing by my side—metaphorically, if not always physically.

What comes after heartbreak?

Fall in love with Katy Upperman's

Everything I Promised You

GOOD FORTUNE

Prologue

WHEN MY MOM WAS SEVENTEEN, she caved to a dare and paid a traveling carnival's clairvoyant twenty dollars to reveal her fate.

Leaving her friends on a dusty footpath beneath a string of glowing bulbs, Mom was led into a candlelit tent. Tapestries embroidered with constellations adorned the walls. The table in the center of the space was blanketed in an ebony cloth. Scattered atop were crystals, celestial charts, seashells, and bones. Cinnamon incense burned in a wooden tray. As Mom got settled, the clairvoyant, who was a cliché in chiffon scarves and silver jewelry, began to sort the items, combining shells and crystals and bones into cryptic groups. She regarded the celestial charts before moving on to Mom's palms.

Once, I asked her if she'd felt uncomfortable.

"The opposite," she told me. "I went into that tent a skeptic, but after I sat down… The fortune teller was a stranger, and she was certainly strange, but I was at peace."

Speaking quietly, in an accent crisper than Mom's Mississippi drawl, the clairvoyant shared what she'd perceived from the seashells, the stars, the crystals, and the palmistry.

"For you," she said, "education is essential. Continue to learn well."

Mom, an insatiable reader with a memory just short of photographic, nodded.

"You seek deep friendships; they're your life's blood," the clairvoyant went on. "Family, too, is important. Your mother acts as your scaffold. You will remain close, though not always physically."

Then she fell into a trancelike quiet, eyes darkening.

Mom leaned forward, confused but intrigued.

The clairvoyant delivered a blow: "Your father will pass before you leave his home."

Mom planned to leave her parents' home the following year; Ole Miss waited. Shaken, she fell back in her seat. She wanted to raise questions, to protest: her daddy was robust, a live oak of a man.

Why was she in a medium's tent when there was a whole carnival just outside? She ought to be with her friends. She could get up and go—she *should* get up and go.

The clairvoyant's somber expression left her heavy in her seat. She blinked back tears and braced for more.

"You'll meet your soulmate after your father's passing," the clairvoyant said. "In her, you'll mine the strength to carry on. Romantic love will find you soon after. Your first impression will be less than favorable, but be open to possibility—open to him." Reaching across the cluttered table, she rested her fingers against Mom's wrist, where her pulse surged. Tingles scattered through her, sparks and shivers alighting her skin. "A nurturer's heart beats within you. You were born to love."

This is the part where Mom always gets misty eyed.

Next, the clairvoyant spoke of me.

"You will bear one child, a flaxen-haired girl with eyes like her father's, blue as the ocean's depths. She will be your greatest joy, and she will walk a path similar to the one you blaze. The woman I spoke of—your soul's mirror—will mother your daughter's fated."

The reading ended, and Mom left the tent.

Outside, the carnival persisted. Bells rang and lights flashed neon. The aromas of hot dogs and funnel cake mingled in the hazy air. She tracked down her friends, who begged her to tell them about her future.

She refused.

She held it close...

...awed as it unfurled before her.

My mom is an educator with a tightly knit circle of friends. She and Grandma talk every day. Prostate cancer took her daddy two weeks after she graduated high school. She met Bernadette— Bernie—on her first day at Ole Miss. They shared a dorm room, and to this day swear that one cannot exist without the other. At a fraternity party a month later, an azure-eyed pledge dropped a watermelon Jolly Rancher into Mom's Zima. They danced two songs before he declared her the love of his life, then puked up Trash Can Punch all over her Steve Maddens.

She forgave him.

They were college sweethearts, and she pinned his rank when the Army commissioned him. A few weeks later, beneath a fragrant magnolia tree, they married. At the reception, to Grandma's chagrin, they ladled Trash Can Punch into Solo cups. They moved, weathered a deployment, and moved again. Bernie married Dad's ROTC battle buddy, Connor Byrne. Not long after, they had a baby boy who weighed a whopping eleven pounds. Connor fainted, slumping into a heap on the delivery room floor. Mom cut the umbilical cord.

Beckett Byrne.

Hair: rusty red.

Eyes: army green.

Heart: promised to me.

Eighteen months later, I was born, as slight as Beck was strapping, with wispy flaxen hair and eyes blue like the sea.

Holding me in her arms that very first time, Mom didn't cry—but not because she wasn't moved, and not because she wasn't happy.

"Because, my sweet Lia," she says, laying her hand against my cheek as she finishes the story she's told me countless times. "I've known you since I was seventeen."

ARMY BRATS

Seventeen Years Old, Virginia

WHEN I WAS IN EIGHTH grade, my dad deployed to Afghanistan for a year. On one of the many nights I couldn't sleep, I opened my ever-present journal and did some calculating: Of my thirteen years, Dad had been away for six. For nearly half my life, he'd had boots on the ground in various foreign countries.

Every time he deploys, I cry rivers. Mom does too. But before long, we settle into a routine. We carry on. We survive.

God willing, Dad will too.

Six months, eight months, twelve months later, he redeploys. Mom and I meet him with posters that boast my bubbly handwriting in red and blue: *Welcome home, Daddy!* He hugs me, smelling of elsewhere, and murmurs, "I missed you, Millie."

Onlookers blot tears, thanking him for his service. He smiles, humble. He's third-generation military. It's not as simple as service; patriotism pumps through his veins.

Tradition dictates that, post-deployment, we swing by Burger King for Double Whoppers and sodas. Then we head home, to whichever house we're renting, in whichever Army-post-adjacent town we're living. Dad drags his dusty duffels into the garage. After a hot shower and a couple IPAs, he passes out in the recliner, jet-lagged and in desperate need of uninterrupted sleep.

I've always been close with my parents. That's the way of most Army brats, I think. We're transient, a family of caribou traversing the land as Dad's orders dictate, our only constants being each other. I've made friends along the way, but when I think of them, I think of fun, blowing off steam, filling time. I don't think *lifelong*.

With the exception of Beck.

Beck was an Army brat too. He knew what it was like to move every few years, to pack up a room and wave goodbye to buddies. He knew how it felt to be the new kid. His dad deployed as often as mine. He'd pulled construction paper links from plenty of countdown chains. He leaned on Bernie in all the ways I've leaned on Mom.

Beck understood.

I grew up vacationing with the Byrnes. FaceTiming Bernie to dish about the angsty TV series we streamed in tandem. I attended Connor's promotion ceremonies, just as I attend my dad's. When I was three-four-five (Beck was five-six-seven), our

398

dads were assigned to the same unit at Fort Bragg. We lived in the same development. When I was eight-nine-ten (Beck was ten-eleven-twelve), it happened again. Fort Lewis. We lived on the same street. When I was fourteen (Beck had just turned sixteen), Dad was given a stint at the Pentagon. Connor was assigned to Fort Belvoir, also in Northern Virginia.

Together again.

Bernie and Mom were ecstatic.

Beck and I fell in love.

PERMANENT CHANGE OF STATION

Seventeen Years Old, En Route to Tennessee

A SENIOR-YEAR MOVE IS MANY an Army brat's worst nightmare.

But not mine.

Leaving Virginia.

Leaving Connor, Bernie, and the twins.

Leaving Rosebell High School.

Our July departure date can't come fast enough.

Escape, flee, withdraw.

These are the words that loop through my head as I tuck my life into boxes. As we embark on our trip to Tennessee. As I watch summer raindrops race across our Explorer's windows. As I fill Moleskine pages with meaningless lists and verbose musings and swirling doodles. As I pet Major, our sixty-pound Pointer pup, who's stretched out on the backseat beside me. As I consume the gas station snacks my parents push into my hands because I'm "not eating enough" and "we're worried, Lia."

It's been one hundred ninety-nine days.

Four thousand seven hundred eighty hours spent navigating a world without Beck.

As Mom and Dad put it: I'm not myself.

How infinitely fucking stupid to suppose I would be.

On the road, my parents fill silences with falsely cheerful chatter. They order peanut butter milkshakes from fast-food drive-throughs. They stretch what should be a ten-hour drive into a three-day trip because "a vacation might make Lia feel better."

Just east of Knoxville, Mom turns to look at me, eyes doleful. "Oh, lovey. Daddy and I miss him too."

I hate when she equates her sadness to mine.

"It's true, Millie," Dad puts in, his gaze trained on the endless highway. While everyone else in my life shortens my given name, Amelia, to Lia, he likes Millie. "Mom and I loved that kid like our own. It's bullshit what happened."

What happened.

No one ever says it like it is: Beck died.

Dad's still talking. "I wish there was something we could do to help you through this. Make it easier for you somehow."

"For Bernie and Connor and the twins too," Mom says.

There's no fixing death, for it is permanent and perpetual.

Those are the words the reverend used at Beck's funeral. He was speaking of the community's love for Beck, but staring at

401

my boyfriend's mahogany casket, surrounded by a veritable field of flowers, with my teary-eyed parents beside me, Bernie and Connor weeping in the pew in front of us, each holding one of the twins, preschoolers who desperately wanted their brother back, it was hard to think about love.

Loss is permanent and perpetual.

While Mom and Dad and Bernie and Connor cried showers, I'd used up my tears. That past summer, they were a drizzle while I helped Beck pack for college. They became a downpour when he left for Charlottesville—for Commonwealth of Virginia University, his dream school and mine—to begin training with the track and field team. I made a rainy season of that autumn. In November, my tears became sleet, icy and dangerous.

And then, that word again: permanent.

A permanent change of station—military speak for "pack your shit and hit the road."

We're off to Fort Campbell, where Dad will serve as Commander of the 3rd Brigade Combat Team.

A fresh start. That's what he proclaims, swinging open the door to our just-acquired rental in River Hollow, Tennessee.

A new beginning. That's what Mom preaches, stacking dishes on shelves she covered with fresh liner.

I don't want either, I tell Beck, retreating to my room-for-now, where boxes stand like mountains in a crowded range.

Dad's already been in here. He hung my bulletin board over my desk, a collage of my life before: ticket stubs, CVU stickers, photos of friends from Virginia and before that, Colorado

402

Springs. Photos of Beck. Seeing him in full color, smiling, *alive,* is like opening a scabbed-over wound, again and again and again.

I shut my bedroom door quietly, with restraint.

That's my grief these days: quiet, restrained.

I, too, am closed off.

Permanently and perpetually, it seems.

MEANT TO BE

Five Years Old, North Carolina

ONE OF MY EARLIEST MEMORIES is set against the backdrop of a popular park in Spring Lake, North Carolina. I was getting ready to start kindergarten, which means Beck was about to turn seven. Dad and Connor, captains back then, were deployed to Iraq, and Mom and Bernie were constantly looking to fill our days. The park, with its wading pool and climbing toys and green spaces, kept Beck and me busy. We arrived early, before the sun got too hot, and staked out a spot from where Mom and Bernie could keep an eye on us while working on their tans.

Beck and I'd been playing in the water, setting up battles waged between his aquatic GI Joes and my rainbow-coiffed mermaid Barbies, when a pair of boys who'd been in his class at school showed up.

He left a wake in his haste to ditch me.

Dolls in hand, I climbed out of the pool and flopped down on a towel beside Mom and Bernie. Mom reapplied my sunscreen. Bernie handed over bunches of grapes, which I ate until I was practically bursting with pent-up indignation. I blurted out that Beck was mean, I hated him, and I'd *never* play with him again.

Bernie said, "Sometimes he's a real stinker. You do you, girlie."

"I think Beck will be sad, though," Mom reasoned, "if you never play together again."

"He's not sad right now," I said, glaring toward the far side of the pool, where he was playing Keep Away with his friends.

"Boys can be rotten sometimes," Bernie said.

"I know!" I crowed, happy to be understood. "Beck always ignores me when his friends come around."

"But *you're* his friend," she pointed out. "His oldest friend. His most special friend."

"You're more than friends, lovey," Mom said. "You're soulmates."

I frowned, circling my arms around my knobby knees. "What does that mean?"

She reached over to tuck a tendril of hair back into my ponytail. "There's a bond between you and Beck unlike any other. A bond that'll last forever."

I squinted up at her. "The same way you and Daddy will be together forever?"

"Daddy and I are married. Who knows—maybe you and Beck will marry one day." I made a show of retching, and Mom paused to laugh with Bernie. "Or maybe you'll stay friends, but *best* friends, like Bernie and me. No matter what, you're a part of each other's lives. You always will be."

"But how do you know?"

"Your mama's been informed of the future," Bernie said, giving Mom's hand an affectionate squeeze. "She knew we'd meet and become forever friends. She knew she'd fall in love with your daddy. She knew I'd have a son, and she'd have a daughter. She knows that you and Beck are meant to be. Like...Mickey and Minnie."

"Or Han and Chewbacca," Mom put in, and I giggled.

"Socks and shoes," Bernie said.

"Campfire and s'mores," Mom countered.

"Peanut butter and jelly," I said, grinning.

Bernie slapped me a high five and Mom kissed my cheek, and I felt okay enough to look over at Beck. I watched him, the monkey in the middle, nick the ball from the air, while I thought of other celebrated pairs: bees and honey; Barbie and Ken; cookies and milk; sidewalks and chalk.

As he was switching spots with one of the other boys, Beck glanced toward where I sat on the lawn. Our eyes caught. "Lia!" he called. "Come play!"

I looked to Mom and Bernie.

"Only if you want to," Bernie reminded me.

"Though it looks like you could show 'em how it's done," Mom said.

I pretended to consider for as long as it took to count to five, then hopped up and ran to join the boys, leaving my towel rumpled on the grass.

406

About the Author

Katy Upperman is a graduate of Washington State University, a former elementary school teacher, a military spouse, and an insatiable reader. Her YA novels include *Everything I Promised You*, *Kissing Max Holden*, *How the Light Gets In*, and *The Impossibility of Us*, which won the 2019 YAVA Award for Excellence in YA Literature by a Virginia author. When she's not writing, Katy can be found baking chocolate chip cookies or exploring the country with her husband and two daughters.